HELLHOUND

A NOVEL

BRIAN DINDAY

Library of Congress
Control Number 2012904619

Dinday, Brian
Hellhound

ISBN 978-0-9852625-0-1

Published by
Mary Dinday
San Rafael, CA

ABOUT THE BOOK

Brian began Hellhound in 1999. He worked tirelessly for months writing this story. When no one was interested in publishing his book—saying it was too literary and well written for mass interest, he put it away forever. Or so I thought.

When I was cleaning his office after his death in 2009, I found a reworked manuscript on his computer. He had almost completed rewriting it, hoping, I am sure, to get it published THIS time.

Brian used his legal experience as a San Francisco attorney in the 1990's to craft the character of Harry Maxwell. Brian was that hard-working, solo practicing lawyer who gave his clients the very best in legal representation because he cared. After his death, his clients, former and current, could not stop telling me what a caring, decent man Brian was. And what a great lawyer. We already knew that.

So here's to you, Brian. Your book in print. You did it!

ACKNOWLEDGMENTS

I want to thank the many people who have helped me in the researching and writing of this book. I especially thank my family for their patience. When I wasn't working at my law practice, it seems I was all too often in writer's seclusion, leaving wife Mary a single parent of Matt, Luke, Alex, and Katie.

Many others have helped. Special thanks to Jim Spellerberg and Susan Lundy, who were my valued critics and pre-editors and who spent many hours catching glitches and making very helpful suggestions. Likewise my profuse thanks to Diane Holland and Betty Rahn for their insights, suggestions, and typo catching. Lt. Dennis O'Leary and Lt. Tom Bruton of the S.F.P.D. were of great help in answering technical questions and providing information. Those wonderful folks at the San Francisco Gun Exchange were generous with their time and expertise to a writer who was not there to buy anything.

My gratitude is also extended to Mr. Andre' Zotoff, food and beverage manager at the Mark Hopkins International Hotel, for his kindness in answering my questions about the Top of the Mark restaurant. I also wish to thank scores of unknown and unidentified people who gladly gave time to answer questions in elevators, on the web, and just in passing. Lastly, my thanks to all the supportive people who encouraged me to "Go for it" on this novel. If there are undiscovered technical errors in this book, it is because I did not ask the right questions of my kind consultants, and the deficits are all mine.

Brian R. Dinday
2009

DISCLAIMER

This is a work of fiction, and all the characters and events are therefore purely fictional. Any similarity to actual persons or events is coincidental. There is a City of San Francisco however, and a Hall of Justice there. As in most counties, there are judges, presiding judges, prosecutors, and homicide details. Also in San Francisco there are in fact lawyers and private investigators. Nothing herein has been intended to reflect upon any actual people living or dead who may have filled those offices, nor should any be inferred.

Brian R. Dinday

CHAPTER ONE

She regained consciousness in blackness, naked, dazed and in pain. The strongest sensation she could feel was the concrete floor sucking the warmth from her exposed flesh. Lurching unsteadily to her feet, she shivered and tried to squint through the gloom of the dank basement. She could see and hear nothing. Only the breathtaking cold beneath her bare feet proved to her that she was alive. Now she could make out a faint light squeezing around the blackout curtain covering the window. She cocked her head toward a strange sound and tried to focus her mind through the pain and dizziness.

She hugged herself in the frigid, musty air, swaying uncontrollably. When she put her fingers to the stinging spot at her right temple, they came away moist and sticky. Twice her arms flailed as she fought for balance, making her Med-Alert bracelet jingle. She could not locate the stairs in the blackness, but there was another sound now, and it was all too vivid: wet, rhythmic, rasping.

She jumped back against the cold wall when he spoke. A hairy spider flailed its legs against her buttocks, and she jumped forward again with a shriek. Yet another sound arose, and she was not sure whether it was coming from her. It was a soft, high-pitched wailing sound, rising and falling. She cringed when the voice again reached out of the darkness.

"C'mere. You're going to make history. Come 'n get it." Then louder and angry, "Move, bitch." Somehow she managed to command her feet to creep forward slightly, even as her torso hung back. Then she retreated again when a shadowy form moved into the window's faint light only ten feet away. Now she knew what the sound was. Saliva oozed through the mesh of the man's stocking mask and then disappeared when he inhaled, making that drooling, rasping noise.

It was his right hand that held her gaze. It held toward her a long silvery object. A faint glint flashed off it, as he slowly turned it left and right. He took a step toward her, dragging his left foot. Again the voice came, and she felt the hairs stand up on her neck.

"I won't hurt you. Just do as I say. I'll explain to you what's going to happen, and what you have to do," came the voice softly now. The mask continued its ungodly noise while the left hand came up holding a hypodermic. She sobbed and then choked out the words "P-please, please...don't kill me here. I don't want my mama to find..."

Through the mesh, the lips smiled.

CHAPTER TWO

Harry Maxwell's leather soles slapped quickly across the wet pavement this misty September Monday morning. He straight-armed the glass door of the Hall of Justice at a run and gave an annoyed cluck when he checked his watch and got in line at the metal detector. While he waited, he surveyed the morning's allotment of characters. Mr. Muscle and Pony-tail sported prison tattoos on greasy skin. Two working ladies braved the fog in hot pants today and were now emptying their purses.

Harry's bright blues peered out from under flyaway eyebrows as he rubbed the scar over his left carotid artery. While he waited, he buttoned the coat of his Pierre Cardin suit. At age 45 he could still fit into its continental cut. Behind Harry was a pucker-faced man with tiny black-rimmed glasses, a forensic expert by Harry's estimate. He hugged a briefcase that might contain expended cartridges from a Mac 11, AIDS-tainted blood, or fingerprint transparencies. Such items could damn or save a criminal defendant, Harry knew all too well.

He checked his watch again as he neared the front of the line. He scanned the gold plaque naming fallen police officers and then studied the patterns in the marble slabs lining the walls. He shook his head slightly and gave himself a weak smile. Where else but San Francisco, he mused, could you find patterns in marble quarried in 1958 that formed a dead ringer portrait of E.T., The Alien, or a curviform cathedral whose contours threw the voluptuous shadow of a woman's breast in the late afternoon?

Now it was Harry's turn, and he slapped down his briefcase, swung open the lid, and slid his metal across the table. Pushing quickly through the detector, he grabbed his items and thrust them back into a coat pocket. Hoisting his briefcase, he sprinted past E.T. up the marble stairs to the second floor.

As he exited the stairwell, he passed Rico Benedetti, a narc police lieutenant who also happened to be his brother-in-law. "So, spaghetti with us this Saturday?" Rico asked the vanishing attorney.

"Huh?"

"Dinner. You coming? On Saturday."

"Oh, uh no. Tell Pat I'm taking you guys out for a change. She can pick, okay?" called Harry as he rounded the corner.

♦

"Oh damn," Harry said, looking at his watch. He rushed into the courtroom and was gratified to see that Judge Vicenzo Alquiza was not yet on the bench. There was nothing that that ex-Jesuit seminary student relished more than taking the bench at the precise stroke of 9:00 a.m. Well, one perhaps. The Mad Monk loved levying fines on Harry for the slightest tardiness. It was rare for him to be late to the bench. Harry took in the courtroom at a glance, and Morton, the bailiff, jerked his thumb over his shoulder toward the holding tank, indicating that Harry's client had already been brought down from the county jail's sixth floor. Harry heard the judge's raised voice through the open door to the security corridor where his chambers were. There was a second voice, more upset, and female.

Harry walked through the doorway to the chambers. There the Mad Monk stood at his desk, a tall man towering over petite Gloria Aberdeen, his court reporter. Angry and harsh as his words were, he was actually smirking as he carried on. Harry eyed the gavel mounted on the wall plaque behind the judge. Whatever it symbolized, it was not in evidence now.

"Oh, just use old Vic's chambers bathroom any time you please. And invite the defendants in to use it too," said the judge with his eyebrows raised. "You must have! It smells like one of them was in there after a three-day burrito binge. Christ, that *couldn't* have been you! That horrible stench has to be at least from a three-hundred-pound truck driver."

Gloria was flushed crimson, her red cheeks framed between long blonde hair and her white ruffled blouse. The tightness in her throat evidently interfered with her attempt to mollify her accuser. "I'm...I'm s-s-sorry, Judge. I didn't know you were here yet."

Undeterred, the judge continued his diatribe, now with a more delighted expression as he realized he had an audience. "Oh, I understand. No one around. Gotta make a little poo-poo. How were you to know it would turn into a toxic cleanup job for the EPA?"

Gloria's eyes began to tear up while she was still trying to choke out an apology. Harry stepped forward. "That's enough, judge," he said calmly.

Alquiza took on a more serious face. "Don't go there, Mr. Maxwell. This is an internal matter of court administration. Stay out of it, before I feel inclined to look into your lateness to court."

Harry glared at the judge, his eyes tightening, but he made no reply. He took two steps to put himself between Gloria and Alquiza and then put two fingers on her shoulder, pushing her toward the doorway. "Let's go grab a cup of coffee, okay?"

"Maxwell, stop interfering if you know what's good for you."

Harry stopped at the door. After a moment he turned to stand toe-to-toe with Alquiza and spoke in a measured voice. "Judge, take a break and let her alone, or discuss the matter with the Judicial Council."

The Mad Monk clenched his teeth, controlling a catch in his voice only partially. "You don't have a lot of respect for this court, do you, Mr. Maxwell?" Harry knew it was too late to stop, even if he were so disposed, which he was not.

"All that it's due, Judge," he said, and walked out with Gloria beside him. As they reached the back of the courtroom, Harry turned to the bailiff. "Storm warning, Morty. Listen, would you ask the Public Defender to stand in for me and request my case to be put over to tomorrow morning? It's just to set a hearing. I don't think the court will be starting for a while. His Excellency needs a time out."

Morton twisted the corner of his mouth, nodding. "Sure, Harry." Then he looked at Gloria. "Glo, you want me to get another reporter to sub for you today?"

She thought a moment and then nodded, tears still on her cheeks. They went into the hallway, and Harry led her to the elevator to go for coffee. She hesitated before entering. "Harry, thank you, but I'd really just rather be alone, okay?"

"Sure. Why don't you just take the rest of the day off? Morton's already got you covered?"

She nodded again and reversed course toward the ladies' restroom.

Harry watched her go and sighed. *The bastard's really losing it.* He tended to two other court appearances, then around ten-thirty he cruised through the lobby toward the door. Walking briskly ahead of him were the imposing figures of two men he knew well. On the left was Homicide Inspector Pierre La Croix, who stood 6'3" in his beret. Harry smiled once again at the contrast between the beret and the massive torso, topped by the puffy face and bushy white mustache. Pierre was walking in step with his partner, Nate Hutchinson, who also stood over six feet tall. Nate wore no hat, and with his grizzled black hair and brown pock-marked face looked more rugged than Pierre.

Their pace seemed more urgent than normal, so Harry did not address them. Then he heard Nate say, "I didn't get a lot, Pierre, just that it was positively him, and that she was seventeen. It was apparently last night, but the grandfather didn't find her until today because she was in the basement."

"I have to go straight to City Hall when we're done," Pierre told him, "so we'll take both cars. What's the address?"

"Twenty-seven, twenty-two Third Avenue. The victim's name is Claudia Wildman."

"Wait," Harry shouted, and both inspectors turned. "Is the grandfather William Wildman?"

Pierre looked at Nate, who nodded. "Yeah, Harry. That's the guy who made the call. You know him?"

"Yeah, he's my client. I represented him in an insurance claim for roof damage at that address. That's how I knew."

"Sorry, Harry. Can't stop," Pierre said. "Time is critical, or the leads get cold."

"If my client is involved in a murder investigation, I'm coming."

"Police business, Harry. No can do," Nate said.

Harry shook his head. "That leaves me no choice but to call him and advise him not to answer any questions until I see him. How cold will the trail be then?"

Pierre looked at Nate and said, "He's got us, Nate."

"All right, Harry," he said. "You come with me."

"Let's go," was Harry's answer.

The three spilled out of the Hall, and Harry followed Pierre to his rebuilt 1973 Chevelle. Harry looked back and saw Nate at the reserved police parking curb, jiggling his key in the door lock of the Department's aging, unmarked Trans Am. They sped to the scene with sirens going. The house was easy to spot with the flashing lights from emergency vehicles marking it.

CHAPTER THREE

Pierre screeched to a stop in front of the house, and Nate did the same behind him. Nate threw Harry and Pierre pairs of latex gloves. The three began pulling them on as they ducked under the yellow tape. Then Pierre stopped and placed his hand on Nate's shoulder.

"What?" asked Nate.

"You're in charge."

"What? Of what?"

"Of the crime scene."

"Why? You've been chasing this guy night and day for, what, eight years? You know him better than anyone, and *I'm* suddenly in charge because…?"

"You want to stay a virgin forever? You've been with me for six months and with San Jose P.D. for fifteen years. You're ready. Anyway, let's see if a fresh eye can find something I haven't been able to, okay?"

"If you say so."

"Eight years?" asked Harry. "You think this is a Hellhound kill?"

Pierre gave a shrug. "Looks like our freelance terrorist got bored."

To the left of the door was a blacked-out basement window partially below sidewalk level. It was surrounded by a semicircular steel well to prevent flooding. They stopped there to speak with the uniformed officer guarding the door. Nate checked his name tag and said, "Serrano, stay out here and don't let anyone but the ID officer and the coroner come in without radioing me for permission first. Understand?"

Harry noticed a quizzical look on the patrolman's face, but he answered simply, "Yes, sir."

Before entering the house Nate asked, "Where is it, Serrano?"

"It, sir?"

"The victim," said Nate with evident annoyance. "The reason we're all here."

"Oh. She's in the basement, sir."

The three walked carefully through the modestly furnished living room to the basement stairs. They descended slowly into the dimly lit basement and made a left at the bottom. A single stark light bulb hung from a rafter. They turned left again, to an open area of unfinished space. The basement was eerily silent. A uniformed officer stood against the wall and gestured silently toward their right.

Beyond and above them was the window they had seen outside, covered with black cloth. Sitting on a dusty chest to their right was an elderly man, whom Harry recognized as Bill Wildman. He did not speak when they entered. He was looking at a girl sitting on the floor. She was sitting stiffly cross-legged, absolutely still, a blanket draped over her shoulders.

Harry went over to Wildman and touched his shoulder. "Bill?" he asked, but got no response. Nate and Pierre spread out to search the room, but found nothing. As they shrugged at each other they began to hear a low whining sound coming from the girl. Now they could see that she was hyperventilating as well. Nate looked suddenly into Pierre's eyes and blurted, "My God, we've got a live..." Pierre scowled and pulled him away from her toward the stairs.

Pierre whispered to Nate, "Good God. They call homicide before the ambulance?"

"I don't like this," Nate said. "Let's talk to Serrano again before we do anything." The two men went upstairs and called in Serrano, while Harry stayed with his client.

Upstairs, Pierre, Nate, and Serrano stood in the doorway talking in hushed tones, but Harry could hear them from the utter silence of the basement.

"What's going on here, Officer Serrano?" Pierre asked. "I got a report of a homicide attributed to the Hellhound. You make that call?"

"Uh, yes, sir, but I never said anyone was dead."

Pierre looked at Nate and then asked the policeman, "Why didn't you get an ambulance here first? Don't they train you to take care of injuries first?"

"Well, of course, sir, but she insisted she didn't want a doctor for the cut on her head. It didn't appear to be very deep, and there were no other injuries."

"If she talked, did she give a description?" asked Pierre.

"Yes, sir. She was terrified, but was talking at first. Then less and less, until she stopped responding at all. Her name is Claudia Wildman. The man down there is her grandfather, William Wildman. The grandfather called 911 and reported that he found his granddaughter sitting naked and cross-legged on the basement floor. I got the call about 8:30 p.m., and when I arrived, there were just the two of them here. The old guy was barely speaking himself. He led me down here.

"I asked her how she got the cut on her head and if she wanted a doctor. She said that he hit her with a flashlight."

"Did she say who he was?" asked Nate.

"That was my next question, and that's when she looked me in the eye for the first time and said 'The Hellhound'."

"How did he get in?" asked Pierre.

"I never found out, sir. She started to cry, but I could still make out that he was a big white man, and that he limped."

From the bottom of the staircase Harry saw Nate and Pierre shoot looks at each other. "That fits the profile," said Nate. "Anything else?"

"Not much. She did say that he told her she shouldn't move."

"One more thing, Serrano," added Nate, "you said there were no injuries. Did you examine her under that blanket?"

"Yes, sir, with Mr. Wildman present. I saw no sign of trauma."

"Call an ambulance anyway, Serrano. She has to be checked over to be sure, and for evidence, if nothing else."

"A live victim. This could be our big break," said Nate.

Pierre shook his head and said, "You don't know him then. He'd never have left her alive if there were anything she could tell us, or if there were any physical evidence. He lets us know only what he wants us to know, and that's likely to point in the direction exactly opposite of the truth."

While they waited for the ambulance, Pierre toured the other rooms of the house looking for the point of entry, while Nate took another look at the girl. She had not moved, but it seemed that her breathing was even heavier than before.

"Claudia, we're the police. He can't hurt you anymore. We'll protect you. Okay, honey?" There was no reaction whatever. Her blonde hair hung in tangles, and dusty tear tracks streaked her cheeks. The face was expressionless, the soft grey eyes fixed.

Nate tried touching her lightly on her shoulder. There was no response to indicate she was even aware of the touch. Nate spoke a bit louder, but still gently. "Claudia, my name is Nate. Talk to me, honey. I'm your friend." She gave no sign that she heard him.

Finally, with nothing to lose, Nate began to hum. He softly hummed, "Rock a Bye Baby." Toward the end of the tune, though she remained motionless, her lips moved slightly. "Police," she said.

"Yes, you're safe now," Nate said. "Listen, we have to take you to the hospital to make sure you're okay. Do you want to get dressed?" She remained sitting rigidly on the floor and made no answer.

◆

Nate and Pierre returned to the living room, where Wildman was now sitting in a chair talking with Harry. Nate spoke first. "Harry, I know your client is still stunned, but we don't have time to wait. Any way you can help get some information out of him?"

"Well, he has started to talk to me. He's not a suspect, right?" Harry asked.

"Right, Harry," Pierre said.

Wildman told them what he knew, which was little enough. He had run an errand the evening before, and left Claudia alone. She had planned no visitors. When he returned, she was missing. There was no note, so he began calling her friends. Then he spent the rest of the night waiting for her to call or come home. This morning he decided to search the house, not really looking for her so much as for some clue where she had gone. He found her in the basement just as she was now, refusing to budge and apparently deeply traumatized.

They heard the paramedics at the door coming in with the stretcher. Harry left Wildman with Pierre while he and Nate went back down to the basement to watch over Claudia as the medical team prepared to transport her.

◆

The two paramedics approached the girl to examine her. Harry watched them for a moment, but then his attention was drawn to Nate, who stood nearby shaking his head and then began to pace. When the paramedics told the girl to lie down so they could put her on the stretcher, Nate closed his eyes and pressed his lips tightly together.

Harry pondered why the girl would sit cross-legged on the cold concrete floor all night, and now, even as the paramedics urged her to lie down, why she refused. Nate began to pace more rapidly, and Harry wondered why he seemed so disturbed. Then Nate stood staring at the girl, his long arms spanning the space between two foundation pillars and his burly shoulders hunched. The paramedics were gently trying to force her to lie down on the gurney when Nate snapped his head up.

"Stop!" Nate shouted at the paramedics. "Don't move her."

"Why not?" one of the startled men asked.

"I don't *know* why, dammit! But make sure everyone at the hospital knows to keep her in exactly that position until they find out why she doesn't want to lie down."

"Okay, but what are we looking for?"

"With that bastard, it could be anything," Nate said.

She was as stiff as a seated jade Buddha when the men picked her up. With Nate and Harry supporting her back to keep her upright, they all went precariously up the stairs. Harry could imagine how bizarre the scenario looked.

Nate called over to Pierre, who was still with the grandfather, "Pierre, you clean up here. I'm going with the girl to the hospital. Have the uniforms take my car over there." He tossed his keys to Pierre while Harry tried briefly to comfort his client. He saw Nate get in the ambulance with Claudia. There Nate braced his feet against the opposite wall and put one arm gently around the traumatized girl to keep her from falling over. The driver moved out very slowly.

CHAPTER FOUR

The ambulance took them to San Francisco General Hospital, which had one of the best trauma clinics in the nation. The paramedics transferred Claudia to the gurney still stiffly upright, and rolled her straight into emergency services. Doctor Barbara Nelson, an attractive young trauma physician already acquainted with Nate, entered the hallway and approached them. As the procession entered the admitting room bearing their seated Buddha, Dr. Nelson stood with hands on hips, looking puzzled.

She drew Nate aside. "You sure know how to make an entrance, Nate," the doctor said quietly. "What have you got here?"

"Latest victim of the Hellhound, Barb. You know he always butchers them or does something else spectacular, but other than a head cut, we have no idea what he did to her to put her into this state." Nate filled her in on what he knew and then said, "I gotta figure there's a good reason she won't move, so I had them maintain her exact position until you could check it out."

"Good move. Put her over there, guys."

Nate stayed with them. An orderly removed the girl's blanket and draped her with a sterile sheet while Barbara began checking her over. She turned the Med-Alert bracelet so she could read the words "Rheumatic Heart Disease," as Nate looked over her shoulder. She shone a light into the victim's eyes to check pupillary reflexes, and then checked respiration, skin color, temperature, and pulse. "Ventricular tachycardia at 150 beats per minute," she called out to her team.

"Oh crap," one of the nurses said. "And she's rheumatic too."

"Got that right. Put her on a heart monitor stat," Barbara called over her shoulder. She turned back to the girl and asked gently, "Honey, do you feel chest pains? Are you light headed?" Getting no response, the doctor looked at Nate.

"She's stopped communicating, totally. I have no idea what's wrong with her," Nate said.

The doctor then began gently and methodically palpating Claudia's body. "It could be lots of things," she said. "Either she's received some hidden physical trauma that's stressing her entire system, or it's emotional. We've got to find out which, with or without her help. Nothing so far, Nate, but I'll tell you one thing. She's either in a lot of pain, or she's getting *more* terrified as time passes. Her heart is pounding and her breathing is accelerated, and that's *very* risky for someone with her cardiac history."

"What *is* rheumatic heart disease?" Nate asked.

"Rheumatic fever is a childhood disease," she said as she continued checking her patient. "It causes inflammation of the heart and can leave the patient with permanent heart damage. How long has she been like this?"

"Forty minutes since we arrived at her home, and something like eleven hours before that," Nate whispered, "and I noticed it too. Her breathing is getting faster, and it was already heavy when we found her."

"If we can't return her heartbeat to normal, she'll die," Barbara said. "Can't you give her a drug to slow her heart?"

"Could, but I won't until I know what's driving her pulse. It could kill her. Airway's clear. LOUIE, blood screen STAT! I want all central nervous system stimulants, psychoactive, and recreational drugs." Nate watched as Louie drew the girl's blood into vials with red, green, and blue tops and ran off.

"LISA," Barbara shouted, "start with the right foot and palpate your way up. Look for any pathology. Sam, take the left foot. GO!" Barbara began kneading the girl's shoulders while continuing to monitor her eyes for any reaction to the palpation.

"Look for any stain or smell indicating possible chemical absorption through the skin; hemorrhage; broken bones; skull damage; any abnormality." She sniffed Claudia's hair and her clothing. Then she began palpating her armpits and chest, and suddenly yelled, "BP?"

"One-seventy over one hundred, and rising, doctor," a nurse called out.

"Pulse?"

"One sixty-five. Rhythm's still regular, Doctor."

"Damn," she said, turning to Nate with a frustrated growl. "If we don't find it soon, her heart will begin to fibrillate, and I'm going to have to defibrillate her and pray."

"How bad is fibrillating?" Nate asked her.

"Fibrillation means the heart is only quivering, it's not pumping effectively. Blood pressure falls; blood stagnates inside the heart; clots can shoot to the brain; stroke; brain damage. *Real* bad."

Turning to the patient, she pleaded, "Come on, baby, TALK TO ME." She murmured to the girl while checking her eyes with a penlight. "I've got a kid sister looks a little like you. Of course, she's not as pretty as you. You play soccer? She loves soccer."

Nate watched the nurse now examining Claudia's neck when he heard her suddenly suck her breath in, then hiss, "Needle puncture over left carotid, Doctor."

"WHERE'S THAT BLOOD SERIES, LOUIE?" Barbara called out, and then dropped her voice to address the girl again. "How do you keep your nails so long, Claudia? Mine split every time one gets even halfway...BLOOD PRESSURE?"

"One ninety over one fifteen, doctor. What is *happening* to her?" another nurse asked.

"Pulse?" Barbara barked.

"180."

Louie rushed back into the room. "They found something, Doc, but they don't know what it is yet."

"What the hell does that mean?" Barbara scowled.

"All they could tell me so far is that she's been given some kind of toxic cocktail," Louie said. "So far they've identified morphine, a nerve toxin in the class of Fugu fish, scopolamine, and more they still can't even classify."

"That makes no sense," Barbara said instantly. "Those are all depressants, and she's reacting like she's on stimulants. We've got to keep looking, and tell them double time on the analysis of the rest of the chemicals. We are *losing* her."

Barbara frowned and slipped her hand around the patient's back to feel over her kidneys and then lower between the girl's buttocks. "Nothing. Spin her around, guys. Knees to the outside." She continued palpating her stomach, left, right, center. She probed softly but deeply, watching the face for reaction. "I don't know," she said. "There seems to be some rigidity in the abdomen, but I'm not sure."

"BE READY WITH THE PADDLES IF SHE STARTS TO FIBRILLATE," her voice rang out again. "Nate, if I have to defib, stay clear, or the electric shock that starts her heart will stop yours."

Nate shifted so he could see Claudia's face, now showing a subtle increase in tension. She was beginning to wheeze in rapid-fire rhythm.

"I think I'm getting warmer," Barbara said and promptly kneeled down on the floor in front of the girl. "Support her back. Bring her hips right to the edge of the gurney." She reached out with her gloved middle finger and gently probed the patient's vagina to the first knuckle. "Nothing. Move her legs." She shifted position and pushed to the second knuckle, bracing her left hand on Claudia's back. Claudia's breath was now sucking in and out frantically.

Barbara called out, "I'VE GOT SOMETHING HERE. It's small and hard, cylindrical, I think. I've got my finger on it. I can get it. Got it!"

She drew out a small tube, which appeared to be a section of pink plastic soda straw, crimped at both ends. She held it up to the light and announced, "It's got something inside, a scrap of paper, I think."

"Open it and read it," said Nate. The nurse took it and unrolled a small spindle of paper with one word on it—"Boom!"

Dr. Nelson stared for a grim moment at Nate and then said loudly over her shoulder to the others in the room, "Anyone who wants to leave has my permission. This could be an explosion zone." No one moved. "Move her legs wider," Barbara said. "I can't get deep enough with her sitting like this."

Nate watched as the doctor closed her eyes and, with head turned, seemed to focus her senses on her fingertips. She pushed her middle finger as deep as she could, as if she were trying to piece together a Braille picture of what was there. "Uh-Oh, I feel something else. It's hard and much bigger."

"X-RAY!" she yelled. An orderly quickly wheeled a portable unit into place, while nurses positioned the film against the girl's low back.

"*Could* it be a bomb?" Barbara asked Nate.

"It could. The technology is there to make one that small." His mouth twisted in dismay.

A technician pushed a button to snap the picture, and Nate heard a buzz while seeing a flash of light. Then a small flume of smoke rose from the unit.

"Shit!" frowned Barbara. "Get another one. NOW."

"BP and pulse?" she called over her shoulder.

"Two ten over one twenty, and pulse is regular at 200."

"Louie, what did Lab give for RBC?"

"A perfect mid-normal red blood cell count, Doc."

"Damn, doesn't make sense," Barbara said through her teeth. Then, "Prep an OR," she yelled. "Possible laparoscopy or vaginal extraction. Type and match the blood, Louie."

"Shall I page the GYN resident, Doctor,?" a nurse asked.

"No. Page Ashton. He's the best. Ask him if he'll come as a favor to me. Tell him it could be dangerous. Oh, and try to find some sand bags for the OR," she glared at Nate.

One orderly began swabbing the girl's stomach and groin with Betadyne solution while another pulled out a shaving kit and prepped to shave her. Nate studied Claudia's face. She was not reacting in the least to any of this.

Barbara suddenly stood up and sat on the edge of the gurney and studied her shoes. The immediate silence was deafening, and was first broken by Nate. "What's wrong?"

"Nothing more to do until the new X-ray unit gets here."

Ten long seconds passed without a word, and then a female voice shouted

"VENTRICULAR FIBRILLATION, DOC. BLOOD PRESSURE FALLING FAST AT...NINETY-FIVE OVER SIXTY-FIVE."

A technician grabbed the defibrillation paddles and leaned in, but Barbara waved him away. The patient jerked and began to sway, and had to be held upright so she did not fall off the gurney. Her eyes rolled upwards. A male nurse braced her back and Barbara began rhythmically pumping her hands on her chest to force her heart to contract. Nate stared in disbelief.

"Why don't you use the defibrillator? You said you could stop it that way."

"Can't use the paddles, Nate. That's 120 volts of electricity in those paddles. If it's a bomb, what do you think would happen?"

"Boom," Nate whispered. "He planned this whole damn drama, didn't he?"

"Think so," Barbara said with a grimace as she continued thumping the heart.

◆

Twenty seconds later an orderly wheeled a portable fluoroscopy unit rapidly into the room. While Claudia continued trembling, Barbara swung the cart into position. She flipped the switch to the screen, and there it was. Nate looked over the doctor's shoulder and saw what appeared to be a closed knife about four inches long. And nothing else.

"It's all the way to the cervix," Barbara said. "FORCEPS," she called out. Nate moved out of the way as Barbara lubricated the instrument with KY Jelly and slowly slipped it into Claudia, searching for the object to get a grip on it. "Have those paddles ready and as soon as I'm clear, hit her," Barbara shouted. Claudia's face was ghastly white, and she was shaking uncontrollably. An intern was poised with a paddle in each hand, arms extended like a hawk's wings in mid swoop.

Nate stood frozen as the knife came out smoothly. It was no bomb. It was a folding knife, and it was closed. Open, it was a vicious weapon, but closed it seemed to be harmless. Just as soon as the knife was clear of the girl, the intern applied the paddles to her chest, and the power button was pushed. Claudia jumped in a violent spasm while Barbara carefully transferred the knife to the stainless steel basin next to the gurney. She released the forceps as two orderlies lunged to keep Claudia from falling off the gurney. The girl collapsed into their arms at the same moment that the knife dropped two inches to the basin with a small clang.

The sound was immediately followed by a much louder clang as the knife jumped out of the basin into the air and catapulted onto the floor, spinning in circles. Now the knife was quite open, and Nate could see that it was a switch blade knife. It had opened so easily that Nate suspected the spring had been tampered with to make the opening mechanism hair-triggered.

♦

Barbara looked at the heart monitor screen and announced, "Normal sinus rhythm. BP rising." Then she shouted to the room full of medical attendants, "CANCEL SURGERY. CANCEL THE OB. CANCEL THE BLOOD." She pulled the fluoroscopy unit away from Claudia and sat next to her, gently putting her arms around her and rocking her for a moment. "You poor baby. You were just so scared. That's why your heart was breaking. But it's all right now. It's okay," she said, stroking the girl's hair.

Nate blurted, "My God, Barbara, if you had used the paddles while the knife was still in her, and she jumped..."

"Shhhhhh," whispered Barbara.

Nate recovered himself, nodded, and asked for a large plastic bag. One was produced, and a nurse picked up the knife with the forceps and slipped the evidence into the bag, handing it to him. Claudia stared straight ahead and did not react.

One nurse shucked her gloves and extracted a cell phone from her pocket. She made a call, waited, and said a little more intensely than she had perhaps intended "Meghan? It's Mom." She forced some calm into her voice and added, "It's nothing, really. I just wanted to hear your voice."

"Geez, Nate, this is one sick puppy," Barbara said, looking Claudia over. She again checked pulse and BP and found that they were returning to more normal levels. "Give her two milligrams of Coumadin to prevent an embolism," she ordered at last.

"Good job, everybody. I'm admitting her to psych when she's discharged from recovery. That's it." She stripped off her latex gloves and threw them on the floor. She and Nate walked to the lounge area.

"This could be a big break regarding the Hellhound," Nate told her.

"Yeah, a catatonic victim. Big break. For your purposes, she might as well be dead."

"I know. I meant the knife. I've never seen a folding knife that didn't collect lint between the blades. You wouldn't believe how talkative a spot of fuzz can be."

"I hope so, Nate. On the off chance that I should get any sleep in the next couple of days, I'm sure it will be a peaceful repose knowing he's still out there." She looked him straight in the eyes, and for the first time showed some indication that her steely courage had limits. Nate paused while she made an effort to speak through a constricted throat. "Nate, I've seen a lot of sick crap in this E.R., but I've never seen anything that scared me as much as this. Get this guy. Any way you have to." She walked away, shaking her head.

♦

Nate's own knees were still trembling as he walked haltingly into the parking lot. He stopped at the uniformed officer standing next to his car, took the keys from his hand without a word, and got behind the wheel just as daylight was beginning to fade. He pulled out and drove nowhere in particular. Some time later, he pulled into the scenic overlook on the San Francisco side of the Golden Gate Bridge. He got out and slammed the door.

San Francisco was nothing if not changeable. The foggy day had evolved into a warm September evening, and crystal highlights shone in the cityscape. It was peacefully quiet.

Nate put his hands on the rail and looked down at the rolling waves. The whispering rush of the swells rose to a roar as tons of brine crashed and exploded into mist on the rocks. Two seals barked at each other somewhere in the darkness below. "Now it starts," he whispered out loud to the seals.

CHAPTER FIVE

Early next morning, Nate checked in at homicide, and, of course, Pierre was already there. If Pierre ever slept, it was contrary to the legend at the Hall. Nate briefed him on the doings at the hospital and began working on his official report. At nine o'clock he called over to forensics and talked to Kendra Singh, the lab analyst on duty. Pierre heard Nate's half of the conversation. "Ken, it's Nate. Did you pick up the drop box stuff yet? Yeah, the knife is mine. I need that ASAP, Ken. It's the Hellhound for sure. I've got to have the analysis right away."

♦

Sixty-five minutes later Ken called Nate and told him to come to the lab, where he handed him his report. In it Ken had catalogued various rare and exotic traces that he found embedded in the knife. "It's all there. Rare Amazonian orchid pollen; Georgia clay; raw petroleum traces; an undyed silk thread; coal dust; a fish scale. You want me to go on?"

"Some of those things are rare enough that we could trace all the places that knife has been, right?" Nate asked. "By a process of elimination we could narrow down suspects who might have been to all those places."

"Forget it, Nate. There's no way all that could have gotten in there by accident. Those substances have been planted."

"You mean he collects these things for months and embeds them in the knife, just so he can laugh at the police stumbling over his false clues?"

"That's how it reads to me," Ken said.

"Yeah, I get it. Disinformation, Pierre calls it. But this isn't just a killer who hates women. This is a guy with a compulsion to prove how smart he is."

"Yes, a man who doesn't mind toiling tedious hours just so we can admire his handiwork."

"Wait a second, Ken. Since some of this stuff is rare, maybe we can trace him by where he had to go to collect it."

Ken's eyes widened. "Yes. If there are only a few places to get them, maybe someone could remember a face."

"Can you show me some of these items under the microscope?" Nate asked. "Sure. Anything particular you want to see?"

"The thread, the pollen, any of the solid objects."

"I'm already set up. Now's as good as ever."

Ken showed Nate the thread under the scope. It was beige and translucent looking, a short piece that was curled and crimped. Next he saw the orchid pollen, a small sliver of wood, and then a fish scale.

"What are those short parallel indentations in the scale?" asked Nate.

"Yes, I see it. I don't know. It's not a normal feature of a fish scale. Circular parallel patterns, yes, but not straight ones."

"Show me the piece of wood again, please," Nate asked.

Ken set it up and gestured grandly to the viewfinder. Nate looked and let out a whistle. There it was again. Three parallel indentations, same spacing, same length.

"Any ideas, Ken?"

Ken grinned broadly. "I know exactly what that is. It's the impression of a pair of tweezers. I have a pair in the lab just like the ones that made these marks."

"I suppose he would have bought a fresh, unused tweezers for this job. No way would he pluck eyebrows or remove splinters with it, getting messy skin, hair and DNA all over it."

"Of course not," said Ken.

The two went very quiet and just looked at each other for a moment. Then Nate spoke. "Total hush, Ken, okay? Report to me personally, and obliterate this report," he said handing it back to him. "No copies. No trace. And don't write anything else."

"Write about what?" Ken asked.

Nate's only answer was a grunt and a nod, and he headed for the door. He returned to the Homicide Office on the fifth floor of the Hall of Justice to find Pierre sitting at his desk. In his civilian clothes Pierre wore his Inspector's badge on his belt, along with his holster with its 40 caliber Beretta semi-automatic pistol.

The room was large by police standards, to accommodate their files. It bore the mark of the paper-intensive nature of murder investigations. Lining two walls were fifteen filing cabinets, upon which were sprawled mattress-thick piles of computer printouts, in no obvious order. These piles catalogued suspects, vehicles, evidence, and case reports.

Pierre's desk could barely hold a computer and a lined yellow pad. Rarely and only briefly, it could also hold the edge of a rookie's butt, but this was not a mistake that was ever made twice. Pierre's left hand massaged his temple as he held an incident report in the other hand. Once more Pierre was poring over unsolved San Francisco rapes and murders, looking for patterns and parallels; looking for the Hellhound, who for eight years had been preying on San Franciscan women in defiance of Pierre's considerable skills.

Nate eyed Pierre for a moment. Pierre was widely considered to be the best homicide investigator in the state, and he did not take failure lightly. Even Nate with his brief tenure had heard the story of how Pierre had cracked the panty rape case. Five women had been found raped and strangled with their panties. Pierre haunted prisons and pumped stoolies until he heard the rumor he knew had to be out there. They bragged sooner or later. They had to. Pierre had "coincidentally" met the suspect in a bar, and began talking to him. Over a series of drinking sessions Pierre began to float woman-hating diatribes. It seemed that Pierre's new buddy was a kindred soul. Finally, after a month of schmoozing the man, the suspect had confided that he liked to choke a woman after "making love" to her. "Oh?" Pierre wondered, "with what?" Once they started making plans to do a team rape, Pierre had enough history and detail to put him away for life.

In twenty-four years with the S.F.P.D. and seventeen in homicide, Pierre La Croix had failed to solve only two serial rape or murder cases. One was the Zodiac, and the other was the Hellhound.

Inspector La Croix had neither wife nor child. His work was his life, and at age forty-four he pursued his career with linear determination. Many cops considered Pierre a humorless social outcast, but all respected his abilities, both within and outside his department.

Pierre pulled out a crime report along with a binder of post mortem photos, and began studying both again.

"How many times have you read that report, Pierre?" Nate asked.

"No idea, buddy."

"You've put his Modus Operandi on the Serial Killer Intelligence Network?" Nate asked.

"Yeah, but SKIN has never made even one match. Apparently this gentleman is all San Francisco's. And why are you suddenly interested in this old case?"

Nate closed his eyes briefly and looked at Pierre. "I guess seeing a victim personally has an impact."

"No shit, and this was the gentlest strike he ever did."

"Yeah, I've heard. How much do you know for sure about him at this point?"

"Damn little. He limps. He's probably white. He takes pains to cause extreme mental anguish to his victims, and he's about 6'0" to 6'2" in height. But for my money, his most distinguishing characteristics are his obsession with grandstanding and his planning for every contingency. If he isn't a chess player, he should be. No matter what goes wrong, he seems to have several backup plans. He's good, Nate. Real good. Once he was cornered in a blind alley by a patrolman."

"So he shot his way out?"

"That's what your average perp might do in that situation. No, our Hellhound just plain vanished. Dozens of men searched the area. Windows, sewers. No trace whatever."

"I've been meaning to ask you. How did he get that name?"

"The father of the second known victim was talking to the press. He was a college professor of literature, and he called him that. It stuck. Every one of the victims was a teen-aged girl. Every one white. These were not kids from the street. Every one was…what?…innocent. Maybe they were selected to suffer just because they were so unspoiled."

"And he always tortures them?"

"No. Usually, but not always. He doesn't stick to any one M.O., except maybe the victim profile. One he cut up and then killed. Another he raped, doused with boiling water and then burned up with gasoline. Another was tied up, raped, and sprinkled with acid. When she worked the gag off and started screaming, neighbors called the police. When they broke the door in, it triggered a bomb that killed the girl and three officers. Blinded another. It was a sophisticated device, so he probably has training."

"I never heard any of that," Nate said.

"For good reason. I do my best to withhold details from the public. I don't want copycats claiming credit. The politicos would love that, so they could shut down the investigation and claim they made the city safe. You know the drill. I also don't want to cause anguish to the victims' families by releasing the details. I didn't even know these girls, and the stuff he does to them keeps me awake at night."

"Yeah, I know. Maybe what you need is a life outside this job. Get a family."

Pierre's face turned expressionless, and he stared at Nate for a moment. Finally he said softly, "I think I got all the family I can stand already," and resumed studying the photo album.

As Pierre was reviewing the photos, a uniformed patrolman walked in to turn in a report on a barroom knifing that had ended in a death. As he passed behind Pierre, he let out a whistle and hooted, "Whooooie. The naked and the dead!"

Pierre spun around and erupted out of his chair without warning. His immense left hand grabbed the patrolman's throat with steely fingers, while his right fist slammed into his midsection. Then he brought up his knee viciously into the helpless man's groin. Nate rushed over and grabbed Pierre by the shoulders, dragging him away. Pierre yelled, "If you ever disrespect a victim like that again, I'll break your fingers one by one."

"Let him be, Pierre. He's just out of academy, and he doesn't know any better." Pierre sat down at his desk again, saying nothing.

Nate helped the patrolman to his feet and supported him while moving him into the hall. He talked to him for a few minutes to make sure he was all right. It took a bit longer to convince him to drop the incident. Nate told him to take the rest of the day off, and promised to square it with his Lieutenant.

As the officer shuffled down the hall toward the elevators, Nate stepped back into the office. He sat down in the chair next to Pierre's desk and stared at him.

"You stuck in a loop, Pierre?"

Pierre sighed and nodded. There had been no break in the case for months. "He almost seems to know when to lie low, Nate. It's maddening. And when he does move, he does it so carefully that he leaves nothing behind. I comb carpets and study door jambs with a magnifying glass and don't get so much as a hair. Never a print. No DNA. No good descriptions."

"Then I've got good news for you." Nate lowered his voice. "Ken Singh found what appear to be traces of DNA on some of the crap pulled out of the knife in the Wildman case."

Pierre straightened up, his eyes opening wider. "What? How?"

"Apparently our boy used some tweezers to plant false clues in the folding knife, but the tweezers had been used before."

"Who else knows about this?"

"Ken, me, and you. He's not even writing anything for now."

"Good work. Keep it that way."

"You've never been able to find a pattern to know when he's going to strike again, or where?"

"On the contrary, I feel like he studies me and anticipates *my* next move. I've never seen anything like it. The only reason the Zodiac got away with it is that we didn't have the technology we have now. You know as well as I do, if Joe Blow walks through our lobby at midnight, we can find a dandruff flake the next morning and use the DNA to ID him. But this guy..." Pierre shook his head.

"All right, Pierre. Relax. I know you won't take a vacation, but take the rest of the day off. I'll cover your other cases. It might be smart to lie low for a bit after that incident just now."

At that moment the corpulent figure of Captain Clifton (Tiny) Ratto entered the room. Pierre and Nate simultaneously swiveled their necks to look at each other. Word traveled fast.

"Pierre, what the hell is going on? You think just because you're some super star you can use patrolmen for punching bag practice?"

"Captain, the rookie made some really crass remarks about a victim…" inserted Nate.

"Stay out of it, Hutchinson, and get back to work. I want a word with Pierre."

Nate pulled out a file to work on and sat down at his desk. Captain Ratto sat on Pierre's desk and glared at him. His big buttocks spread out and lapped over the edge of the desk, and when he turned his head his cheek wattles wiggled. He wiped a bead of sweat from his hairline and grunted, "I give you a lot of slack, La Croix. I know what you can do, and I respect that, but that don't give you license to freak out. Get it?"

"I do my job."

"Nobody ever said you didn't. You do more than your job. That's not what I'm talking about, and you know it. I'm talking about you working night and day for years trying to catch that asshole, and getting burned out."

Pierre looked up silently, measuring the fat man.

"Look, Pierre, I've always given you a long leash. You work harder than anyone else in the P.D. I know that. You breaking up on me? If you are, I got a right to know."

"No. I'm all right. It won't happen again." Pierre smiled faintly and got up. Setting his beret on his head, he walked out without a word.

Nate watched him go, and then Tiny lumbered out after him, shaking his head in displeasure. Nate saw that Pierre had left the photo binder open on his desk. As he reached to put it away, he caught a glimpse of the worst pictures he had ever seen. The victim looked to be about sixteen or seventeen. A straight razor lay beside her nude body. Her lips, ears, and nose were gone. Even in death the face revealed that these things had not happened post-mortem. Nate shut his eyes and fought nausea. He slammed the binder in the drawer and locked it up. Then he sat down and choked back tears.

CHAPTER SIX

The next morning Harry Maxwell paused a moment at the door of his office building at Boardman Place. He glanced to his right at the eight-story granite facade of the Hall of Justice and then at the wispy clouds floating above it. He trudged up the stairway, where he could smell Bridget's coffee already brewing.

"Morning, Bridge," he greeted her as usual.

"Morning, Oaf," she greeted him as usual, and as usual it made him smile. He remembered three months earlier, when this Cockney girl fresh from London came seeking a job. Harry figured there were hundreds of secretaries with adequate skills, but someone who was sharp and fun to work with was a prize worth gleaning.

The "Oaf" business arose when Harry would just walk out without a word to her. He could remember her voice clearly when she would call out after him, "Are you off, then?" Except that in her accent it sounded like "Are you Oaf?" Harry had answered, "Yep, that's me. I'm the Oaf," and it stuck. Bridget worked Tuesdays, Wednesdays, and Thursdays. On Monday and Friday the office seemed awfully empty.

He walked back to the kitchen, found the cups and spoons where they were supposed to be, and poured himself a cup of coffee. He returned to the front room and waited by her desk for her to finish. On her desk were neatly arranged her appointment calendar, message pads, and a small framed photo of her adopted stray cat. Two lush plants hung over her desk. He overheard her bright, lilting voice dealing with someone on the phone, a skill for which he valued her considerably.

"Oh, well, that's not going to work then, is it? No, I should think not," he heard her inform someone. "Well, what's needed is for you to bring the stationery over yourself this afternoon, isn't it? We can't be sending out threatening letters to people on paper towels then, can we?"

When she "rang off," Harry stood before her sipping coffee, and waited until the wide blue eyes looked up. "Well then, that will do nicely, won't it?" he said.

"Yes, luv, happy to oblige," she rejoined with a bright smile. "Oh, and your investigator called and wants to hear back this morning."

"Which investigator?"

"The boozy black man who always flirts with me."

"Don't they all?" Harry said.

"Not with the same degree of skill, I shouldn't think."

Harry chuckled. "That would be Tyrone Washington. If you don't mind the high octane breath, he does a great job."

◆

Harry opened the door to his office, a room in which Bridget's ministrations were forbidden. He walked in and saw that all was as he had left it. There were a few thousand pages of paper stacked about, with corners jutting at 360 different angles. The telephone peeked out from under a deposition transcript. He plopped down in his leather chair and saw a smear of Man Hung Hu's lobster sauce on the glass front of the photo of Alissa, Yvonne, and himself. He found a napkin, cleaned it off and then polished the glass. When it was clean, the eight-year-old smiled out at him, with Harry behind her holding both arms around her. He traced his finger over her face and put the picture back down.

He took the deposition transcript off the phone and tossed it into the bookcase on his right. It landed on the third shelf and knocked over another photo. He reached over to right it and flicked his fingers to throw off the dust. Harry's father looked out at him glumly from an aged garden chair with a drink holder on the arm. As his eyes lingered a moment on the photo, his father's voice lived again. "Harry, you dipshit, you spilled my drink."

Harry picked up the phone and hit the button marked "Tyrone." While he listened to the dial, he looked across to the wall of plaques. Maybe he should let Bridget in to clean them. His Colombia Law School degree was thick with dust, as were his California Bar certificate and Phi Beta Kappa award. Tyrone answered after seven rings.

"Hey, Tyrone. Harry here. What's up?"

"Hi, Harry. You get my proof of service on the security guard in Watkins?"

"Yeah. Thanks." Harry frowned. "Umm, there wouldn't be any other reason you called, would there?"

"Well, yeah," came a voice that Harry could tell came from a broadly smiling mouth. "I...see...I got me this deuce, man. An' it's bullshit. See, I wasn't drunk, I had just two beers, but I like got this bad cold, so the dude that pulled me over thought..." Harry put the phone in his lap and cleaned his fingernails. Then he checked his calendar for the day's appointments and sorted the stack of phone messages. Then his instinct told him it was time, much as a Labrador retriever will sniff the wind to know that winter is coming on, so he picked up the phone again to hear Tyrone say, "You hear me, Harry?"

"Of course, Tyrone. Bring me the citation and a copy of the arrest report. and I'll see what I can do."

Harry could hear a rush of gratitude in the man's reply. "Oh, thanks Harry. I owe you big for this one."

"That's right. You do," Harry said. "That it for now?"

"Uh, yeah. Thanks again, Harry."

"Right, bye." Harry hung up, shaking his head. As soon as the phone hit the cradle, Bridge buzzed him.

"Oaf, Inspector La Croix called while you were on the phone. He said you could come over and pick up an autopsy report any time you want."

"Thanks, Bridge. Now's as good as ever." He grabbed his briefcase and made the short hop to Bryant Street and the Hall. Up ahead at the corner he saw his favorite beggar, Osmund, sitting in his accustomed place. "Hi, Oz," Harry said. Harry loved his outfits. Osmund did not have a lot in his life, but his wardrobe had style. Today he plied the pavement in dark slacks, red suspenders, and a white ruffled shirt with frayed sleeves and a missing button. He was definitely the classiest looking panhandler on the street.

"Hey, Harr. How's that cute little girl of yours?"

"How do you know I have a daughter?"

"The great and powerful Oz sees all and knows all. I see her dropped off some Fridays. Cute kid. Looks smart too."

"So true. Makes her old man look dumb. Gotta run, Dude." As Harry started to leave, Osmund gave him a quiet nod, a small smile, and a tip of an imaginary hat.

Harry caught the unspoken hint and stopped. "Oh, want to play a game, Oz?"

"Howzit go?"

"I hold this dollar by my fingertips just so. You hold your thumb and forefinger right below mine as close together as you want but without touching. When I let go, we see if you're the kind of guy who lets money slip through his fingers."

"OK," Osmund said in a serious voice.

Harry looked into his eyes while Osmund watched the bill. When Harry released it, Osmund quickly squeezed his fingers together but closed on thin air as the bill floated to the ground.

"OK, Oz, that was practice. Ready?"

"Go," Osmund replied, biting his upper lip thoughtfully.

Harry set the trick up again, and again the greenback slipped down through the other's finger tips before he could pinch them closed. Harry picked up the bill and set it up one more time. Again the bill floated downward, unsullied by Osmund's fingers, while Osmund frowned with frustration.

"OK. That's it," Harry declared. Let's see...that was one practice and two wins. Here are your two dollars."

Osmund looked at Harry with confusion, and then asked tentatively, "But I lost, didn't I?"

"No, I said we'd find out if you're the kind of guy who lets money slip through his fingers, and you sure are. I can't think of anyone who needs a couple of bucks more than someone with that problem. See ya, Oz." Harry was gone. Reaching the far curb, he took the Hall's steps two at a time.

◆

Harry took the elevator to the fourth floor and walked into the Homicide Bureau. He didn't recognize the middle-aged female receptionist. He saw a magnet in the "IN" column under Pierre's name on the status board. "I'm expected," he said to her with a wave of his hand, and walked past her without waiting for an answer.

Nate was there at his desk studying some photos, and at the next desk two feet away Pierre sat reading a transcript. Harry waved to the two and greeted them cheerfully, "I'm impressed. You guys are always so hard at work earning my tax money."

"Hi, Harry," Nate said. "Not Pierre. He just got back from a leisurely lunch."

Pierre twisted his lips and said nothing. Harry walked over and positioned himself between the two desks facing Nate. The receptionist stormed in and began to explain that she had not admitted this man who had disturbed them. Her mouth froze in mid-sentence when Harry parked his behind on the edge of Pierre's desk. She had been present before, when young uniformed officers had done the same thing. Pierre had said nothing, but carefully placed his foot on the center of the top edge of his desk and then pushed suddenly, sliding the desk out from under the chiropractic candidates.

"Hi, Harry. Coffee? It's good stuff. I made it myself," Pierre said.

Harry knew that meant he used expensive beans, but it would be like mud, because Pierre let it cook all day. It would be particularly wretched by now. "Thanks, Pierre, but I'm tanked up."

"Harry," Nate asked, "have you met Julie? She's our new receptionist and filing clerk."

"A pleasure, madam," said Harry. Julie offered a confused smile and then quietly retreated. Nate slammed his lower desk drawer with a loud bang and swung his legs around just as Pierre asked Harry, "So you're after an autopsy report?"

Harry did not respond. Instead, his eyes went blank, and he stood as if frozen. Pierre always got an embarrassed look on his face when Harry got like this, and most everyone knew the cause. The loud bang had begun replaying memories in Harry's head. They were of another day and another loud report, followed by two more in rapid succession. A day when the ground came up fast at Harry, he was screaming, and holes were torn in his neck right over the carotid artery and in his shoulder. He was lying on top of another man, pressing the heel of his palm into an arterial spurt from the man's shoulder. With the other hand, he scooped up the loose gun. Then the deafening reports came again and again.

The wounded man's arms were splayed out to his sides in crucifixion position, and blood squirted out of his shoulder and puddled on the concrete. His head fell to the left, where it lay like a brick. Harry was shouting, "Fuck you, assholes. Come and die." The pistol in Harry's hand fired repeatedly into the parking lot. One gunman darted behind a concrete pillar supporting the freeway next to the Hall.

The gunman's pistol flashed again and again. Motes of concrete shrapnel hit Harry's face and that of the man he was trying to protect. The gunman was falling back, yelling to his accomplice to run. Harry whirled, keeping one hand sealed to the victim's geysering wound but letting his own blood flow as he fired again at the assassins. Then came the sound of feet running. Harry was still blanketing the man, his face close to his, grabbing his chin in one hand and screaming, "Don't you crap out on me." Then, toward the building and the Northern District Police Station, he screamed "AMBULAAANCE."

♦

Then Harry quashed those thoughts and was back in Homicide again. Nate was still staring quizzically at him as he moved to look over Nate's shoulder at the photos being reviewed.

"He's tall. About 6'1" to 6'3", and he's left-handed," Harry said.

"Thank you, Dr. Maxwell," Nate grunted.

"He's close, Nate," Pierre said. "How did you arrive at that, Harry?"

"Easy," said Harry, pointing to the bloody color picture. "Look at the depth of the slash on her throat. If he had been facing her, the deepest part would have been in the middle, where it sticks out the most. The deepest part is at the upper throat under her left chin. That's the part at the end of the slashing motion where his knife has had a chance to dig in deeper as he held her head still. The shallow part is at the lower right throat where he started. When he drew his knife to the outside, his arm naturally rose up, creating the lower to upper slash path. That means he was considerably taller than she was. She looks to be about 5'7". He had to reach down to bring his knife across her throat."

"A quick death then, Harry?" asked Nate.

"Afraid not. Look at the edges of the cuts. They're jagged. He started and stopped the knife more than once. My guess is that he taunted her as he slit her throat by degrees," Harry said. "There aren't too many that sick out there. Is this the Hellhound's handiwork?"

Nate frowned, silent. Pierre spoke, "Yeah, but keep this to yourself, Harry. Anyone else out there knows the details of this guy's work, and we'll have to close up shop and just record confessions until we collect our pensions."

"Don't tell me he's struck two days in a row?" Harry asked.

"No," Nate said. "This is an old case, the Roberson killing of five years ago."

"What did he do to the Wildman girl? Claudia. The newspaper accounts were vague this morning," inquired Harry.

"You don't need to know that, Harry," Pierre said. "In fact, the less you know about this guy, the better off you'll be. It doesn't involve you."

"Gee, Pierre, do you really think I'm the Hellhound's type?"

Pierre's only answer was, "Harry, leave it to the professionals."

"Well, I don't know about that, Pierre," interjected Nate. "That was an amazingly insightful photo reading he just did."

"Oh, sure. Anytime we need lawyers to do our jobs for us, we'll raise the alarm," Pierre said.

Harry was suddenly hearing different alarms of long ago, and staring off blankly again. Pierre's head dipped, and he sighed. On the day Harry was reliving, many alarms had sounded, and highly shined black boots had come running. Radios dueled, and men screamed for stretchers, panic in their voices. Harry still lay shielding the man the assassins had cut down, the gun still in his hand roaming left and right. His hand was bloody, and his face and collar. Harry held his face close to the other man, eyes half an inch from the other's, and implored, "Don't die on me." But Harry could see the light fading from his eyes as he tried to speak. Only a hiss escaped his lips. Harry leaned close and turned his ear to the other's lips, but no strength seemed left for speech. Then the other lifted his lips a micro-inch and kissed Harry's cheek.

"Are you okay, Harry?" Pierre asked. "Harry? Yo, Harry, are you all right?"

Harry looked up and smiled. "Yeah, I'm fine."

"Just stay clear of the Hellhound mess, Harry," Pierre continued. "You have no idea who you're dealing with."

"I think I do," said Harry. "He's a psychotic little moron who loves to terrorize, rape, torture and kill women, and he goes in for flamboyant escapades."

"NO," shouted Pierre, crashing a palm down on the desk. "No, he is NOT a 'little moron.' He hasn't managed to stay ahead of me for eight years by being stupid, and he is capable of anything. Stay out of this..."

They were interrupted by shouting and the sound of running footsteps coming down the hall. The noise entered the outer office, and they could hear a voice clearly now calling "Pierre! Pierre!" It was Lieutenant Gene Behrens of the Cyber Sleuths. His squad patrolled the Internet to catch pedophiles who tried to entice children into meeting them.

Behrens skidded into the room and laid his laptop computer on Pierre's desk. It was fitted with a modem for internet access. "He's online, Pierre," he said excitedly.

"The Hellhound? How do you know it's him?" Pierre asked.

"He knows some stuff you told me that no one else should know. Here, read back." Gene moused to the chat room's dialogue box, where all the occupants of the room could read each other's comments. He scrolled backwards so Pierre could read the dialogue that had been transmitted earlier. Nate, Pierre, and Harry all crowded around the screen, and read the title of the chat room, "DADDY'S LITTLE GIRLS."

"Oh man," said Nate. "I got a feeling I'm *really* not gonna like this."

BOPEEP15: Are you going to make your little girl behave, Daddy?
HARDGUY42: I always do, Sweetie. But you've got to obey completely.
HELLHOUND69: My little girl wears a knife in her pussy.
DADISGRL17: What the hell?
HARDGUY42: Ignore him, Bo. He's just a sick Hellhound wannabe.

*HELLHOUND69: Are you sure, Softguy? Why don't you give me
your name and address? You'll be safe, since I'm not the guy.*
*HARDGUY42: What's this about a knife? You trying to scare the
females?*
*HELLHOUND69: I really don't think you know what scared is,
asshole.*
MASTERRICH: This is no game. I'm calling the police.
HELLHOUND69: That would be good.
MASTERRICH: What's that about?
HELLHOUND69: Boom!

"That's it?" asked Pierre.

"Yes," said Gene. "From there on he hasn't talked anymore.
But the chat room members who didn't run away are talking about
him."

"But his name is still listed among the room occupants,"
Nate pointed out.

"That's right," said Gene. "It's like a phone connection is
still open, but you're not talking for a while. It must be him. No one
else would know about the 'Boom' note or the knife."

"He's waiting for us," Pierre said. "He left his calling card
and then waited for us to be alerted. He wants to play, or to gloat."

"Can we get online into this room?" Pierre asked.

"I already am," said Gene. "I'm SUITE15. It's how I found
him."

"Good," said Pierre. "Gene, get him talking while I trace
him. Nate, call into Mr. Chat and get the subscriber's ID and
address. Radio the address to me when you get it."

"Right, Pierre, but you don't really think he'll be waiting for
you, do you?" Nate asked.

"Probably not, but we can't pass up any chance. I'm gone."

Pierre rushed out the door while checking his Beretta,
slapping the clip back in.

Gene grabbed the phone, saying "I've got a hot line for
telephonic search warrants, and I'm pre-cleared to receive
subscriber information, so let me do it. Here, you talk to Mr.
Psycho," he said to Nate.

Gene got the warrant in two minutes, and was on the phone
to Mr. Chat. "Problem, Nate. The membership database is down.

They have to do a manual search." They sat and waited as the minutes passed. Then:

HELLHOUND69: Boring. Guess I should go kill some virgins.

"You'd better type something that will interest him before he boogies," Harry said. Nate rapidly typed:

SUITE15: And where will you find them, Hellhound?

A moment later came back:

HELLHOUND69: At last. Good afternoon, officer. I thought you were going to be silent and coy forever.

Nate and Harry turned to look at each other at the same instant.

SUITE15: Okay. What do you want?

"No," said Harry. "Don't follow him. Take the lead."

HELLHOUND69: Where is La Croix?
SUITE15: In San Francisco, just like you.
HELLHOUND69: If you don't stop boring me with dull-witted attempts like that one, I'm leaving.

"I'm blowing it, Harry," Nate said. "I don't know what to say to him."

"Here, let me try," said Harry, reaching for the keyboard. "He wants to play. If he gets caught up, he might reveal something about himself."

SUITE15: Why does someone with a pole as short as yours stand so tall among psychotics?
HELLHOUND69: Ah, is there a bull mastiff among the bitches? Who do I have the honor of addressing?
SUITE15: Call me Ishmael.
HELLHOUND69: I'll call you Morbid Dick.
SUITE15: Well, you're the expert on morbid, so who am I to argue?

"Christ, Harry," hissed Nate, "Are you *trying* to provoke him?"

"Absolutely," Harry muttered. "Same technique you use on suspects, right? Get them pissed, and listen to them babble."

HELLHOUND69: Where is La Croix?

SUITE15: Out catching criminals that are man enough to victimize adult males. He snagged me, the janitor, to tend to you.

HELLHOUND69: Ahhh. An armchair-shrink janitor. Well then, perhaps you can tell me something about myself. Which would I choose between—driving a rose's thorns into a young girl's breasts, or taking her toe off with a bolt cutter? And why, Dr. Morbid?

SUITE15: Let's see. The toe.

HELLHOUND69: Excellent, but why?

SUITE15: The rose would symbolize an association between the beauty of the rose with the beauty of the girl. You hate women, so you'd pick the toe.

HELLHOUND69: A+, Dr. Morbid. Spoken like a man of some expertise with women.

SUITE15: My ex might disagree with you.

"Gene, what's holding them up?" Nate asked. "Tell them it's crisis urgent." Nate picked up the radio and got Pierre on. "Pierre, we've got technical problems. Mr. Chat's membership database is down. We're waiting on a manual search. I'll send the info as soon as I have it. Stand by until then."

Pierre's voice came back, "Acknowledged, Nate. Am proceeding to the entrance of the Duboce on ramp. That'll give me options for I-80, I-280 and 101. When you get it, have three back-up units meet me there on silent approach and await my arrival. Over and Out."

At that moment the chat room picked up again.

HELLHOUND69: And which would I prefer between these? Whip stripes on a girl's naked back, or a refreshing splash of boiling water?

SUITE15: The whip, because seeing the blood is the only way a pathetic piece of shit like you can get it up.

HELLHOUND69: I sense that you're feeling a bit of anger and frustration, Ishmael.

SUITE15: How would you know? Your intellect is more of a submarine than a rocket, just like certain other portions of your anatomy.

Gene shouted, "I got the name and address of the subscriber, and it's in San Francisco." Nate relayed to Pierre that he should highball it to Precita St. to talk to a Mr. Albert Wessells.

HELLHOUND69: You are the one who has gone too deep without any reserve tank. You will learn the price of that error. Thanks for helping with my quandary. Adieu for now.
MR. CHAT SAYS: HELLHOUND69 signs off.

"Dammit!" said Nate.

"Don't sweat it, Nate," Harry said. "When Pierre arrives, he'll barge in on some nerd whose online identity and password were stolen."

"Harry, do you realize that you told him that you're divorced? You left a trail, Harry. Not good, since you also pissed him off enough to get him interested in you."

"Guess I got caught up in it. What's done is done. If you want my input in the future, I'll be glad to help."

"Just keep it quiet. The less said about your involvement, the better. Okay, Harry, time for you to go," said Nate. Harry nodded.

He went back across the street to his office, where he worked on files the rest of the afternoon. At rush hour Harry glanced out at the sidewalks beginning to fill with scurrying people. Darkness gradually infiltrated the SoMa, the South Of Market Area, and the crowds faded. Then the night players emerged, like so many nocturnal crawdads scavenging the shallows for whatever might sustain them. As Harry packed his briefcase to leave, he glanced at the smiling picture of Alissa, Yvonne, and himself, from what seemed ages ago. With only three people, the house had always seemed so full.

CHAPTER SEVEN

It was Thursday morning. Two chattering birds and Harry Maxwell were up at four o'clock while most of the City's other life forms slept. Harry put his feet immediately on the floor to avoid the danger of oversleeping. He could see no glimmer in the sky, but the birds' clock seemed to know that morning was imminent. He pulled on his shorts, tank top, and running shoes, and went jogging in the dark. When he returned home, he checked his watch and hurriedly changed into his gee. His Karate instructor hated it when he was late, which was every time. Harry looked forward to the sessions, because they were energizing. He wasn't so sure how much he had learned in three years, but it was fun.

At 6:43 a.m., Harry arrived at his office. He fired off correspondence and did legal research on an illegal seizure of evidence in a drug case. At 7:00 a.m., he decided it was a good time to go visit some new clients in the sixth-floor jail before the jailers got busy unshelving prisoners to stock the morning court calendars.

After signing the visitor's book and having his briefcase checked by the entry guard, Harry got to the first interview room. He smiled when he read an inmate's graffiti scrawled on the lower wall. It neatly summed up the author's ability to describe his concerns: "For a good time call Rosie. For a lot of time call my lawyer."

Harry interviewed three clients charged with sales of crack cocaine; rape; and assault with a firearm. Only the rape defendant claimed to be innocent. The "innocent" clients were the ones Harry's piercing stare drilled straight through. He was usually right, and he always felt that knowing the truth when you see it, is easy. The hard part is believing enough in it to stick your neck out.

When he was done, Harry signed out. He waited until the door lock buzzed, and then pushed hard against the heavy metal slab. He went through, and the door swung closed with a heavy slam. He thought it might be a good time for a shoeshine, if he could intercept Rick Hansen's wanderings.

On the first floor Harry spied Hansen's stooped shoulders right away. He was kneeling at the motorcycle boots of a California Highway Patrol officer outside Department 4. Hansen was a good looking, Nordic-type guy of about twenty-four, with eyes having more depth than one might expect from one in his occupation. He told Harry that he would be next. Harry sat on a bench nearby and scooped up the morning paper that Rick always provided for his customers, a touch that along with his great shines made him popular at the Hall.

While Harry sat submerged in the newspaper he became vaguely aware of someone sitting down next to him, so he absently shifted over to make room. A hand came to rest lightly on his elbow, and he turned to see Pierre's face close to his. Leaning forward further, Pierre whispered into Harry's ear, "After you finish, can I see you upstairs about the little Web interview you did yesterday?"

Harry nodded, and Pierre stood up and walked toward the stairs. Pierre always took the stairs.

Not much later, Harry entered through the door marked "Homicide" and saw Julie rising with an outstretched hand to prevent his invasion of the inner offices. She buzzed Pierre, and in a moment Pierre appeared at the door. Harry started toward him. "No," Pierre said. "In the interview room down the hall." Harry fell in behind Pierre, with Nate following.

Pierre held the door, and when the three were inside, he closed and locked it. Turning his massive torso to Harry, he began without prologue. "What was the last thing I said to you yesterday, Harry? I told you that you were out of your league and to leave it to the professionals, didn't I? Damn! Do you have any idea what you've done?" Pierre turned and favored his partner with a glare that singed Nate's eyebrows. Still looking at Nate, he told Harry "If my *partner* here hadn't been present and allowed it all, I would arrest you for interfering with a police investigation."

"Ah, come on Pierre, I was just trying to help a buddy."

"Stow that buddy shit, Harry," Pierre growled. Harry glanced sidelong at the locked door and understood why they were in the interview room for this tea party instead of Homicide.

"You don't see that you've endangered yourself, me, and others, do you?" Pierre lowered his voice. "Harry, if someone stumbles accidentally across this guy's path, he reaches out in ways you can't predict. You cross him on purpose, and it gets to be a point of honor to screw with you. He's a game player with severe rules, Harry. The penalties are death and torture. Why on *earth* would you roll those dice?"

For once Harry was dumbfounded, but he was rescued by Nate, who interjected, "We didn't plan that, Pierre. Harry was there and had some good ideas to draw the guy out. It seemed to work."

"It doesn't matter, Nate. You don't involve civilians."

"We do it all the damn time," said Nate. "We consult UCSF professors, doctors, voice stress analysts, firearms experts, and even goddamn psychics when we need to."

"*But not Harry*," Pierre shouted. Harry heard the echo of his own name as the only sound in the still of the room. Nate looked at Harry, who was studying his brightly shined shoes. He looked at Pierre, perplexed, but Pierre was now looking down too. Nate turned back to Harry, who was now regarding the wall of the room, his eyes distant. When Nate spoke, Harry did not react. Pierre shook his head and pressed his lips together. In his mind Harry could hear running footsteps again, and shouts. Suddenly Harry was rolling off the body of the man as his pistol clattered to the pavement. Through the ringing in his head and the dizziness Harry was unaware now of the blood spurting from his neck into the face of the other bleeding man. Two stretchers were laid down, and the two bloody men were placed on them while a red light flickered across their faces again and again. Harry Maxwell was placed in the ambulance on the left and Pierre La Croix on the right.

But now Harry was back in the interview room, while Nate was addressing Pierre. "Your personal life is not my concern, sir, but what affects the case is my business. Is there something I don't know that I should know?"

"Not like you think, Nate," Harry answered after a moment. He told him the short version of the story. "It's not a secret, Nate. Most everyone in the department knows our history. I guess you just haven't listened to Hall gossip much since you came here from San Jose."

"I don't have the time or the inclination," said Nate stiffly.

Now Harry addressed Pierre. "Listen, Pierre, I appreciate your concern, but I think you're overstating the danger. You can't represent criminals without accepting the risk that one will take a loss personally and come back at you, but it's as rare as it is for them to go after an officer for doing his job. It just hardly ever happens."

Pierre sighed. "There's just no talking to you, is there, Harry? Okay. Here it is. Knowing you, I thought I might have to go this far." He reached into his coat pocket and drew out some scraps of newsprint paper and laid them out on the table. There were eight of them, each bearing a penciled sketch of a hangman's game in various stages of completion.

"He leaves me these," Pierre said, pointing at the drawings. Pierre looked at Harry and Nate and said softly, "He's been leaving them for me for years. I won't get one for a year, and then two in a month. He started with the bare scaffold years ago. Then one by one, they came with more parts added. I got the last one after the Claudia Wildman case. This one."

Pierre pointed to a slip of paper that had seven body parts drawn in—the head, neck, two arms, torso, one leg, and one hand. There were only four elements missing—the other hand, one leg, and two feet.

"What does it mean?" Nate asked.

"I think it's a countdown, or rather a count-up. When he finishes the body, I think he's going to kill me. It's personal. He leaves them in my car, at my apartment, in my desk at work. He wants to make sure I know he can take me any time he wants. Why do you think I kept you off this case as much as I could, Nate? You've got family. Why do you think I've been working this file night and day for eight years? I didn't want anyone else to get sucked into this whirlpool."

Harry's Adam's apple bobbed. He opened his briefcase and took out a piece of paper vibrating in his hand. On it was drawn a scaffold and a body with *eight* elements finished. Moisture appeared on Harry's forehead as he groaned, "Shit, I think I just jumped the queue. I found this in my briefcase this morning."

"God, Harry, this is exactly what I didn't want to happen," Pierre said. He took Harry's head between his hands and shook it gently. "Why wouldn't you listen?"

Nate reached into his own shirt pocket and slowly brought out a hangman with *nine* elements done, missing only a hand and a foot. "I found this in my shirt pocket this morning when I got dressed. Damn, this bastard even knows what shirt I'm going to wear? And he gets into my home? Who else gets these?" Nate asked.

"No one that I know of. Until now, I was the only one," Pierre said.

"What's his game?" Harry asked. "I'm brand new to this case yesterday, and he jumps me ahead of you on his murder list within twenty-four hours. How does he even know it was me on the chat line?"

"For all I know, he's tapped into the police department," Pierre said.

"I told you that you were giving him as much on you as you were getting from him," said Nate.

"Shit!" said Harry. "That means he knows all three of us. He knows what day Nate wears which shirt, that I'm divorced, and when and where Pierre sleeps."

"Yep," Pierre said.

"How much time do you think we have, Pierre?" Nate asked.

"I don't know. Suddenly he's changed the whole game. The attacks are coming more frequently now. The victims are closer together, and the hangman drawings are sure going into high gear."

"If I'm a target, I want in on finding him," Harry said.

Nate and Pierre looked at each other. Both nodded. Nate sighed. "I don't think there's much reason to refuse your help now, Harry."

"There isn't any choice anymore," said Pierre. "Harry, I know you've got a knack for investigation, and having a non-police viewpoint could help. At least if you're working closely with us, it'll be easier to protect you."

"I don't see why he'd go after me first, and then Harry," Nate said. "I don't fool myself into thinking I'm as smart as you, Pierre. No offense, but what sense does it make not to kill you first?"

"It's clear to me, Nate," Harry said. "Fear doesn't enter into it. He wants to kill us first so Pierre can squirm while watching us die. Why checkmate Pierre early and ruin the fun?"

"Gentlemen, don't assume from the hangmen that Nate is first. It's just like him to reassure the next victim that he's not next. What's the Bible say? 'And the first shall be last and the last first'? Oh, and I'm going to ask Captain Ratto to get Chief Tanaka to issue Harry a permit to carry a concealed weapon, assuming he wants one."

"'Want' is a strong word, but let's say I begin to feel the need," Harry said.

A loud, insistent beeping broke into their discussion, and each man began fingering his belt. "It's me," said Nate. "It's a 911 code message from Julie. I'll go check in and come back."

Four minutes later, Nate returned, shut the door, and sat down hard. He sat biting his knuckle for a few moments, then looked up and said, "Harry, I'm sorry. I didn't know. I didn't suspect."

Harry's face took on a look of panic as he asked, "Not Alissa? Not my daughter?"

Nate looked confused and then said, "Oh, no. No. Not your daughter. She's fine. It's...he struck again. While he was on line yesterday, apparently. Pierre was right. I shouldn't have involved you, Harry. I'm sorry."

"Well, stop saying you're sorry, and tell us what happened," Harry said.

"A seventeen-year-old girl was staying home alone while her parents were out of town at a funeral," Nate said. "She was found this morning in her bedroom when her parents returned. She had whip marks on her back and a toe was cut off. She also had 'Thanks, Ishmael' carved into her stomach. The neighbors heard nothing. She was gagged and strangled to death."

Harry buried his face in his arms on the table top. Pierre rested his forehead in his palm and whispered, "He was doing her while you were talking to him." A moment later, he said, "Something is very wrong here. He knew who Ishmael was almost immediately. He's got to be listening."

"We'd better sweep and be sure," Nate said.

Then Pierre was on the phone to the Electronic Surveillance Unit requesting that they come by to sweep the homicide bureau, the interview rooms, the lab, and the radio dispatch office. E.S.U. could not oblige him today, but they promised to come in the morning.

Pierre grabbed his hat. "Well, time for the sanitation crew to go clean up the bastard's latest atrocity." He sighed and added, "The parents will be the worst part. They always are. Nate, stay with Harry and see that he gets home all right. Get him a doctor if he needs it."

"You got it," Nate answered, but before Pierre could leave, Harry rose to his feet.

"I'm fine. You should take Nate with you. Go on. I'll be all right. Honest."

"Okay, Harry, if you're sure. Call us tomorrow."

♦

Nate rode with Pierre to the murder location. They did not notice the car following them. On their arrival at the front door of the apartment house, Harry walked up behind them and pre-empted their protests. "Look. It was my doing. If I can't face this, what good will I be during the investigation? And...I need to do this." Pierre glanced at Nate, exhaled deeply, and led the way inside.

The bedroom was torn up with signs of struggle and blood splattered high and low. The body appeared as it was found, bound to the bed posts. She was secured to the bed with duct tape and gagged so tightly that it must have been difficult for her to breathe. There had been copious bleeding from lash marks on the girl's back. Her right big toe was cleanly severed, and it lay on the carpet near the foot of the bed. Arterial sprays of blood flecked the wall to the side of the bed, and there were puddles on the carpet where blood had seeped off the end of the mattress. Dr. Watkins Barstoff, the Medical Examiner, turned the toe over with his forceps and showed them the marks at the edge of the bone.

"These marks show that the toe was chopped off by a wedge-shaped blade pressed against a flat surface, probably an anvil pruner or a bolt cutter," the doctor said. No such device was found, however. Pierre pointed out that the girl must have lost a critical volume of blood even before the killer finally strangled her, and the doctor concurred. Pierre carefully turned the victim's head with his gloved hand. It lolled unnaturally, the neck broken for good measure, no doubt.

Harry studied the room and the corpse while tightly gritting his teeth. He did not share his thoughts with Nate and Pierre. Nate went off to check the other rooms and question the family while Pierre and Harry checked the entry door. It was a good solid core door, with a security peep hole, a normal key lock, and a chain lock as well. None of them were forced. "Nate," called Pierre, "Come look at this. There's no sign of force at all. The Hellhound can't know all his victims. Why do they always trust him and let him in?"

"Some ruse, I guess," Harry said.

"What, then?" Nate asked. "A fake medical emergency? A smoke bomb in the hallway and a fire fighter's outfit?"

"It couldn't be," Harry said. "He needs quiet and privacy for his work." The neighbors, of course, had heard nothing.

They continued looking over the premises until a uniformed officer led them to another bed room. Bright, blue wall paper with clowns, drums, and hobby horses adorned the walls. A crib stood against the far wall.

"Sirs, this is strange. I checked out this room and found these gift wrapped packages next to the crib. We were instructed to check the house carefully for booby traps, so I asked the mother about them. She couldn't answer, so I asked the father. He says he never saw them before. It's not the four-year-old's birthday, either."

"Did anyone touch them?" Nate asked.

"No, sir."

Pierre began to give directions. "Set up a cordon for a half block on all sides. Evacuate each apartment in the building. Nate, get the bomb squad ASAP. All the uniformed officers are to search the apartment and the entire building to make sure everyone's out. I want an all-clear before I let the bomb squad touch those packages. Everyone understand? Okay, go."

Lieutenant Marc Aston's bomb squad arrived within ten minutes. Harry watched the slim Lieutenant, with his groomed red moustache and his flack vest, pointing, directing, and ordering his people to move into place and to set up equipment. Pierre, Nate, and Harry went outside to hunker down and wait behind a sand bag barrier while Aston's crew wheeled and carried into the building several boxes, machines, and electronic gizmos, the nature of which

Harry had not a clue. Within thirty minutes the team was ready to begin neutralization.

Lt. Aston maintained radio contact with Pierre, who relayed progress reports to Harry and Nate. The squad used a metal detector; an electronic bug detector to spot electronic timers and circuitry; and an inductive magnetic field sensor to detect any current flow around the boxes. Nothing. From time to time, an armor-clad team member ran out of the building to the truck and ran back in with additional equipment. Both an explosive-sniffing dog and an electronic explosive sniffer were employed with similar results. Finally, the bomb squad carefully unwrapped the boxes, using plastic scissors and blades.

At last Lt. Aston told Pierre that it was safe to enter. They found Aston tossing a teddy bear up and down in his hand. "Can you believe this?" he asked them. "Just toys."

"Is that it?" Nate asked. "Nothing else?"

"Nothing else," Aston said. Lying at his feet was a toy robot that actually walked and a portable video game with a real TV screen. "Could these have been left by some uncle or grandparents to surprise the parents?" Aston asked.

"No, Marc," Pierre replied. "We checked. The gifts appeared when the killer did."

"If this is the Hellhound's idea of a sick joke, it's an expensive one. These are top-of-the-line toys," Nate said. "What's his game?" The three exchanged glances, but no one had a theory to offer.

♦

At last Pierre went home and unlocked his apartment door. Then he used another key on the dead bolt. He took a very short step inside and flipped on the light, then stooped over and examined the floor in front of the door, where he had left a light dusting of flour. There were no foot prints, so he went in, locking the door behind himself. He checked the table tops and inside the refrigerator and then whipped back the cover on the bed. Finding no drawings or anything else amiss today, he undressed and laid his pistol on the night stand. He stared at the ceiling. He did not sleep.

CHAPTER EIGHT

Friday morning, as soon as the clock ticked off seven-thirty, Harry called Alissa. She had just sat down to breakfast as usual. Yvonne asked if anything were wrong.

"No, I just missed her a lot yesterday and promised myself I'd talk to her this morning. Would you put her on?"

"Uh, sure, Harry. You sure you're okay?"

"Fine."

"Hi, Daddy. What's wrong?"

Harry gave a weak laugh. "Well, I guess my women have my number. But everything's fine, sweetie. I just missed you so much," he said to his eight-year-old.

"Are you still going to take me this weekend?"

"Wouldn't miss it for the world, Lissa. I just needed to hear your voice. I sure love you."

"I know that, Daddy," she said in her serious voice.

"Put Mom back on, Lissa."

"Harry?"

"Yeah. Well, I guess there's no fooling anyone. I visited a really nasty crime scene yesterday. Another girl opened her door to the wrong person. You've warned Alissa about that, haven't you, Yvonne?"

"Of course, Harry."

"Do me a favor? Tell her again. Use the newspapers as a reason. It's in there almost every week. Make sure."

"All right. Anything else?"

"No. That's it."

"Well, I've got something, Harry," she said. "Today is October third, and no check. Why do you always have to be a few days late? Amusement? My bills are due on the first too, and I get hit with finance charges when you're late."

"Oh, sorry. So busy. I'll send it right out."

"Right," she said in a tired voice. He heard her breathing, but she said nothing for a long moment. Then she whispered something into the mouthpiece of the phone.

"What, Yvonne?"

"Nothing."

"Yes. Something. Say it and get it over with."

"Why do you do this to yourself?"

"I've just been busy. I'll mail it. I'll mail it."

"It's not just that. I mean everything. You go so far out of your way to fail, don't you?"

"Can't anything ever just be inadvertent?"

"Give me a break, Harry. You live by your calendar. You look at it and write in it ten times a day. It's impossible for you not to know when the first of the month is on you. And it's your law practice too. It's getting your suits cleaned. It's letting yourself win. It's like you hate yourself."

"Actually, I kinda thought I was a nice guy."

Yvonne's end of the line went quiet again, except for the staccato sigh. "Bye Harry."

"Bye."

♦

Harry stopped in at Homicide before going over to his office. He was not there five minutes when a cop in plain clothes entered. Pierre introduced Eddie Petrie of E.S.U., and apparently Nate already knew him. "Are you done?" Pierre asked him.

Eddie looked at Harry dubiously, but Pierre said, "You can discuss this in front of Harry. He's assisting us with the investigation now."

"Yes, sir. I just finished the other interview rooms," he said. "I've been waiting outside until you finished."

"Eddie, did you mention this job to anyone at all?" Pierre asked.

"Nope."

Pierre went on, "With this guy always staying one jump ahead of me I had to consider the possibility that he's been listening. We don't have a routine sweeping protocol, a glitch I've called to the Chief's attention. I'm hoping a bug will be found, maybe even with a print on it."

"Sorry to disappoint, Pierre," Eddie said. "You called me on the phone to request this sweep. You were probably talking to the guy who planted the bugs."

"You found some?" Pierre asked.

"Not exactly. I opened up the phones in Homicide. I didn't see anything, but when I blew a fine cloud of dust inside the mouthpiece, it stuck to a small circular film of adhesive residue. The circle was just the size of a button transmitter typically used inside a phone."

"Any way of knowing when it was removed?" Pierre asked.

"Unfortunately, no. I also checked the main switching box in the basement. One wire had a small length of insulation stripped on the back side facing the rear of the box. It was just big enough to allow this small alligator clip to contact the bare copper, though the leads were detached from the alligator clip." At that, he handed Nate a small alligator clip. "Scratches on the copper were shiny enough to have been done within the last three or four days. The wire led to the lab's main incoming line."

"Anything that can lead to who did it?" Nate asked.

"Afraid not. Who has access? Every cop in San Francisco? Every sheriff's officer? Out of town police? Bicycle messengers, lawyers, cleaning staff…"

"All right, I get the picture," nodded Pierre. "Did I have to be on the phone for him to listen in?"

"Negative. He was in the room with you all day long."

"Thanks Eddie, and remember this job never happened."

◆

When Eddie had left, Pierre turned to them. "Obviously, he knows we've discovered his bugs. That's why he removed them. He doesn't seem to have any trouble wandering around the police department."

"So should we profile our suspect as a cop now?" Nate asked.

"I don't know. He could be, but an outsider could have done all this too. Using Harry as an analogy, he knows almost as much about criminal investigation techniques as we do, and would have access to plant a bug in someone's office. So could the janitor or the floor waxers."

"Then can we screen all the personnel records of people who have police department security clearance?" Nate asked.

"Would that include Harry?" Pierre asked. "The Chief's brother? Your wife? Telephone repairmen? Thousands of people traipse through here every week."

"All right," Nate said. "This is getting us nowhere. We need to plan for personal security and for security of information. If he's been keeping ahead of you all this time by electronic surveillance, he's likely to try it again. Our homes, cars, and personal phones all need to be swept too. Then we need periodic sweeps in case he tries to plant us again."

Pierre sighed. "Gentlemen, we can't afford to continue making mistakes like I did by calling E.S.U. on a compromised phone. If we continue to be careless, we're going to start dying one by one."

Harry asked "Once our homes and cars are swept, who's going to do the periodic sweeps to keep us clean?"

"I can borrow a sweep device from E.S.U. on permanent loan, and we can each sweep our own places and trade it off. It's not complicated. That should keep us clean. Oh. About Harry's piece, I spoke to Tiny this morning about going to the Chief for Harry's permit to carry, but he refused. Actually, he more than refused. He blasted me for letting a civilian get involved. Ummm, he also wants a talk with you about that too, Nate, but don't freak out. I went directly to Chief Tanaka this morning, and he's backing me. He's issuing a permit for Harry to carry. Harry, you can use my spare piece until you get your own."

"Pierre, I'm not a cop, but isn't going over your superior's head a big no-no in the P.D.?"

"Yeah, it is, Harry," answered Nate. "This means that we'll have Tiny Ratto on our necks from now on. So be it. Now what about the direction of the investigation?"

"I guess Nate knows quite a bit about what's gone on so far," said Harry, "but I don't. I don't want to underestimate him again, so I'd like to read all the past investigative files."

"That's a year's worth of reading," Pierre said.

"Then how about I start with just the original incident reports, and ask for more if I need them?"

"Makes sense. I'll have it for you this afternoon."

"What *is* the profile of the typical victim?" Harry asked.

"White, sixteen to eighteen years old, fair hair, and always 'Nice Girls', innocent ones, never Juvenile Hall bait. He goes for the innocent ones. That's it. No other patterns. He usually invades the home, and always seems to know when they'll be alone. He usually gains entry without force, but we don't know how. He has entered and then waited for the victim to come home. The perfect bogeyman hiding in the closet."

"Harry, brief Pierre on what you learned yesterday in the chat room." Nate said.

"I kept tweaking his ego. Since he's enamored of himself, I challenged his sanity and virility."

"So? Did you learn something useful?"

"I think maybe so. The best clue was at the end when I really pissed him off. What'd he say? When I mentioned a submarine, he countered me with scuba diving, saying I'd be going down without a reserve tank."

"And again I say 'So?'"

Harry went on. "They haven't had reserve scuba tanks for years, so he's from the old school. We now know he's well read, and no dummy."

"Swell. Hope it does us some good someday." Nate scowled and added, "Someday soon."

"We're done," Pierre cut in, "so why don't we meet back in homicide at 5:30 p.m.? I'll have those reports for you then, Harry, and your piece too."

Harry made his way back to his office. On the way, he gave some pocket change to Osmund.

This being Thursday, he was greeted by Bridget cheerfully, "Well, the wayward Oaf makes a cameo appearance?"

"Hi, Bridge. Miss me?"

"Never, but Judge Kellogg seems to have."

"Oh, no. I was so caught up in…things. Damn! Of all judges to no-show for. Is there an order to show cause for contempt?"

"No, luv. The judge's clerk called me, so I let her know of your 'personal emergency' this morning. The motion was continued to next Friday. Two things more then. Is there something I can do to help? Among your occasional faults, you've never been one to miss a court appearance."

Harry gestured for her to follow him, and he led the perplexed woman down to the street and the coffee shop. "Bridge, I've got to let you in on something. The police will be coming here soon and..." He was interrupted as Bridget began to speak in a pitch considerably higher than normal.

"I knew it. I knew you were in trouble. We won't let them do it though, will we? I know you didn't do anything wrong. You can trust me."

Harry saw her eyes suddenly redden.

"Bridge, relax. No, I didn't do anything illegal. Let me finish, okay? The police will come to conduct an electronic sweep of the office. I wouldn't let all this happen without warning you." Harry paused to let her further collect herself before he went on. "Bridge, I suppose you might want to consider resigning."

"So you don't trust me then?"

"I trust you, Bridge. I'm just not sure I trust me with your life. It's a long story, but to make it short, I sort of pissed off the serial murderer they call the Hellhound. You've heard of him?"

"Have I heard of him? Have I heard of Jack the Ripper?" Her face took on a peeved expression, and she said, "Well, that's not an easy thing you've accomplished now, is it? I mean you just can't go walk up to the most notorious urban terrorist and murderer on earth and smack him in the chops now, can you? I should think it took considerable effort to make an enemy of someone whose identity no one knows. Did you take out an advertisement in the *Chronicle* daring him to a fight perhaps? Question his manhood? Tell now. You've certainly piqued my curiosity."

"Are you sure you're done?"

"Not quite. Have I somehow let on that I'm quite the coward? That I'd cut and run at the first shot? Is that my reputation?"

"Bridge, you're not making this easy. I don't want to see you go. I want even less to see you sliced and diced. This guy is pure psychosis, and he has no end of hatred for women. Now it looks like he's disposed to go out of his way to get me, and yes, I did sort of challenge his manhood. It wasn't smart. I had reasons, but it was a dumb move. People have already gotten hurt because of me, and I don't want you getting in his way when…if he comes for me. And anyway, I won't even be here most of the time now. I'll be working with Nate and Pierre trying to catch this guy before he catches us."

"Oaf, isn't that all the more reason you need me to stay on? I'll have to hang about and patch things together while you're off tracking down this coo-coo clock, won't I?"

Harry breathed deeply. "Bridge, you have no idea how much I want to have you stay, but maybe you should know what my mistake cost. Because I taunted this man, he whipped a young girl's back raw, cut off her toe, and then strangled her to death. Now do you see why you might want to leave?"

Bridget's eyes went wide and her complexion got redder, if that was possible. Harry watched her breathing with some sign of distress.

"Has he made some move or some threat toward the office or toward me?" she asked.

"No, but he particularly likes to play mind games and he hates women, especially young, white, sweet innocent ones."

"Well, bloody hell! That's not me then, is it?"

Harry laughed. "Well, maybe not, Ms. Brash, but he might also target anyone who's close to me just to make me suffer."

"And has Mr. Hellhound already wire tapped our office?"

"Since I only blundered into his life yesterday, I don't think so. I'm just being extra cautious."

"Well then, he doesn't know how we get on at all, does he?"

"I don't know what he knows, but we suspect that he might even be someone that Nate, Pierre and I all know. He could be someone who's been in this office. We just don't know."

"But I've only been in your office less than three months. Do you talk to other people about me?"

"No."

"Right, then. I can't think of any visitor who's seen us all warm and fuzzy, so why can't we show any listeners that we're not overly fond of each other? You STUPID MAN!" she shouted angrily in his face.

"Huh?"

"Just practicing. Really though, don't you think we can just put on a show of barely tolerating each other until this is over? Why would he target me then? I'm not your typical quiet, shy virgin, and if we're not friends, then he'd have no interest in me, would he?"

Harry noted that she had passed entirely over the question of whether she would stay, and was piecing together how. Harry had to admit that he would need her competence now more than ever.

"Bridge, I can't believe you're doing this with the risk involved. You...you aren't sweet on me, are you?"

"Ohhhh," she groaned. "You egotistical, short-sighted fool." She pushed her face close to his and continued. "You think every woman is hot for your body? I've got a boyfriend, and he's not old enough to be my father like you either. Sweet Christmas! Haven't you ever had a friend, Harry?"

Harry squeezed his lower lip between his fingers and exhaled. "Maybe not like you," he said softly. "Thanks." Then he gave her a hug.

"You DIRTY OLD MAN!" she shouted, and then slapped his face. "If you ever lay those geriatric hands on me again, I'll not only tender my resignation, but sue you for sexual harassment. Is that understood?" In a lower voice she added, "Wasn't very wise to do that on the street, now was it?"

"Uh, right. Sorry. I guess I was overcome." Then he said loudly, "I didn't mean anything by that. It won't happen again, I promise." Bridge turned and walked quickly back to the office. Harry stood on the pavement with palms raised, exclaiming "Women!"

♦

He watched her go and decided to take a walk around the block to think. He thought of Lissa. He could not be sure that she and Yvonne were not in danger too. His mistake on the Web had changed everything. His life's familiar streets were unchanged physically, but now they hid uncertainty in a dangerous game whose rules he did not know. When Harry looked down the block again, it was with a feeling that he had never been so alone.

Back in the office he looked out the window directly into the building across the street, whose windows were also unshaded. Harry twisted the rod that closed the blinds so that he could be neither observed nor cross-haired. By the time he was done with the mail and drafting a complaint, it was 5:15 p.m., so Harry closed his briefcase and left for his meeting with Pierre and Nate. He arrived five minutes early to find Nate and Pierre waiting in the newly sanitized and bug-free Inspectors' office. On Pierre's desk was a cardboard box containing a score of folders with new photocopies of files.

Next to the box was the pistol, and under the pistol was an envelope labeled "Permit." Harry withdrew the pistol from the holster. It was the clip-on type of holster that attached to the belt, and the weapon was a nine-millimeter Glock semi-automatic. The semi was similar to ones he had fired. It had a ten-shot magazine, a half-cock safety, and of course a positive safety switch. He dropped the empty clip into his palm and put it on the desk. Then he pulled back the slide, while Nate and Pierre watched him intently. He let the slide go forward and then pulled it again, looked inside the chamber, and let it go forward again. Then he replaced the clip and put it back into the holster. Nate and Pierre smiled and clapped.

"What's that for?" asked Harry.

"Nothing, Harry. We're just amazed that you didn't point it straight at us," Pierre answered.

"I appreciate the vote of confidence, but you should know I qualified Expert with the Colt .45 and the M-16 in the Army. I know how to handle a weapon. Does a 9-mm. round have much stopping power?"

"It won't knock him down, if that's what you mean," Nate said, "but it will definitely stop him. If you have to use it on the guy we're chasing, empty the clip."

"Ummm, not to be critical, but there is this old-fashioned legal concept of using only as much force as is necessary to effect the arrest," Harry observed.

Nate looked over at Pierre, who said, "Harry, I understand your training. I understand the perp's rights. But by now I would have thought you'd understand that you're not in the court room. You're in a fight for survival. This gentleman we're hunting will kill you with a smile if he gets the chance, and he'll torture you first if he has the time. If you're lucky enough that he gives you the excuse and the opportunity to cap him, for the last time Harry, *don't underestimate him*," Pierre ended in a loud voice. "You should not assume that he will conveniently fall dead with the first bullet. He's insane. He's tough, and he's full of rage. You need every advantage you can take. You show him mercy, and your dying word will be 'oops.'"

Harry realized that he had again misjudged. "Full clip," he echoed.

Pierre slid a box of fifty cartridges across the desk to him, and Harry put them in his briefcase. Nate slyly asked, "I gather you got the memo guaranteeing a moratorium on killing you when you leave the building today?"

Harry's Adam's apple bobbed a moment, and then he took out the box and extracted ten shells. One by one he slid them into the clip and slapped it home into the pistol, but did not chamber a cartridge. He installed the holster onto his belt.

"Harry, I'm not sure we're doing right bringing you in. You aren't equipped to fight this fight," said Pierre.

"You're probably right. If I had to choose a third partner for your team, I'd be the last person I'd pick, but it was *his* choice, not ours."

There was no disagreement. After a moment Nate asked, "Pierre, what's our next move?"

"I'm open to suggestions from the new blood."

"I've given it some thought," Harry said. "You started chasing him about eight years ago, 1990. Computers were not as universal then as now. Some of the databases that exist now didn't exist then. How about a database elimination?"

"Which is?" Nate asked.

"Once I've studied the case records of the past crimes, I'll know better what we know for sure about this guy. My idea is to take each known fact about the Hellhound and see if he appears on an existing database because of it, like California DMV for example."

"Swell," said Nate, "we'll just arrest all male licensed drivers in California and interview them."

Harry pursed his lips and went on. "Obviously we won't use just one level of elimination. The next step might be the database of Social Security records for our boy's age bracket. The result of combining the two lists would be a third list, shorter than either of the two we began with. A third database would shorten the list further, and so on. When we've narrowed the remaining list to a workable number of suspects, we concentrate on investigating them."

Pierre was interested. "If we got it down to a hundred people," he said, "we could match their movements against the times of the crimes." Nate nodded. "We might not need to, though, Harry. Our lab confirmed that our boy left us some DNA. When we've narrowed the suspect list, all we need is a DNA sample from each to run the tests."

"Yeah, like he's going to sit still while we wait for the lab report," Harry said. "As soon as we take a DNA sample, he'll be in Tierra Del Fuego."

"Who says we let him know?" Nate said. "Suppose we get warrants to search the suspects' homes when they're out, and just take a hair off pillows? He'd never know, as long as we don't break his lock on entering."

"Hmmm, devious mind," Harry said. "I like that. What's the status on the electronic sweep of our homes and my office?"

"Tomorrow. Keep your pager on, and E.S.U. will co-ordinate with you. When the initial sweep is done, E.S.U. will leave the scanner with Nate, and we'll rotate it among ourselves. Even when we've been cleared, a good rule is to assume he's listening at all times."

"Damn it all!" Nate said. "You mean I've got to deal with the Hellhound's listening in when I'm making love to my wife?"

"I dunno," Harry said. "Pierre, what does the psych profile say about the Hellhound's boredom tolerance?" Nate curled his lip, Pierre sighed, and Harry asked, "Speaking of which, can I get a copy of the psych profile? It might help me understand who's stalking me."

"Yeah," muttered Nate. "I'd kinda like to know something more about the guy too."

"I consulted psychiatrists early in the investigation years ago after the first couple of killings, but there isn't a written profile," Pierre told them.

"Well then, let's get a new profile based on all the crimes to date," Nate said.

"I've dealt with the crime-shrinks more than you two," Harry said. "Can I suggest we use Doctor Paschov? He always struck me as insightful."

"He's all right with me," Pierre said. "I expect what Dr. Paschov will need is what's sitting in this box here. Harry, can you just copy it all and give it to him?"

"Okay. Can I borrow the photos too?"

Pierre went to his desk and pulled out a large envelope full of photos and gave them to Harry. "You'll have to run off two sets and get these back to me, Harry. Will you take care of getting one set to the doctor?"

"No problem."

"Are we done?" Nate asked.

"Not quite," Pierre said. "Advise everyone who has to know about Harry's participation to keep it to themselves. I don't want it to become general knowledge."

Harry staggered out of the Hall under his new burden and returned to his office. In one hour he had the file duplicated. He sat down and reviewed the photos for each of the murders. They were more horrific than any he had ever seen. He scanned page after page of artifacts that were found with the bodies: pliers, knives, razors, dowel rods, and heat-discolored fireplace tools. As he studied the pictures, no answer came to his one agonized question: Why would the killer do these things?

CHAPTER NINE

On Friday morning Harry eased into his desk chair. The pistol caught on the chair arm, so he shifted the holster toward his back, but could not get comfortable with it. He worked on some case files until 7:45 a.m., when he went across to the jail to see a few clients.

At the sixth floor, he showed his ID and walked in. He checked his weapon into a locker and then opened his briefcase for inspection. Eventually he passed through the check point. In time his clients entered an interview room the size of a telephone booth. Harry heard their confessions, granted them plea bargains, and gathered his papers. Then he retrieved his gun and waited at the elevator until the guard finally pushed the button that released the last barred gate. It slammed closed with a hollow boom, followed by an echo that seemed unfamiliar.

Harry entered the elevator and punched the lobby button, then decided to check in with Pierre and Nate and punched the button for the fourth floor instead. He began to hear the loud racket of alarm bells as the door opened. He entered the fourth-floor hallway and saw a large dust cloud moving toward him from his left. People were running and shouting. Then Nate appeared to his right. "Harry, it's forensics. A bomb."

Harry took off down the hall toward the dust cloud. Nate followed close behind him as if they were on a tandem bike. Halfway down the hall Harry heard Nate shouting in his ear, "Harry, stop. Wait for the bomb squad."

But Harry continued running into the dust cloud, yelling over his shoulder, "Hell no. There may be people dying."

They were twenty-five yards from the area where the blast debris spilled across the hallway when Nate yelled again, putting his hand on Harry's shoulder to slow him, "Stop, Harry." Harry's first knowledge of the second blast was not the noise but the feeling of being pushed violently backwards into Nate. The two flailed through the air, slammed into the wall on their left, and tumbled hard onto the linoleum as an ear piercing roar invaded Harry's consciousness.

His ears rang as the echoes of the explosion faded. He couldn't feel his body at first, so the degree of potential damage was a mystery. Slowly he and Nate began to groan and try to move body parts, complicated by the fact that their respective parts were all tangled up. Nate rose to his knees and put his hand on the wall to steady himself, but fell again to the floor. Then he staggered to his feet while Harry still lay on the floor with his eyes shut. Nate grabbed Harry's collar and tried to drag him away, but he fell again. Suddenly strong hands were grabbing both of them and dragging them speedily back over the linoleum the way they had come. Harry jerkily watched his heels cruising over the floor, but in the smoke he also saw what remained of the hallway—tangled girders, pulverized sheetrock, and powdered glass.

As he was lowered to the floor near the elevators, his rescuer knelt down next to him. It was Pierre. Harry tried to lift his head, but it wanted to bob and weave like a lazy fly on a summer night. He rolled onto his side and saw Nate in similar condition, but Nate was also bleeding from a cut on his head and from his nose, as well as from cuts on his hands and through a hole in his pant leg. He seemed to be staring at Harry, who heard the other's voice as through an echo chamber—"*You loooook awfullll...*"

Pierre laid Harry back down, placing his head on a chair cushion. He said, "Lie still until the doctor can check you. You could have a brain injury or hemorrhage. Don't move, man, okay?" The officer who had dragged Nate clear laid him back down and put a folded jacket under his head. Harry put his hand to his head to rub a painful spot, but Pierre caught his wrist. "I don't think you should touch that." As Harry's hand came into his field of vision, it was dripping blood. Perhaps lying still would not be so bad after all, he thought.

Nate groaned. Harry groaned. He was amazed at the number of places on his body that were suddenly sore. His head checked in with a screamer of a headache, his back ached; so did his neck, fingers, scalp, and ears. He was sure even his blood was somehow bruised.

Harry turned his head. "Nate, how you feeling?"

"Oh, shit. The only thing that don't hurt is the air in my lungs." Harry laughed. Then his lungs hurt.

The paramedic crew, arriving within three minutes of the second blast, began to work on Nate and Harry. The bomb squad arrived with dogs and ran them down the hall to sniff for any more devices. Once the dogs had cleared the area, Lt. Ashton was waving an all clear signal, and a second paramedic crew ran down the hall to check for other survivors. Meanwhile the first crew shone lights into Nate and Harry's eyes, poked and stretched various tissues, and make inquisitive rumbling noises in their throats.

Within two minutes the second paramedic crew returned and joined the men tending Nate and Harry. Harry winced at the realization that either no one had been in the lab, or more likely, no one there needed help any more. One of the second crew whispered to Pierre, who closed his eyes and sighed. Ken Singh was someone with whom Harry had on occasion shared a pitcher of beer. Another victim.

When the paramedics pronounced them safe to move, the two men were taken by portable gurneys in the elevator down to the waiting ambulance. Soon Nate was back at San Francisco General's trauma unit, this time as a patient. As he was wheeled in, he was surprised to see Dr. Barbara Nelson. "It's not your shift," he remembered.

"Covering for a friend. Nate, anytime you want to see me, just make a little scrape on your knee. Don't overdo it."

"Harry, Doc. Doc, Harry. Harry likes being first at disasters."

Barbara was briefed by the paramedics but repeated many of their tests anyway. After a thorough exam, she pronounced their injuries superficial. The cut on Harry's head was the only one needing sutures. "Scalp cuts bleed rivers," Barbara told Harry. "Four or five stitches and you'll be fine."

While supervising the cleaning and bandaging of Nate's wounds, Barbara ventured, "Let me take a far-out, shoot-me-if-I'm-wrong guess, but this wouldn't by any chance be the work of the guy who did the catatonic girl, would it?"

"Forgive me if I don't admire your wit," Nate moaned.

"You're taking the rest of the day off, Nate," she told him while flicking her fingernail on the barrel of a hypodermic syringe. "This'll kill the pain, but make you sleepy. I'll give you a prescription for some tablets to take with you."

"And are you offering cocktails only to Nate, or do I rate too?" Harry asked.

Harry looked up at two of the brightest brown eyes he had ever seen and heard her say, "I'm buying a round for the house. Any friend of Nate's is a friend of mine." She gave Harry an injection, and he laid his head back. Barbara returned to Nate's side, speaking in a low voice, "Let me say this while you're still coherent. Anything in the medical field you need to help catch this guy, you call me day or night, okay? If I can't get it or don't know it, I'll find someone who can help." She slipped a card into Nate's pocket with her pager number on it and patted his arm.

"Thanks. Pierre or I will call you for sure if we need help. Oh, and Harry too. He's working with us."

"Sure, Nate. You got it."

The nurses finished bandaging Nate and Harry at about the same time. After the paperwork they were discharged. A nurse brought them their prescriptions, and a patrol car was waiting outside for them. A uniformed officer asked Nate, "Where to, sir?"

Nate asked Harry "You still live alone?"

"Uh-huh."

"We're supposed to be under observation for concussion for twenty-four hours. You should come home with me."

Harry turned two glassy eyes to Nate and couldn't think of any arguments, so he nodded. Nate gave the officer the address and sat back.

"Um, does your wife know what happened, Nate?"

"No, I'll explain it to her when we get there."

Harry blew out air between his teeth and reached into his coat pocket for his cell phone. "What are the odds that this still works?" He was amazed to hear the dial tone. "Nate, call her and tell her there's been an accident, but you're fine and you're coming home early with a friend. She'll be upset if you surprise her."

"I don't need your advice on how to run my marriage. And who told you that you were a marital advice guru anyway, your divorce judge?"

"Some people do learn from mistakes, Nate. Call her."

"Mind your own business. Anyway, if I did need advice, it wouldn't be from the idiot who dragged me into a bomb blast."

They rode in silence the rest of the way, and the officer pulled to the curb in front of Nate's door. When they had dislodged themselves and closed the door, the driver pulled away with an odd smile on his face.

"I'll just wait out here until things settle down," Harry said.

"Suit yourself. I'll come out and get you later, if I feel like it."

◆

As the door closed, Harry put his back against the house and slid down into a sitting position. He crossed his arms on his knees and put his head down on them. A cat snooping at the curb suddenly jumped straight up and hid behind a trash can when a high-pitched shriek bored through the door.

Harry's mind fogged up and his surroundings faded until a soft voice roused him. He looked up into the smiling face of a beautiful woman who was helping him to his feet. "I'm Selma Hutchinson. Come in, please." She gently guided him to the living room couch. He sat facing a wall mirror, which gave him a disappointing reflection. Nate sat in a stuffed armchair opposite the couch.

Harry looked away from the bloated mummy in the mirror and at Nate with his bandages and his glass of scotch on the rocks. For a moment they just stared at each other, and then Harry started to laugh. In a moment Nate joined him. Selma came in and put down another glassful of amber near Harry's hand. She shook her head and said, "Oh, aren't you two a pair? Looking so very fine, and you're just amused as hell."

Nate turned serious and crossed his arms over his stomach. "Damn, even my bladder and guts are sore." He got stiffly to his feet. "Be right back," he grunted. Which of course he was not.

Selma sat down near Harry, her face troubled. "I know you must think I'm..."

"A lovely and loving woman," Harry said. He took a swig of the scotch and told her, "Listen, I'm not going to stay awake long. Between what they gave me at the hospital, being half dead, and this booze, I'm scheduled to crash." He took a breath, and it hurt. "But I want to tell you something. Nate should have called you, I know. But it's just male disease."

"Oh, this is going to be good. Tell me more."

Harry exhaled and continued. "He didn't keep you in the dark because of lack of trust or not wanting to share his life with you. He sees keeping this from you as a way to protect you. He loves you."

"Well, Mr. Wise Man Harry, what if it doesn't make any difference if I know that? From my perspective, I'm shut out, and that hurts. Sometimes he shows up at 3 p.m., sometimes dinner time, or even after 9 p.m., and I never hear a word about his work. Now he's spending even more time at it."

Even in his befuddled state, Harry knew that to say any more would be to go too far. "I'll make up the bed for you in the spare bedroom," she said. "The instruction sheet from the hospital says that I'm to check on the two of you every couple of hours to make sure you're not comatose, so don't mind me stirring you."

She showed him to the guest room, where he dragged off his outer clothes and crawled into bed, immediately going blank. The next thing he knew, it was 6 a.m. What had awakened him was still attached to his elbow, Nate's hand. "What?" he asked sleepily.

"Come on man, gonna sleep all day?"

"Go away. I'm still tired."

"Harry, you've been sleeping for seventeen hours."

That came as a surprise. But all in all Harry had the feeling that he must have enjoyed his rest. "Okay, I'm up."

Harry put on borrowed clothes and took painful steps to the kitchen, where Nate handed him a cup of coffee. They both downed pain pills and sat in silence except for slurping and groaning. Then Nate scrambled some eggs, while Harry inhaled more caffeine. Selma was elsewhere in the house working on business on her computer.

"What'd we get ourselves into, Nate?"

"Shitload of trouble, I'm thinking. Want to bet on what evidence got destroyed?"

"I don't bet on sure things. Did you hear anything this morning concerning mortalities?"

"Yes," he said after a moment. "Ken Singh got it. He's always in the lab. This doesn't do it, Harry. We gotta take the aggressive for a change. Now that I'm on his list, I'm a believer in the pro-active approach. The son of a bitch wants me? I want *him*."

"Damn, you're sensitive. A guy blows you up just once, and you get cranky."

"Harry, does everything have to be a joke with you? This asshole nearly kills me, and you toss off one-liners? You better grow up fast, Harry, or you're gonna die before mental puberty sets in."

"All right. I'm sorry already. I'll do everything I can. Don't worry."

"Worry? You're damn right I'm worried. You may be smart, but that don't mean shit out on the street. Hell, you sit in that cheap-ass office and live your life just half trying, and that's good enough for you. You let your marriage die; you let the other lawyers grab the big cases; you don't return calls half the time. Watching life go by may be good enough for you, but not for me, not when the game is staying alive." He glared at Harry and turned away. But minutes later he said, more quietly, "I'm sorry, Harry. I didn't mean any of that. I'm just pissed off."

Harry looked at the table for a moment, then Nate. "It's all right, Nate. If I have one skill in life, it's that I know the truth when I hear it."

They ate their eggs in silence, and then Harry blurted, "I've been thinking. Why not do a second database elimination on the victims? We could draw up a questionnaire and ask everything possible about the victims' families. They'll cooperate. Then we feed all that data into a database for each victim, and let the computer find factors in common. Maybe knowing how he selected the victims will give us a reasonable trail to him."

"I like it."

♦

After Harry took pains to thank Selma for her concern, the two men made their way outside. Nate's car was sitting in the driveway with the keys on the visor. "Pierre's really something, isn't he?" shrugged the officer as he slid into the driver's seat. He dropped Harry off at his office, as instructed, but instead of going directly up to his office, Harry went to the phone booth at the corner. It was still early, and this was Saturday, so Lissa would probably still be home. Yvonne answered.

"Is Lissa home with you?"

"Yes, do you want me to go get her?"

"No. Don't, but I need you to take her and get to a public phone and call me, please." Then he gave her the number. This instruction was met with a long silence.

"Now?" she said.

"Now."

She hung up. Ten minutes later the pay phone rang. "Yvonne?"

"Yes, what is all this about?"

"If you could wait, I'd like to talk to her first."

Yvonne put the young girl on. "Hi, Daddy. Are we coming to see you today?"

"No, honey. But I need to talk to you about something important. Try to pay close attention. You know I defend criminal cases, right?"

"Oh duh, Daddy!"

"There is a very bad criminal out there who's mad at me."

"Oh Daddy, you come here, and you and I will fight him off."

"I knew I could count on you, Sweetie, but the police don't know who this criminal is. He could even be someone we know. You follow me, honey?"

"Yes."

"Since I don't know who he is, I also don't know whether he'd look for me at my office, my apartment, or even at your house. He's not a guy we'd like to let in the house, is he?"

"I won't, Daddy."

"But Lissa, there's a problem keeping away from him, isn't there?"

"Yes. If I don't know who he is, how can I know who to stay away from?"

"Ah, that's my smart girl. So what you need to do is not to let anyone into the house except Mommy and me, and never go anywhere with anyone who comes for you saying that Mommy or I sent him to get you. Will you do that?"

"I promise. What about Christie and Luanne? Can't they come to play with me?"

"Yes, they can. You have to ask Mommy or me for everyone else. Everyone, understand honey? Don't even unlock the door. Can you remember all that?"

"Yes."

"But Daddy, what if you were hurt and couldn't come and really sent someone to get me?"

"Well, aren't you smart? That's just why I told your Mom to go to a pay phone, to give you a secret password. Do you remember the oriental dagger I brought home from the office? Now, don't say what I cut, but do you remember that I cut something with it?"

She giggled. "I remember."

"If I ever had to send someone else to get you, you tell them 'dagger' and they have to say the thing I cut. Don't say it on the phone, Lissa. Do you follow what I'm saying?"

"Right, it's like secret agents. If they don't know the right password, they're traitors."

"Bless your little soul. Put Mommy back on, okay?" Harry shifted his weight and rested his elbow on the telephone ledge to ease the fire in his back. Yvonne came back on.

"Harry, what was that all about?"

"Trouble, Yvonne. You and Lissa have to be on guard. It's not good."

"I guessed that. What's wrong?"

"I received a sort of death threat from the serial killer the papers call the Hellhound."

"Oh, you have got to be joking."

"For once I wish I were. You know about the bombing at the Hall yesterday?"

"No, I was in meetings all day and haven't picked up today's paper yet."

"The bomb was set by the Hellhound. We think he's targeting Nate Hutchinson and me. We got injured in the blast." Harry could hear her breath come faster, and when she spoke her voice had risen.

"Oh, my God. Is it serious?"

"No. Just cuts and bruises."

"Harry, how could even you enrage someone who's never even met you?"

Harry gave her a short version of the chat room incident. "This guy knows so much about the investigation, that he's either bugging us, or he's someone we know. I can't rule out him looking for me at your house."

"Oh no, Harry. Alissa!"

"Don't let people other than Lissa's little playmates and your immediate family in the house, and don't let her go anywhere with anyone else for a while, even though you know them."

"He's after *her*?"

"He's a raging criminal lunatic. We have to assume the worst. I'm working with Pierre and Nate trying to find him first. You guys have to stay away from me for a while. Please explain to her that it's for her protection?"

"Harry, I don't want her to lose a whole semester, but I'll move away from here if you say I should."

Harry pondered the question, which might have terrible consequences if he decided wrongly.

"Call a locksmith to come out today and put extra dead bolt locks on every door, including the bedrooms. Does your brother Raymond still keep guns?"

"Yes. Maggie has never stopped complaining about them. I don't know if I could do that, Harry, I mean…use one."

"Yvonne, I know you better than you do yourself. If it came to him or Lissa, you could. Ask Raymond to take you to the firing range tonight to learn to shoot it."

"And Alissa?"

"What about her? Oh, you mean teach her to shoot?"

"I don't know, Harry. Should she?"

The line remained quiet for a long time. "Take her along and teach her, so at least she'll know how not to kill herself with it. Make sure she knows not to tell anyone about it."

"I can't believe we are actually discussing teaching our daughter how to kill someone. It's hard to believe this is the same planet I was on when I woke up this morning."

"I've had the same feeling myself lately. Oh, and tell her to teach you the secret password, but never speak it out loud in the house or on the phone. It would be prudent to assume that your home, car, and phone are bugged. I don't really believe they are, but he could do it if he sees a need."

"Harry, is there anything else I should know?"

"Yes. We think he is tall, white, and maybe has a limp. He's smart and vicious. Alert her school so that no one comes for her under a pretext. He has no mercy and no feelings. Believe me, he doesn't."

Her voice was tense but steady. "I understand."

"One last thing. Warn Alissa again. Somehow he manages to get girls to open their doors to him. We have no clue how. For all I know he comes dressed as a priest. Or a doctor. Whatever."

She exhaled. "Good luck, Harry."

CHAPTER TEN

Harry hung up the phone and went up to his office. He looked up the home address of Dr. Serge Paschov. It was a rare name. Harry found him listed at an address in the St. Francis Wood area, one of the richest neighborhoods in San Francisco. He reached for the phone, but thought better of it. If he had any chance of convincing the psychiatrist that this was urgent, it would not be by sitting in his office calling him cold on the phone.

It took him only twenty minutes to drive to the address. He painfully lifted the carton of files out of his car and carried it up the wide front walkway of a house styled with the look of old adobe Spanish architecture. It was a big building with arches, no doubt worth over a million dollars.

Harry set the box down and rang the chimes. A Latino woman in her fifties came to the door. With wide eyes she looked him up and down, and then asked what his business might be. He handed her his business card, told her that it was a police emergency, and that he needed to see Dr. Paschov right away. As she disappeared back into the house, he remembered what a sight he must be in his bandages.

Inside the house Harry heard some conversation, and then Dr. Paschov materialized. "Mr. Maxwell, we've met before, haven't we?" he said, extending his hand pleasantly.

"Yes, Harry Maxwell. Kind of you to remember me. We've had a case or two in common over the years."

"What brings you to my *home* on a weekend, Mr. Maxwell? And since when do the police send private attorneys on police business?"

"I'm working with Homicide Inspectors Pierre La Croix and Nate Hutchinson to narrow the search for the serial murderer called the Hellhound."

"Ah yes, Inspector La Croix. A remarkable man. I have had several cases with him. Come in. Come in, please."

Harry entered a large foyer, where the green Italian marble floor glowed richly with the reflection of a crystal chandelier. The walnut wall panels were glossy with wax, and the small French Provincial table to his right was probably a couple of hundred years old. A plaque on the wall from a publishing house suggested one source of wealth, but Harry smelled family money behind the carefully arranged house.

Dr. Paschov took his hand from his prosperous-looking belly and stroked his silver beard. The leather patches on the elbows of his woolen cardigan completed his image of comfort and affluence. He led Harry into the living room, where Harry parked himself in a beautifully upholstered wing-backed chair. "What can I do for you, Mr. Maxwell?" queried the doctor.

"It's urgent, as you might guess."

"Well then, I suppose I'm to cancel my weekend activities and work on your file?"

Harry absorbed this quiet rebuke from a gracious man, yet firm enough to let his resentment at intrusion be known. Not someone you bulldozed into doing anything. Harry bent his head, and then lifted it again to look straight at Paschov. "I wouldn't ever tell an expert how to do his work, and you haven't yet agreed to do anything for me, sir. I know I am imposing, but I hope you'll hear me out and decide what urgency this case might have."

The words seemed to mollify the psychiatrist somewhat, so Harry went on. "The Hellhound has recently stepped up his activities. He did a particularly brutal torture-murder while online in a chat room verbally jousting with a police investigator and me. Yesterday he bombed the forensics laboratory to destroy some ID evidence. I think he's assigned all his investigators expiration dates."

"I take it from your bandages that you were unfortunate enough to be in the vicinity of that bomb blast?"

"Yes, along with Officer Nate Hutchinson."

"He wasn't the one killed, was he?"

"No, that was a forensics lab technician named Ken Singh. But Nate was injured about as much as I was."

The doctor looked thoughtful. "Wasn't there something about you and Inspector La Croix years ago? A shooting, I think."

"Yes, the other time in my life that I was in the wrong place at the right time."

"A question about that has tugged at my curiosity for years."

"Go ahead. Ask."

"Is it true that you shielded his body with yours, while firing back at a gang of gunmen?"

"The press exaggerated that. There were only two gunmen."

"You must have been very close to Inspector La Croix."

Harry looked down a moment. "Well, no. That was the first time I recall meeting Pierre."

The doctor's eyebrows jumped a bit, but his face reflected clinical fascination. His gaze slowly turned into a smile. "Can I offer you a cup of espresso or some codeine? I am a medical doctor and can prescribe, if you are in pain."

"No, I'm fine. Thank you."

"Well then, you were about to tell me what you need of me," Dr. Paschov said, pushing his cardigan sleeves up his forearms to display weathered wrists.

Harry responded quickly, "We need an updated psych profile. The Hellhound's game plan seems to be changing. His pace is getting faster and his crimes wilder. We're afraid we may not have much time before more people die. Maybe Nate. Maybe me. We'd like you to study these files and give us some insights into what drives this guy, where he's headed, why he's changing, and how can we get a jump ahead of him. Copies of the crime photos are being made for you. Compensation would be at the usual police consultant rates."

"Would I be at risk?"

Harry had never considered that possibility, and was now afraid he might lose this valuable man's assistance. "Well, the Hellhound seems to get inside information, either through wiretaps, personal connections, computer hacking, or who knows how. He was never predictable, but now he changes the rules daily. Frankly, it's just the impossibility of predicting him that brings me to you. So your answer is that I have no idea."

"Well, I appreciate your honesty, Mr. Maxwell. Now I am afraid I must show you to the door." Harry sighed, then thanked the doctor and stood to pick up his box. As he turned toward the door, Paschov spoke again.

"You'd better leave that here. If I'm to spend all day and half the night on these files, you'd better be on your way," he said with a mischievous smile. Then he called loudly into the other room, "Melinda, please call Karl and Dr. Bennett and tell them I have an emergency and won't make the tee time. And I'm eating home tonight and all day tomorrow."

Harry beamed with one of those unharnessed smiles usually seen only on children. He thanked his host profusely as he began to leave.

"No, Mr. Maxwell. I thank you. It is not often that I get to assist in something this urgent and fascinating. You see, dissecting personalities is my vocation, but my hobby is also dissecting personalities." His eyes seemed to widen with satisfaction as he went on. "It has always been my belief, in both my professional and private life, that every human being has a depth and intensity to his or her psyche that can be overlooked upon the first dozen meetings. Then one day a door may open, and the observer may be able to see something really intriguing. Now you have come to me and offered to let me peek into two of the most fascinating personalities I've ever encountered."

"Who's the other?"

Dr. Paschov threw his head back and laughed, then ushered Harry out with a pat on the shoulder and closed the door. Through the door Harry heard yet another unfettered laugh. But he began to feel his failure to take any pain meds for several hours, and groaned as he eased himself behind the wheel of his car.

He punched the number Pierre had given him for the E.S.U. into his cell phone. He asked the man on duty if anyone was available to "visit" his office, since he had not been available on Friday. The officer said, "How are you doing, Mr. Maxwell?"

"Not bad, considering. Thanks."

"Well sir, I show that your matter was taken care of yesterday. You're clear."

"It couldn't have been. No one was in the office yesterday."

"Well, it was, sir. You must have left your office unlocked."

"I never leave my...oh," said Harry, suddenly understanding. No officer used pick locks without a warrant, of course, but with Pierre, necessary things got done. "Thank you very much," Harry said, and rang off. He drove to the Hall and went up to E.S.U. He found one young officer at his desk.

"I'm Harry Maxwell," he said, showing his driver's license. "Was it you I just talked to?"

"Yes, sir. Alvin Chu. Is there a problem?"

"Not at all, but I'd like you to do my ex's home and car. My daughter lives with her, and..."

"I understand, sir. Write down the address, and I'll do it this afternoon. Be sure to notify her, right?"

"Right." Harry thanked him and left. He called Yvonne from his cell phone and left her a message that he had arranged for the telephone repair men to come today to fix the phone problem. Finally, he could go home and clean up.

As he approached his place, no one loitered nearby, so he went on in. He took a detour into the den, punched the computer power button, and went to run the shower water. In ten seconds he was out of his clothes and into the hot shower. When the bandages were thoroughly soaked, he lifted them off and dropped them on the floor. The one on his head was particularly sticky with the blood caked in his hair, but he carefully cleaned himself up. After toweling off afterwards, he put large bandages on the cuts that had begun to bleed again and pulled on a pair of old blue jeans and a T-shirt. Then he put on the tea kettle and went back to the den to check his e-mail.

Apparently he was the lucky winner of an opportunity to get rich. He hit *delete*. Someone wanted to entertain him at an "adult site." *Delete.* Alissa told him "I love you, Daddy." *Save.* He switched to word processing and then reconsidered. He keyed up the e-mail screen again and erased the message from Alissa. He made a mental note next time he talked to Yvonne to tell her not to let Alissa do that again. The Hellhound was a hacker. It was best not to let this hound sniff out a trail to his daughter.

CHAPTER ELEVEN

Refreshed and fed, Harry returned to his office to try to keep some cash flowing. Ninety minutes later the phone rang, and he heard Yvonne's distraught voice. "Oh Harry, I'm glad I found you. There are two men here who say you sent them."

"I guess you didn't get my message." He reassured her and added, "Oh, before I forget, I think it would be a better idea if no one sends me e-mails for a while."

"Oh, that will go over...not too well."

"I know, but it's necessary."

"I understand."

"How is she holding up?"

"It hit her a half hour after you talked to her, but still, she handled it well. She's mostly worried about you."

For a few moments Harry could not say a word. Then, "And what about her mother?"

"She can do this."

In her last words Harry could detect a familiar rush of emotion, which he knew signaled teary eyes. "Take care of yourself, Harry." Suddenly she was gone.

◆

He watered and weeded a couple of accident cases that he hoped to harvest soon. Two hours later Harry's hurts were acting up enough to distract him from work, so he called it quits. He hit the street and looked up and down the alley, inhaling the cool air. Three breaths later, he could hear a distressed voice, and then a second one. Two women were arguing, apparently in the building directly across the street. The volume and intensity of the voices rose. An older woman was shouting at a younger one.

"Do you understand? Never, never let anyone in. He loves to get little girls like you." Harry heard a loud smacking noise and then crying from the younger voice.

"But I didn't, Mama," came the labored answer.

"Don't lie to me, Lettie. You think I don't know what goes on around here when I'm at work? He loves to sneak in and hide in the closet, and then he'll get you. He'll whip you raw, and then cut your throat." Harry sighed and walked to his car.

♦

It was mid-afternoon when he jammed his key into the door lock, and suddenly a deafening explosion assaulted his ears. He flung himself to the ground and immediately realized that both he and his car were in one piece. He looked up and saw the Blue Angels flying in close formation directly over the Hall.

Yes indeed, thought Harry, as the roar stopped rumbling in his skull and moved off a mile to the south. Early October, and it must be Fleet Week. It was a San Francisco tradition popular with tourists, but an annoyance to the locals. The famed precision pilots buzzed the city, thundered low over Civic Center, under the San Francisco Bay Bridge, and finger painted the sky with their smoke trails. Harry sighed and drove back home.

He snacked on crackers and old cheddar, and then arranged himself on the living room couch. He lay with a lined pad on his lap, the fingernails of his left hand keeping a cadence raking the leg seam on his blue jeans. He began reading the incident reports from the past murders and attacks and recorded those facts about the Hellhound that seemed reliable.

On the first pass through, he read only the original incident reports. After that he went through the supplementals. Soon he was seated cross-legged in his socks on the carpet with the reports spread in a circle around him. Saturday afternoon became Saturday night. Hunger became Chinese take-out, delivered to his door. Saturday midnight yielded to the gentle glow of Sunday sunrise, and still he studied files. When the sun got higher and beat through the window, he undressed, showered, and napped. Then he wolfed down some corn flakes and toast with peanut butter and jelly, and again immersed himself in pages of paper, like a dog stretched out in the grass.

By five o'clock Sunday afternoon Harry felt ready to contribute to the database elimination discussion. He began work on the victim questionnaire and invested forty-five minutes in setting up macros, so that with one punch of a key he could spit out a commonly used phrase like "Give the name and address of all the places where you have _____". In this way he sailed through the questions rapidly, spewing out queries that would chronicle a family's social, business, religious, and incidental associations. Many of the questions were deeply personal, but he had studied what the Hellhound had done to these parents' children. They would answer. He had no doubt that each family would give its best to dispatch the Hound back to Hell.

At 10 p.m. Harry was beat. He forced his rubbery legs to carry him to his TV recliner to try to unwind before sleeping. He played with the remote and came to rest on a woman holding a microphone. Solemn-faced, she was telling of a teen-aged girl now in the custody of the juvenile authorities after she had shot her younger brother. Home early from soccer practice, he had apparently been snooping in her room. When she arrived home, she had expected to be alone but heard rustling in her closet; she had taken out her father's pistol and ordered the intruder out of the closet. A sudden noise made her fire through the door, killing her brother instantly. The reporter wore a distant expression as she repeated what the girl had said when they locked her into the patrol car: "I thought he was the Hellhound!"

Harry's feet felt for the floor, but not on their way to his bed. He was still keyboarding when the sun rose. The word processor had automatically numbered four hundred and forty-three questions. He saved three copies of it to disk.

He set his alarm for two hours later, 8:15 a.m., and slept. When he woke, he remembered lunging toward the pillow but had no memory of actually reaching it. He dressed and hustled over to the Hall, shouted a quick greeting to Oz, and ran in. He tended to his court appearances for that morning, and then stopped in at Homicide to check in with Pierre. Harry let him know that he was ready early with his thoughts on the database elimination, and that he had a victim survey. They arranged to meet at 2 p.m. to conference it.

♦

At the Clerk's Office Harry researched Friday's missed court appearances, the day that he was bombed. He learned that the Public Defender had covered for him on one case in Department 2, and the judge had covered him with a brief continuance in Department 6. Alquiza had not even been in on Friday, and all his cases were continued. On inquiring, Harry learned that Alquiza had called in sick with the flu on both Thursday and Friday. He couldn't help smirking at the judge's convenient absence while the Hellhound was doing his chat room murder.

Harry ran back across the street and spent some time tidying up his office and returning documents to their correct files. He whirled around suddenly when he heard a noise at the window, but it turned out to be only the wind blowing a telephone wire against his window frame. He closed the blinds and sighed. His mind drifted to the breezy summer that he, Yvonne and Alissa had spent at Lake Berryessa. Images appeared...of five-year-old Alissa tickling him, and his pretending to be overcome, whereupon Yvonne joined in and tickled both of them...Good times...good times, he thought.

He picked absently at the mystery crust on his suit lapel and wondered if he had tried harder to be neat or punctual, to accommodate Yvonne's craving for order, might there have been fewer arguments and snarls, and more smiles and snuggles? As always when these thoughts racked his brain, he wondered: Could he be different, even if he tried? He blinked back the mist in his eyes and busied himself on a pressing discovery deadline.

CHAPTER TWELVE

At 11:30 a.m. there was still time to run a hardware errand. After checking the yellow pages for the address, he drove to Dunn's Guns, on Third Street.

He entered a longish store with glass cases lining each wall from front to back. To his left were dozens of varieties of knives. Then came the hundreds of makes, models, and varieties of guns. The handguns included antique Derringers, modern plastic pistols, revolvers, frontier-styled six-shooters, small .22 automatics, and .45 magnums that could penetrate a truck's engine block and still kill a moose.

Harry approached an older clerk with a beard, who wore a name tag reading "Walt."

"Can I help you?"

"Yes, I have to return this borrowed gun, and so I need to buy my own," Harry said, showing his permit.

"What are you interested in, Mr. Maxwell?"

"Something semi-automatic and unlikely to jam."

"How about this Beretta Model 96? It's a .40 caliber semi-automatic pistol with excellent balance, and is tops in reliability. It's very similar to the standard S.F.P.D. sidearm."

"Isn't the Beretta the gun that Ian Fleming had jamming on James Bond all the time?"

Walt smiled. "The same company, but if it did, it's not a problem today."

"Just the same, I'd rather have something smaller. This borrowed Glock offers only two choices: wear it at the side and snag things, or push it to the back for a kidney caress."

"I can certainly find you a smaller pistol, but I recommend a shoulder holster for better comfort. How about this Heckler & Koch model USP? It's a .40 caliber semi with a 3 1/2" barrel for $665."

"Does it have good knock down power?"

"If you mean will it knock someone off his feet from the momentum of the bullet, no. If you want real power, you need to go to a .357 or a .45 magnum."

"But then we're talking humongous cannons again, right?"

"Well, let's see." He put the H&K back into the case, and drew out a Smith & Wesson .357 magnum, Model 640 with a 2 1/8" barrel. He cleared the weapon by pulling the slide and inspecting the chamber, and dropping the magazine out and inspecting it. Then he put the weapon into Harry's hand. It fit well, and was considerably smaller than some of the others. The price was $477.

Harry hefted it again and sighted along the top. "I'll take it."

"Shall I show you some holsters?"

"Not yet. I'm thinking of an ankle gun as well."

"How about this model here?" He brought out a very small .380 Colt pistol called a Pony Pocketlite. It had a 2 3/4" barrel, was silver gray in color, and cost $493. "It's double action only, and is unlikely to fire accidentally."

"Double action only means what?"

"You can fire it only by pulling the trigger, which cocks the hammer at the same time it fires the round. You can't pull the hammer back with your thumb and then pull the trigger."

"What's the advantage of that?"

"No external hammer means no snagging on your pant leg." He cleared the weapon and gave it to Harry. "Try the action."

Harry pointed it at the wall and pulled on the trigger, with no result. He pulled harder and the internal hammer drew back stiffly and then snapped forward. "I can see this gun wouldn't go off accidentally, but if I needed to use a hideaway gun, I'd probably already have a fight on my hands. I don't need a second one with the pistol."

Walt smiled, put the Colt away, and led Harry down to the end of the counter to a silver colored S&W revolver. It was a .38 with a stubby barrel. On one side was stamped "Model 642", and "Airweight" appeared on the other side.

Harry held the weapon, and was amazed. It was well named.

"The frame is aluminum, but the barrel and cylinder are steel, of course. That saves a lot of weight. The cylinder holds five shots. This revolver is double action too, but try the trigger action."

Harry did so, and it fired smoothly and easily. The top rear of the weapon featured only smooth curves, and no hammer. With a 2-inch barrel, it would be easier to draw in tight quarters. "How much?"

Walt flipped the tag over and said, "$405. For a clutch gun, you don't want a semi-automatic. You wouldn't have time to pull a slide to chamber a round. Now I'll get you the holsters." He brought out two, fitted them to Harry, and adjusted the straps.

"You can leave a deposit today so we can start the Department of Justice check, and then pay the balance when you pick up, okay?"

"Fine. Thank you." Harry paid the deposit and filled out the paperwork before leaving.

"Good luck," came Walt's voice after him.

♦

Hurrying back to the Hall to meet with Pierre and Nate, Harry arrived with a few minutes to spare. Harry had his list of Hellhound characteristics, as did Pierre. On some items they all agreed. The past incident reports established the height at 6'0" to 6'2".

"What about age?" asked Harry.

Nate answered, "The McMasters girl told us two things before she died. He was about 6'0" to 6'2" and was about 38-44 years old. That was two years ago, putting his present age at 40-46."

"How much faith should we have in that?" said Harry dubiously.

"It's OK for me," Nate said. "Claudia Wildman told her grandfather the man was about forty-five before she clammed up."

The process continued for over an hour. Harry kept track of items on two lists, one with traits they were sure of and the other a list of probable traits. Eventually, they had listed as positives:

California driver's license
Subscription to a San Francisco newspaper
Height: 6' to 6'2"
Has social security number
Age: 40-46
Has a telephone, probably unlisted
Subscribes to an Internet Service Provider
Lives or works in San Francisco

"That's still way too many people," Harry said. "We need more identifiers."

Pierre said "I'd like to discuss whether we can further narrow the last item. Why not change it to 'Works at the Hall of Justice'? We know he keeps close tabs on this investigation. Considering his ability to leave a crime scene sanitized under difficult circumstances, he obviously has detailed knowledge of police investigatory techniques and tests. It's inescapable, isn't it? He's involved with the criminal justice system."

"A cop?" Nate asked.

"Maybe, but not necessarily," Pierre said. "Maybe a probation officer, judge, lawyer, or prosecutor. All of them would have picked up a lot of police procedure over the years. I mean, you get handed the best distillation of expert opinions and procedures listening to a trial, don't you Harry?"

"It makes sense," Harry said, "and it would explain how he could evade Pierre for eight years. But I don't know, I still think that someone could get all that expertise in places other than this building. Other counties. Other times, even. He could have worked here but retired two years ago and just visits now, or maybe his police experience was in Fresno."

"We'll see. Let's divide up the databases to collect and begin assembling our master list," Pierre said.

They divided up researching and collecting databases from Social Security, the Division of Motor Vehicles, newspapers, and so on.

"We haven't discussed the victim survey yet, Pierre," Harry pointed out. "Nate and I discussed sending a survey to the victims' families to see if we can figure out how he selected his victims. I have copies of a questionnaire I did for both of you."

"That's great," Nate said. They began making calls to their assigned organizations, and Pierre began looking for a programmer to splice it all together.

Finally Harry jumped up and told them, "I've got to go. I have to pretend I'm earning a living once in a while."

♦

He took the elevator to the lobby and was on his way to the door when he heard

"Shine, Harry?" An arm extended beneath rounded shoulders pointed to his scuffed shoes.

"Uh, yeah. Sure." Harry sat down. Hansen always did a thorough job. Harry watched him instead of reading the newspaper and was intrigued by the obvious intelligence in his face. Why was he shining shoes?

"So, do you do other work besides this?"

"Nope. Why?"

"Oh, I just figured a bright guy like you might either have another business on the side or be going to school to move up."

"I've been up."

"Meaning?"

"I went to college. It's no secret. Police checked me out before I got the vendor's license for the Hall. They know about my drug convictions too."

"Lots of people beat drug habits and go on to have good careers. You could do better than this, couldn't you? I mean you do a great job, and you arrive reliably during the same work hours every day. No complaints here, but you could be selling office supplies, driving big rigs, or have other well-paying jobs, couldn't you? I'd guess your family could use the extra income."

"Not married. No way."

"What work did you do before you got into drugs?"

"The job I liked the best was office manager-bookkeeper in an advertising firm. I got fired when some petty cash vanished."

"I'm sorry. Drugs make you do strange stuff, I know."

"Yeah, they do. 'Cept I didn't take that money. Funny, the secretary who said I did, got my job soon as I was fired."

"I don't guess I could do anything to straighten that out or to help you look for a new job..."

"Look, I like this work. It suits me, okay?" The tone of voice told Harry that he was trespassing, so he shut up and read the paper. As he fished out the bills to pay Hansen, Harry's pager went off. He gave him an extra buck tip like always, and dialed the number. It was Homicide. Nate answered and let Harry know that the disk he left was blank. Harry checked his briefcase and found that he had left the wrong one, so he told Nate he'd bring it right up.

When Harry entered the office, both Nate and Pierre were on the phone again, so he waved the disk at them and placed it on the desk near Nate. As soon as he had set it down, the third phone rang and rang. Pierre gestured to it, and Harry answered. He winced when the voice identified itself, but he still fielded the call from Lola Wildman. He listened to her aching pleas to catch the Hellhound and tried to reassure her that they were doing everything possible to get him. She kept telling Harry what a good girl Claudia had been and then began weeping uncontrollably, begging to know "Why her?" Harry tried to share her pain until she could bear to say goodbye. Then he quietly replaced the handset. When he took out his pen to make a note on the phone call, it was vibrating annoyingly in his hand.

CHAPTER THIRTEEN

The following Wednesday Harry learned at Homicide that several layers of database information had been screened to eliminate outliers and produce a working list of possible suspects. Pierre had scored a programmer from the Department of Justice named Veronica Atkins. Pierre made the introductions. Ronnie was about thirty-five, tall, and very attractive. Better still, she had applied an eagerness and competence to the task that was a happy surprise to the three investigators.

It seems that 11,683 of California's drivers fit the physical, gender, and age parameters. Ronnie had further narrowed the field. Only 9,508 of these had Social Security numbers, and of that group, only 4,000 subscribed to either the *Chronicle* or *Examiner* or both. Exactly 1,825 of those lived or worked in San Francisco. Eliminating those who had no telephone pared the list down to 1,647. Ronnie pointed out that someone like the Hellhound might choose to list his telephone under a fictitious name, in which case that elimination would exclude the Hellhound. They decided to back up and undo that elimination. Then Ronnie eliminated those people without an account with an internet service provider. The murderer had to have a service provider to log onto the internet, whether he stole an identity or not. This reduced the list from 1,825 to 671 people.

Nate then thought of checking with Social Security for another elimination. Anyone receiving SSI for blindness or total physical disability could not be the murderer. With Social Security cooperation the number then stood at 604. The three investigators came to a consensus that this number was still too large to embark on a suspect-by-suspect search, but the list was getting promising.

Harry wondered out loud whether Claudia Wildman had ever spoken again since she was hospitalized. Nate gave him the home phone number, and Harry called Dr. Barbara Nelson. She told him that Claudia had been committed to a small San Francisco private mental hospital called St. Teresa's. Harry asked if she knew if Claudia had begun talking again, and she offered to call and ask.

In five minutes she called him back. "Harry, I spoke to the director, and she said that three days ago an orderly and a nurse were near Claudia talking, and they heard her speak one word as if it were a question, 'Nate?'"

"Anything else?" Harry asked her.

"That was all she said. The resident therapist tried to get her to open up some more, but got nothing out of her."

"Can you hold on a second?" He covered the phone and asked "Nate, the girl said your name. How about we go out right now and try to talk to her?"

"He can't," said Pierre. "I'm leaving for an appointment right now, and Nate has to man the office while I'm gone."

"But Pierre, shouldn't we move immediately on this? We might not get another chance."

"Right, Harry. So you go. You've already met Dr. Nelson and the Wildman girl too. See if the doctor will take you there."

Dr. Nelson readily agreed, and he told her he'd pick her up. It took Harry only ten minutes to arrive at her apartment. She was waiting outside when he pulled to the curb.

"Hi Doc."

"Hi, Harry. You realize that the one word she uttered might have been the last one she'll ever speak?"

"Maybe, but something made her surface for a moment, and I figured that while that was fresh might be our best time to try to get more. Will it be a problem for me to get in with you?"

"No. I'm sure it won't. What is it you hope to get?"

"Anything about the Hellhound we don't already have. One more fact could narrow the list of possibles from hundreds to less than a dozen."

♦

On arrival at the hospital Barbara had a brief chat with the director of medicine, and they were then conducted to the ward where Claudia was housed. She was seated in a stuffed chair near the window as they quietly approached her. She sat very still in her white hospital gown, staring straight ahead. Barbara checked her pulse and found it was normal. Since Claudia seemed in no apparent distress, Barbara nodded to Harry to begin.

Harry spoke in a low, soft voice. "Claudia, I'm Harry Maxwell, Nate's friend. Claudia, we need your help. Please try to remember. We need to know something about the man who hurt you. Can you tell us anything about what he looked like? His eye color? Complexion? Beard? Scars? Anything Claudia, anything at all." The two looked intently at the girl, but there was no reaction.

Harry tried again. "We met at your house the day Nate came and took you to the hospital. Do you remember Nate? He's the policeman who helped you, Claudia. I'm Nate's friend. Remember? Nate? The black cop?" Harry saw her brow furrow ever so slightly, as if she was trying to remember.

"Claudia, we need your help." Barbara put her fingers on the girl's wrist to get her pulse, and reported to Harry that it had elevated a bit. He tried again, using the name that had roused her from her trance, however briefly. "Nate needs your help, Claudia. What did the bad man look like?"

Her brow twitched again, and then her lips tightened a little as her face began to turn from side to side. The lips pursed, and she emitted a stuttering sound, "B-b…"

Barbara spoke now. "You remember honey? Tell us. Please. You're safe now. You can tell us."

The girl swallowed and resumed the "B" sound. "B-b…black."

Harry asked, "Who? Who was black? The bad man?" But there were no more answers. She began to emit a soft whining noise from her throat and to sway back and forward. The eyes were blank.

Barbara put her hand on his arm and drew him back. "That's all, Harry."

♦

They walked back to Harry's car without speaking. He started the drive back downtown, and after a few minutes Barbara asked, "Was that worth it?"

"I don't know. I was asking her about both the Hellhound and Nate. Now I don't know which question she was answering. If she was talking about the Hellhound, it changes everything. We've assumed he's white, because all his victims are white."

Harry pulled to her curb and let her out. "Thank you, Barbara. I appreciate your help. Even with what little we got, it could be important later."

"Good luck Harry. Call me again if you need me."

Harry returned to Homicide and found that Pierre had also returned. Harry briefed his colleagues on the results of the Wildman interview, and Pierre declared that it changed nothing. "We can't change any of our assumptions, when we don't even know whether she was talking about the Hellhound. Nice try anyway, Harry."

Lacking any other elimination facts to use, Ronnie suggested trying out Pierre's suggestion that the Hellhound was someone who worked at the Hall.

"I thought we agreed that a retired cop or someone who visits from out of town could as well fit the profile," Pierre said.

"I'm sure they could," Ronnie said, "but until you give me more elimination factors, doesn't it make sense to see who's on the local list and maybe work on them until we get a better list?"

No one disagreed. After teasing the database, she found that there were seventeen defense lawyers who fit that profile, two prosecutors, three public defenders, eighteen San Francisco police officers, seven California Highway Patrol officers, four judges, one probation officer, two clerks, one interpreter, and five "miscellaneous"–an even sixty people. Four heads crowded around the computer monitor, all eyes riveted to the list. On it appeared the names of Judge Alquiza; Rick Hansen, the shoe shine guy; Harry's narc brother-in-law, Rico Benedetti; the Medical Examiner, Watkins Barstoff; Harry's investigator, Tyrone Washington; Clifton Ratto, the Captain of Homicide; Nate Hutchinson; and Harry Maxwell, among fifty-two others. They looked up and grinned at each other, all except Ronnie. Ronnie whispered to Pierre that she wished to speak to him in private.

"Pierre, you've got to pull those two off the investigation," she fumed. "It's a blatant conflict of interest, and it's dangerous."

"Stay cool, officer. You're forgetting that this isn't a list of suspects. It's a list of people who have not been excluded by height, job, or age. Computers don't create suspects in this office. I do. Your database elimination just helps me decide who is NOT a suspect. Anyway, the last victim was tortured and killed while on line in a chat room, while Harry, Nate, and another officer were together the whole time monitoring the chat. Neither of them could be him."

"Oh. I see. I'm sorry if I overreacted."

"No problem. It's only good police work to raise a possible conflict."

"We've gotten two victim surveys back already," said Ronnie. "I'll begin the merge as soon as the others come in."

Rejoining Nate and Harry, Pierre sat down. "Gentlemen, I want to pick out two or three of these people on the list to begin looking at carefully. Nominations?"

"Judge Alquiza," said Harry immediately.

"Harry, just because he busts your chops and you can't stand him, doesn't make him a primary suspect," Nate said.

"Maybe you just don't know him as well as I do. He has some heavy duty emotional problems. His wife killed herself, and his daughters don't even see him on Christmas. He has a reputation for hating women, and he called in sick the day that we had our little chat room Tango with the Hellhound. I would love to know what the Judicial Council has in their file on Alquiza, like psych records maybe?"

"Forget that," Pierre said. "You know how strong the psych privilege is, Harry, and besides, how keen will any judge be to order disclosure of another judge's psych file on a cop's hunch? But I think the good jurist rates a second look."

"So, who else?" Nate asked.

"Tiny Ratto. We've got to do him right up front," Pierre said. "First of all, he's not been a big help in getting approval for the permit, the programmer, or extra funds. I had to go over his head. If we investigate him, it takes him out of the way."

"But it couldn't really be him, could it?" Harry asked. "He's tall, but too heavy, and he doesn't fit the part to me."

"Tiny made his rep in the department by cracking skulls on the street. He holds the department record for the number of excessive force complaints made against him, and the number of lawsuits settled for brutality."

"By that standard, we have two hundred Hellhounds in San Francisco," Harry said.

"Well, he was…ummm, imaginative shall we say? He threw one suspect up against the patrol car to search him. He positioned the guy's hand so his pinky overlapped the door jamb and then slammed the door. The worst was an interrogation of a meth dealer. He was trying to find out where their cash was. He cuffed his hands behind him, knelt on his chest, and went to work on his groin with his baton. Rumor has it that Tiny put a down payment on a new car the next day."

Harry shook his head in disgust.

"That's only part of it," Pierre said. "He also had his peculiar attitudes toward women. He patronized the working girls, but they usually got paid in fists. A rape victim once complained that he had her pose spread legged, so he could 'photograph the evidence.' More recently, female subordinates have complained to the union that the men under him always get the promotions."

"You can't be serious?" Harry asked. "And they *promoted* him?"

Pierre shrugged.

"I see one big problem here," said Harry. "With Nate and me also on that elimination list, Ratto can trash us and get us taken off the investigation too."

"Not a problem. He'll never see the list. It's confidential, and after the unfortunate leak to the press, I don't think Tiny will have much credibility. I'm on my way now to formally notify Chief Tanaka that Tiny is a suspect."

"Will he suspend him?" Harry asked.

"No. I'm only asking him to transfer Tiny out of the building to Juvenile until the investigation is over. That will take him out of my hair. Be sure all copies of the list are "unavailable" until I come back with a written order barring him from the Hall. Anyone else?"

"I think so," Harry said. "Rick Hansen may be a good choice for spot number three on the list."

"Harry, he's one of the more ridiculous names on the list," Nate said. "The guy shines shoes, for Pete's sake."

"Listen and judge for yourself." Harry related his recent conversation with Hansen.

"Well, a drug abuse history and lack of ambition are poor grounds to make him a top level suspect," Pierre said.

"Think about it though. He pretends to be dumb, but just look in his eyes and you can see he's not. He comes and goes throughout every department in the Hall, police, courts, D.A., Probation. Shit, he even does the Chief's dress shoes."

"And mine," said Nate. "He's been in here lots of times."

"It's a sweet passport to any office he wants to enter," Harry said. "He can't help but hear a lot. People treat him like furniture while he's shining shoes."

Pierre interjected, "Harry, do you remember where you were when I whispered to you that I wanted to talk to you about your chat room escapade?"

"Yeah, I was in the lobby getting...getting my shoes shined."

"Within twenty-four hours the Hellhound knew it was you taunting him in the chat room. Anyone know if he's married?" Pierre asked.

"He says not," Harry said. "And when I suggested he might have better career potential than shining shoes, he said he liked it. Then the atmosphere got distinctly frosty."

"All right, Hansen is number three. Well guys, it's been fun, but I've got to work on other cases too," Pierre said. "Take off, Harry." He lifted his hand as Harry got up to leave. "Oh, and Harry," he said, "stay away from Alquiza in this investigation unless I clear it. Nate and I will check him out. All you can do is screw it up by raising issues of personal vendetta."

"Whatever you say, Pierre," Harry called over his shoulder as he left.

♦

He headed for Department 6, where Gloria Aberdeen was now the court reporter. She hadn't worked in Alquiza's department since he humiliated her. They had apparently finished the morning calendar early, and Harry found her in the reporter's room. It was small, but at least it had a door, which Harry closed.

"Hi Gloria."

"Hi Harry. How's business?"

"The morally challenged still need my help as much as ever." Gloria laughed, but it was not her accustomed free and easy laugh.

"I need your help, Gloria."

"If this is about Judge Alquiza, I'd really like never to think about it again."

"I know, but I hope you believe that it has to be important for me to raise this with you."

"He was horrible to me. I don't want to ever see him again."

"And I don't blame you. But can you manage answering two questions to maybe help other women avoid even worse grief?" She was silent for a time, looking down at her lap. She seemed thinner than he remembered, and her face was pale. Finally, she raised her head and nodded slightly.

"How long did you work for Alquiza?"

"Two years."

"Second and last question. Did you ever get the feeling before that incident with you, that Alquiza was capable of hurting women physically?"

This time she purposefully raised her chin and expelled the protracted word "Yesss…"

He nodded, and said goodbye.

♦

At his office Harry went through his mail. He fielded a couple of phone calls that Bridget could not handle and reviewed some more Hellhound case files. Midway through the afternoon Bridget buzzed Harry to announce the arrival of Amos and Ila Cobb.

"Did I forget something?" Harry asked.

"No, luv. You don't have an appointment. Mr. Cobb says you represented him once and they wanted to just say hello for a bit."

"Okay. Show them in please."

A light knock came at Harry's door, and Bridget pushed it open to usher them in. Old Amos stood there in his Stetson, silk jacket, gold cuff links, and polished brown boots. His rough-hewn auburn face shone with a warmth that apparently no hardship could extinguish. His wife Ila stood next to him, her ample bosom pushing out her bright flowered dress. Her brown eyes crinkled as she hefted a deep dish apple pie and handed it to him. "I baked this just for you. I hope you like apple."

"We don't mean to hold you up, Attorney Maxwell," Amos said, "but I do say that I know you will like it. No one makes pie like Ila."

"That is so wonderful of you," Harry said.

"You saved my life, Mr. Maxwell. Ain't a day go by I don't remember you in my prayers," Amos said in a gravelly Louisiana accent."

Bridget's eyebrows twitched at Harry, and he said "Well, that's a bit of an exaggeration."

"Don't you believe him, young lady," Ila said emphatically. "Three years ago my husband was wearing an orange jump suit in the jail across the street. I couldn't get him out on account of the bail was half a million," she said a little louder.

"Oh, Bridget gets bored with hearing about old cases."

"No such thing," she said brightly. "Do tell."

"It was because that terrible woman Amos worked with accused him of raping her, but he never done no such thing. Why, Miss, she was just setting up their employer for a big law suit. Can you imagine? She put my Amos in jail just so she could win a big..."

"This pie smells incredible," Harry interrupted. "Bridget, why don't you get a knife, so we can have a taste?"

"Oh hush, Oaf," Bridge said with a scowl. "Go on, Mrs. Cobb. I want to hear this."

"Harry ain't never told you about Amos?"

"Not a word."

"Amos never had so much as a jaywalking ticket, and that woman had a criminal record, but the police and prosecutor believed her anyway. Thirty days he sat in jail. The Public Defender couldn't get him out. I don't know if he ever really believed Amos. I called Mr. Maxwell and he went and talked to Amos. We didn't have all the money to hire him, but he believed us and took the case."

Amos took over. "Young lady, your boss kept bird-dogging that prosecutor and investigating that woman until he proved she was a fraud. He got me out of jail. Then he got the charges dismissed, and then got me a court order sayin' I was actually innocent. The judge signed that. I won't NEVER forget what he done." On the word "never" Amos took Harry's hand and squeezed hard.

Ila took Amos's elbow and said "We've taken enough of Mr. Maxwell's time, Papa. We'd best be going now. It was a pleasure meeting you, Miss."

The Cobbs took their leave and made their way down the stairs, as Bridge favored Harry with a broad, wide-eyed smile.

"What? What?" he asked her helplessly.

She continued smiling wordlessly as she returned to her desk. Harry's private line began to ring, and he went back to his office to pick it up. It was Pierre.

"Harry, I've got a lead that might amuse you."

"I presume this lead would relate to the Hellhound."

"You presume correctly, Wise-ass. Let's see. It's 6:30 p.m. I'll pick you up at your home at 8:30 p.m. Is that all right?"

"Well sure, but what's it about?"

"Oh, let that be a surprise."

Harry sighed, "Like I always say, I love surprises."

CHAPTER FOURTEEN

Harry was surprised when Pierre rolled up at 8:15 p.m. instead of 8:30 p.m. "You really love this stuff, don't you Pierre? Don't you ever just go home and read or watch a game on TV?"

Harry could almost see the excitement illuminating Pierre's eyes. "Are you kidding? There isn't anything on that tube to match the dysfunctional dimwits' daily drama."

They slid into Pierre's 1973 Chevelle, and when Pierre lightly touched the accelerator, the car leaped from the curb to the traveled lanes. Pierre drove southwest on Market Street. At Dolores Street, Pierre hung a left, goosing the Chevelle into broad-jumping the intersection ahead of the oncoming downhill traffic.

They passed a colonnade of old palm trees which stood sentinel on the wide boulevard's median island. As they cruised along, Harry heard parrots squawking from the fronds. He recalled reading how the escaped pets had set up housekeeping in those trees. They were now a small colony.

Harry stifled his urge to ask again what this was about. In mid-block, Pierre suddenly screeched to a halt, bent over the wheel.

Harry finished rebounding from the dashboard to ask, "What's wrong?"

Pierre abruptly leaned back into his seat and punched the gas pedal. He swung over two lanes and skidded sideways to the curb. He jumped out. "Stay here," he said, without looking back at Harry.

Harry stayed and watched. A man in his thirties wearing a dirty T-shirt and a kerchief for a headband was yanking a child by the arm from a doorway. She appeared to be no more than six and was crying loudly, "Papa, you're hurting me." His steps were unsteady and his eyes glazed. Harry could make out only part of his slurred, rapid Spanish, something about her mother not ordering him around. Then he twisted her arm and screamed louder at her.

When Pierre reached them, he detached the man's hand from the child's arm in a movement so quick Harry could not follow it. The arm swung violently up, and the man fell back with the momentum. Pierre carried the little girl back to the stairs the two had just descended, watched her go up for two seconds, and then stepped purposefully back to the father. His right hand snaked out and seized the drunk's left wrist. With a graceful twist, the man's hand went up behind his shoulder blade. As Pierre rushed him into the narrow alley between the two apartment buildings, Harry saw the officer pull a sap out of his back pocket.

Thirty slow seconds passed. Then sixty. After a fidgety ninety seconds Pierre emerged from the alley, briefly glancing left and right as he straightened his beret and marched to the car. He buckled up and commenced backing up, until Harry caught his eye and he stopped.

"What did you do, Pierre?"

"I promised him I would return every month and find out from the neighbors if he's touched her again. Why, Harry, did you see something unusual?"

Harry inhaled a full breath and then exhaled slowly, muttering "No. Nothing, Pierre. Nothing at all."

Pierre pulled away, and neither of them mentioned the incident again. Near the southern end of Dolores, Pierre hung a right, and the old hog began to climb. This was a neighborhood into which Harry had never ventured, a fact he shared with Pierre.

"No? This is Glen Park. Wait until we get higher into Diamond Heights. Some of the best views in the city are here." Harry swayed right and left as Pierre climbed the serpentine lanes up the hill. Near the top Pierre pulled his car to the curb and killed the lights.

"Watch that house over there, Harry." He pointed at a Victorian house with turrets and a tri-color palette of elaborate woodwork. Pierre's face was animated and intent and a hint of pleasure gleamed in his eyes as he spoke. Harry was amazed at the abrupt change in mood. "Now look across the street from it and a few doors downhill. See that car?" Pierre pointed out a silver Lexus. Inside was the shadowy silhouette of a man, who appeared to be watching the house. A passing car's lights fleetingly illuminated the driver. It was Vicenzo Alquiza, without any doubt.

"That house is the secret meeting place of a support group for people with an emotional problem, Love Addicts Anonymous. Recently, members noticed that someone has been following women when they leave. One woman got a partial license plate reading and turned it over to the police unit on sex crimes, who cross-matched the partial against all silver Lexuses in San Francisco. Our friend was one of only three matches."

"His Honor the predator? How sick is that?"

"The bonus question is: Does he get any sicker than this?"

In twenty minutes, people began to go to their cars. "Harry, when I pull him over, you stay hidden. If I bust him, you slip away and take a taxi home."

The house continued disgorging men and women, young and old, ragged and regal. A Caucasian woman with classical cheek bones, looking to be about eighteen, made Alquiza sit up. When her Ford Escort pulled out, he fell in behind her. Pierre did likewise to him. When they reached the flats, they spotted Alquiza cruising up Dolores behind the Escort.

At a stop sign the Lexus pulled up beside the Escort. Harry could see Alquiza's left arm stuck out the window showing her something and gesturing for her to pull over. The two cars pulled to the curb just short of the intersection of Dolores Street and Day Street. Harry laughed as Pierre pulled over about fifty yards behind them.

"What's funny, Harry?"

"Dolores and Day. Dolores means 'pains' in Spanish. Oh, I'd say this will be a day of pains for dear Vicenzo."

Alquiza could be seen speaking for a minute into the young woman's window, and then she recoiled. "That's it!" Pierre said. He took off his trademark beret and got out of the car. He walked up the sidewalk at a normal pace, keeping his head down. Ten feet from the Lexus, he cut left into the street, and in a second was standing behind Alquiza.

"Step away from this car."

"Don't you know who I am, Inspector La Croix?"

"Yes. Who and *what*. Step back from the car window." This time the judge did as instructed. Pierre led him by his elbow to the rear of the car. At the back bumper, he spun Alquiza around and pushed him face-down onto the Escort's trunk and searched him. The judge was not armed, but Pierre pulled a leather folder out of his coat pocket, Inside was neatly mounted a gold Inspector's star. Pierre slipped it into his own coat pocket.

"You're making a big mistake, Inspector La Croix."

"How original. Look, you stand straight up, right here, and don't move a muscle until I get back. You move, and you go straight to the tank."

Pierre walked back to the driver's window, and the young woman looked out at him from behind the glass. Pierre motioned for her to roll down the window. As it slid down, the interior released the smells of Shalimar and fear.

"Ma'am, I'm Police Inspector Pierre La Croix." He showed her his own star and picture identification. "Did that man show you this gold star, ma'am?"

She did not answer him, but shriveled back in her seat. "Ma'am I believe that this man posed as a police officer. I stopped him to protect you, but I understand why you're still scared. Is that a cell phone sticking out of your purse?" She nodded and tried to mouth "yes" but the word was choked.

"Then please call 911 and tell them a man has stopped you, but you are not sure he's really a cop, and he wants to talk to the dispatcher. She can verify who I am. OK? Will you do that?" She nodded and punched 911.

In a moment she had done as he said and then handed the phone to him. "Hi Carla," he said. "Busy tonight? Listen, this lady's not sure that my ID is real. Tell her the physical description of Pierre La Croix and verify that you recognize my voice, will you? No. No backup, thanks." He handed the phone back to the young woman. As she listened to the dispatcher, she looked Pierre up and down and incongruously nodded in agreement with the description that the woman on the phone gave her. Then she said, "No, it's OK now. Thank you." She clicked the power button to "off".

"Now ma'am, did he show you this ID and claim to be a cop?"

"Yes. He said he was a police inspector, and that he was investigating reports of a man stalking some women attending my, ummm, meeting. He said he was assigned to protect me, and that I should follow him, because he had a lot of questions for me."

"He said he was a police officer? Can you swear to that?"

"Yes."

"Ma'am, I'll be honest with you. This man is a Superior Court Judge, and I'm sure he'll hire an expensive lawyer if he's prosecuted. You would have to testify, and he will definitely delve into your personal life to discredit you. I'm telling you this not to protect him, but to protect you. I will happily arrest him if that's what you want. Do you want to press charges?"

The young woman looked horrified. "The last thing I want is to get dragged through the courts and have his judge buddies protect him anyway. But it gives me chills imagining that criminal sitting in judgment of other people."

"Agreed, and I'm going to use this incident to force his resignation. If that's agreeable to you, I will still need your name and address and phone number so that we can go forward if he gets cold feet about resigning."

"Do as you say, but just stop him."

He took down her identification information, and then said she could leave. Her car jerked from the curb with wheels spinning, leaving the judge coughing in the exhaust. Pierre led him to the sidewalk and sat him on the fender of his Lexus.

"What did that girl tell you?" grunted Alquiza.

"No. I ask the questions. You shut up and listen."

"I don't know what she said, but it's my word against hers and…"

Pierre leaned forward and raised his voice, "Shut the hell up! *Get* this, Vic! You stepped off your safe little bench, and you wandered into my venue. You're mine. I say you get charged with kidnap and attempted rape, and you get charged. Clear enough?"

"I hear you, Inspector. Whatever that woman says, I didn't touch her. You can't make a case out of this."

"Damn. You still don't get it. You used false police ID to stalk those women. And you know? I look at all those murder cases clogging my office. And I just wonder why all those young girls, like this one, for some unexplained reason, opened their doors to the Hellhound. Do you think maybe he used false police ID?"

Alquiza's face contorted and his eyes grew watery. "My *God.* You aren't serious. The Hellhound? Me? I'm not him. You can't believe that."

"Can't I? You're my number one suspect right now. Where were you going to take her, huh? Got a room set up somewhere? Oh, no. I forgot. You like to do them in their own homes."

"No. Stop talking like he's me. I didn't do those things. I never killed anyone."

"I see. You're just a kidnapper and rapist, but not a bad person, right? You know Vic, maybe I might believe you if you were just some guy in therapy with an emotional problem, and the shrink could assure me your problem isn't of that scope. But that's not the case."

"Yes, it is. Yes it is. I can prove it. God, please don't arrest me. Give me a chance to prove I'm not that guy before you ruin me."

"Trouble is, Vic, I don't trust you. I let you go tonight, and tomorrow I get nasty letters and threats from your attorney. I don't think so."

"No. No. You can trust me. I'm not lying. I've never hurt any of these girls. I mean …Oh, shit."

"The only way I'd believe you is if I walked away from here with your irrevocable authorization to get all your medical and psych records from your doctors, with a list of their names and addresses. You willing to do that?"

"Yes, Yes! I'll write it out for you. I've got a pad in my car."

"I'll get it. Give me your keys. You sit right here." Pierre went into the Lexus and searched it. He found a pair of handcuffs and some sexual lubricant in the glove compartment. No mask. No rubber gloves. No gun. Kink, not Kill. He had Alquiza write out the authorization, and then list his doctors.

"You'll see. I have, uh, problems, but I don't hurt anyone. Check it out. You'll see."

"Vic, whatever it shows, you're done. You're what? Two years from retirement? You don't have to work. I have good news for you. You're taking an early retirement. If what you tell me checks out, you retire with both your pension and your name intact. But understand this; the entire department will watch you anywhere you go at night. You'll never run this scam again." Pierre threw up a hand in dismissal. "You're free to go. You have a copy of your signed resignation on my desk no later than 8:45 a.m. tomorrow morning. If you don't, at 9:00 a.m. I'll be handing Judge Beale your arrest warrant, which she will sign at thirty seconds past nine."

The Judge's eyes went wide when he heard Becki Beale mentioned. Everyone knew how she felt about him. Then he nodded and wiped his eyes. Pierre found Harry hunkering down low in the Chevelle, as directed.

"Well? What happened?"

"It's not him."

"Hell, he's stalking and abducting women. He's a woman hater. How much more do we need?"

"We need to get the right guy. He didn't have a gun on him. Our boy doesn't go out on a job unarmed, and he wouldn't cry and cave in when caught." Pierre outlined his deal with Alquiza, but seeing Harry's distaste gruffly inquired, "What's wrong with all that, Harry? You didn't get your pound of flesh?"

"I guess I was always taught criminals should go to jail," Harry mumbled.

Pierre's face lit up with delight. "And so of course, you became a defense attorney?" It was several seconds before he stopped laughing.

"Maybe you're right. The Hellhound wouldn't have folded so easily. He'd have used a silenced gun on your spine the moment you approached him, then calmly gotten into his car, which would turn out to be stolen."

"Exactly. If you ever met this guy, he'd take you out while juggling on a unicycle."

"What about you? If it had been the Hellhound, you'd be dead too."

Pierre reached into his coat pocket and pulled out his own pistol. Then he gently lowered the hammer and put on the safety. "I had my hand in my pocket, finger on the trigger, Harry. He might have gotten me if he were doing the same, but I'd *damn* sure have had him before I hit the ground."

They were silent while Pierre drove Harry back home. As they drove up Dolores Street, even the parrots had settled down for the night with their mates and babies. Pierre deposited Harry at his apartment block, then pulled away rapidly. Harry supposed he had more missions to accomplish that night.

CHAPTER FIFTEEN

As Harry walked up the two flights of stairs, the faint smell of mildew wafted up from the vintage stair carpeting. He opened his apartment door only twelve inches wide and squeezed through the opening. He flipped on the wall switch and stooped over to examine the carpet. There he found the bobby pin he had inserted vertically into the pile two feet from the door jamb. If anyone opened the door more than two feet wide, it would knock the bobby pin over. Even if it were noticed, the intruder could not know that Harry oriented the bobby pin so that the keyhole end formed a gunsight toward the window opposite the door. Today all was well.

Harry nuked a frozen enchilada and sucked on a bottle of Sierra Nevada Pale Ale. He threw the Glock onto the couch, sank down into the stuffed chair, and used the magic wand on the TV. The ten o'clock news featured the mayor and Board of Supervisors squabbling over funding, and citizen groups in conflict over legalizing marijuana. Big surprise.

Finally, a story of some interest. An undisclosed source had revealed that Police Captain Clifton Ratto was a suspect in the investigation of the crazed terrorist/murderer called the Hellhound. As a purely precautionary measure, the Chief of Police had transferred him out of Homicide to other duties. Harry took a sip of his beer and marveled at how fast Pierre could work. The reporter didn't name Ratto's successor. Harry rolled the cold, nutty flavor around on his tongue and surmised that as far as the Hellhound case was concerned, it would not matter. The example made of Ratto would discourage anything but enthusiastic support from above for Pierre's investigation.

Harry coasted along with a chop-socky movie for a bit, and when sleep began to overcome him he sank into his mattress into welcome oblivion.

The alarm brought him awake with a start, and a vague feeling of fear until he found the bobby pin standing tall. Thursday morning and one more day safe. He skipped breakfast, clipped on his gun holster, and got to the office.

Later, Bridge arrived, acting her usual amiable self. "I'm glad you're in early," she said immediately. "We need to talk. The commercial account is running on empty, and you aren't settling enough cases to meet expenses and still provide income. You can't keep dipping into savings to pay office expenses and living expenses for you and your family every month. You've got to spend more time on your own cases, luv."

"I just don't have the time, Bridge. Everything I wind up doing on the Hellhound case is on an urgency basis. It's just not leaving enough time. You've packaged a lot of settlement cases for me, right? You know what the adjusters need: bills, police reports, medical reports, a narrative of the accident, and a demand. You could do that yourself, couldn't you?"

"I suppose so, but I couldn't take responsibility to decide what settlement should be demanded."

"Heck Bridge, I've heard you on the phone with suppliers and creditors, and you're a natural negotiator. Just assemble the package and do the framework of the settlement demand letter, and leave the amount of the demand blank for me to fill in. You can follow up by telephone and relay their counter offers to me. That would work, wouldn't it?"

"I don't see why not. It's how the larger firms operate every day. Am I to be a paralegal then, Oaf?"

"I guess so, Bridge. Umm, congratulations?"

"I was thinking more of 'Umm, raise?'"

"How much?"

"How does fifteen percent strike you?"

"Reasonable."

"That was easy, wasn't it? Maybe I should have..."

"Oh gosh, Bridge, I'm so strapped, I can't afford a raise. I've got three starving wives and a child to feed."

Bridget snorted, and Harry added, "I'll leave you a list of the files ripe for closing, and you can start right away."

"I presume you'll be out most of the day?"

"Looks like it." Harry thought of Tyrone's place on the database elimination list, and then about the handful of cases on which Tyrone was working for Harry. "Bridge, even though Tyrone works for me, he's not to be privy to any information about the Hellhound investigation, okay?"

"You didn't have to tell me that, Oaf. That's my rule with everything that happens in here."

"Good. I'll be off to the Hall to meet with Pierre and Nate in a little bit."

"Shocked I am, truly."

♦

Harry worked files until eight-thirty, and then ambled over to the Hall, slipping Osmund a dollar without stopping. Harry had no sooner sat down next to Pierre's desk than Alquiza barged in and slapped an envelope down on the desk. He glared at Pierre and walked out without a word. Pierre opened the envelope, nodded to himself, and handed the paper to Nate. Harry read over his shoulder.

"I've filled Nate in on last night's activities. I'll send this resignation over to the Judicial Council with copies to the presiding judge and the press. No comments to the press, gentlemen. I'm leaving it like this for the moment. "Personal reasons" were the only reasons cited in the resignation letter."

"When's Dr. Paschov coming, Harry?" Nate asked.

"He said 10:15 a.m."

"Good," Nate said, "because we have some stuff to go over." He opened a file on his desk. "First in order, I was able to get a history on Rick Hansen. He was born in Redding, California. He was a straight-A student in grade school and most of high school in San Diego. Then he started to do drugs. He nose-dived academically, but still went to college at U.C. Santa Cruz with an electrical engineering major and a minor in English lit. In his second year, he dropped out. Then he entered a drug rehab program in New Mexico following a misdemeanor conviction and cleaned up his drug use for a while. Next we find him attending, get this, a police academy in Louisiana. He scored high marks in virtually everything. He completed academy, but never applied for a police officer position anywhere in this country. Then he dropped out for a couple of years and I can't find any record of him anywhere. He has a Social Security card, but it doesn't show any earnings under that number for two years. No arrests. No license applications. No speeding tickets."

"In prison?" Harry asked.

"He never went. Minor jail terms only. Then he shows up in San Francisco ten years ago and we have minor drug possessions, parking tickets, odds and ends. He begins shining shoes at the Hall here five years ago. As far as Social Security and the IRS know, he doesn't exist for the last eight years."

"So he evades taxes. I'll worry about that another year. Parents?" Pierre asked.

"Both dead."

"What does he do with his life when he's not hanging around the Hall?" Pierre asked.

"We don't know. I canvassed the neighbors and he's one of those 'Nice fellows'. Keeps to himself kind of mystery man. One neighbor recalled a marijuana smell from his door once, but otherwise he remains inconspicuous."

"Any known psych history?" Harry asked Nate.

"None we know of. What I'd really like to do is take a peek in his apartment. Think we can get a warrant, Pierre?"

"On the marijuana possession? It'll do. I agree with the look-see on his apartment. Nate, will you work it up using the citizen informant as the probable cause? Harry, do you think the probable cause will hold up?"

"Yes, a citizen informant is the best P.C., and anyone is competent these days to recognize the smell of pot. Some judges would reject a warrant for mere possession, but maybe you could flesh it out with numerous visits at odd hours, and an expert opinion that this is consistent with dealing? Anyone would sign then."

"Unfortunately not," Nate said. "He has no visitors."

"Then pick the judge carefully. Who's the best on marginal warrants?" Harry asked.

"Alquiza," Pierre said. All three men laughed.

"Who after him?"

"That would be Kellogg, the Presiding Judge," Pierre said, "He'll do it for me, but on this one it'll have to be on a 'trust me this time' basis."

"When will you serve it, Pierre?" Harry asked.

"I'd like to do it this afternoon if we can, while Hansen's still at the Hall shining..." Pierre was interrupted by a loud door slam. Tiny Ratto swaggered, or rather waddled, up to them, his neck flab pushing at his collar. His face was flushed.

"You prick, La Croix." He then looked at Nate and Harry and said "You two get out. I'm gonna talk to La Croix in private."

Harry stood up, and Nate shifted in his seat. Pierre waved his hand and countermanded Ratto's order. "Stay where you are, gentlemen. I want witnesses to this."

"I'm a Captain; you're a Lieutenant; and Hutchinson is a Sergeant. This is a direct order."

"Yes," Pierre agreed, "an illegal one in direct violation of the Chief's order that you stay out of here. That's why I want witnesses to this conduct."

"Fuck you, La Croix. I'm trying to give you the command courtesy of dealing with you in private, but you want to grandstand, don't you? Okay, you got it. You think you're ready to move up to my Captain's bars? You think framing me and slandering me is gonna get you a promotion? The only rank it will get you is top rank on every command officer's shit list. No one will ever trust you again. The first time you screw up, my friends will take you out. You hear me?"

"Oh, yes," Pierre said with a little smile. "I'm always surprised but pleased when someone warns me that he's going to come after me. Now get out, or do you want to trade in your transfer for a suspension?"

"Oh, eat shit, you sanctimonious son of a bitch. I'll leave when I'm done."

"If you're not out of here in five seconds, I'll have the Chief suspend you for compromising a murder investigation by coming here in violation of direct orders."

"You got no pull. I've been on the force thirty-five years."

"One."

"You're mental, Pierre. You wreck my career? For what? For nothing? You're paranoid."

"Two."

"Eat my Guinney ass, you piece of shit. Carmen was right about you. Just watch your back, asshole. You screwed with the wrong guy."

"Three." Ratto's face looked about one red blood cell short of apoplexy.

"Four."

Ratto bolted, and his wobbling buttocks just cleared the door jamb as Pierre spoke the word, "Five."

"Geez," Nate said, "the idiot really swallowed it."

"One thing I've learned about Pierre over the years, Nate," Harry said, "is that when he sets limits, he always means it, right down to the inch and the nanosecond. Tiny knew that too." Pierre sat in silence as the two mused as if he were not present.

Nate asked, "If you had gotten to five just one second before he reached the door, would you have reported him?" Pierre did not answer.

"Nate, three years ago, a perp was brandishing a little pocket knife at Pierre from five yards away. Your partner here warned him not to take one step farther. The moron decided to play with Pierre, and took that one step, just to show he couldn't be intimidated. Pierre shot him through the knee for the same reason." Just the slightest smile stretched over Pierre's mouth. He seemed happy with the story.

"Where were we?" Harry asked. "Oh, the search. You want me out of this, right?"

"Afraid so, Harry. Just stay clear and we'll brief you tomorrow."

"Okay."

"Well, that's it for now," Nate said. "I'll work on the Hansen warrant until Dr. Paschov gets here. Harry, could you work on getting the Alquiza records, using this authorization?"

"Sure, happy to oblige," Harry said. He set to work copying the consent form and using Pierre's computer to generate the correspondence to accompany the records requests. Then he made phone calls to expedite matters.

♦

Soon Julie buzzed Nate's desk and Harry answered it. "Send him in," Harry said.

The portly Doctor Paschov walked in and sat down. He began without prologue. "Your man is, of course, a very intelligent person. The fact that he is able to kill repeatedly without being caught rather disqualifies the marginally witted. That is not news to you, I am sure. There is clearly a rage against women which motivates him. That is a given as well. That he was abused as a child is probable, also rather standard. What I found that is not routine is that you are seeking two people, not one."

"No, Doctor Paschov," Pierre said. "There is only one."

"You must listen, Inspector La Croix. I will tell you why it is so. The killings and rapes fall into two distinct categories. There are repeated themes and techniques in a number of them. I can easily attribute them to the same man. However, there is another group of cases which bear a markedly different flavor, and in my opinion, they cannot be the work of the same man. The motivations are inconsistent and incompatible."

"Doctor," Pierre said, "with all due respect to your expertise, I have been chasing him for eight years and have studied the files for many hundreds of hours. I am certain it is all the same man."

Doctor Paschov gave him a look combining annoyance and perplexity, but went on without commenting on Pierre's interruption.

"One set of crimes is typified by extremes of brutal torture and gratuitous infliction of suffering. No lust is evident in these, only hatred for women. The other group is set off by the obvious pursuit of sexual gratification for both him and the victim. This is seen in the absence of the torture and disfigurement, and also in the autopsies. There was always genital engorgement at the time of death, meaning that the killer first performed foreplay on the victim, though probably against her will. The presence of fresh vaginal lubrication in these cases confirms this. In no way could the first killer have behaved like this. He would be no more aroused by a woman, than you or I would be aroused by a rabid dog. There are two killers at work in these cases. Perhaps that might account for the inability to narrow the suspects by their movements and alibis."

"Well, you'll have to re-evaluate the evidence. The incidents are all the same man," Pierre repeated.

Doctor Paschov looked at Harry, and then back to Pierre. "I will do no such thing," he finally threw back at Pierre. "I do not mold my opinions to suit the investigator's theories. If you disregard my theory just because it is not what you expected, then you have wasted my time. Would you like to tell me why you insist they are the same man, when the evidence is to the contrary?"

Pierre looked from Doctor Paschov, to Nate, to Harry. His face registered a decision being made, and he said "Okay, I've held some evidence back from you and from everyone, to avoid any copycats fooling us. Not even Nate and Harry knew this, so please mention it to no other breathing person. At each one of the Hellhound crime scenes was hidden a hangman drawing. I found the first one when I was alone, and kept it quiet. After that, I always made sure I was the first one to search, so that no one else would ever know. It was the only way I could rule out confessors and copycats. That's how I knew the drawings were a death sentence when we got them, except ours come in stages."

"But Inspector La Croix, that changes nothing. I never suggested that these killers were independent. We are talking about a partnership. Of course they both leave the same calling card."

"Doctor, do you know how few of the serial killers in the history of the world worked in pairs? It almost never happens."

"I do know that. That is why I can understand your rejecting that theory, but it does happen, and I believe this is such a case. You must look for a mismatched pair. We have one dominant one, and one who obeys, a stooge. To accommodate both men's different depravities, they take turns deciding how the crimes will go. You must bear in mind that the crimes usually increase in brutality and frequency. It is a form of addiction, and with time, it takes more to get that same 'high' that they used to get."

"Now it's making sense," Harry said. "He can be in two places at once, so it's been impossible to figure out his movements."

"Thank you, Doctor," Pierre said. "I apologize for not giving you the full background. There were good reasons, and I had no clue that the twelve women were not all victims of the same man. If I had suspected it, I would have shared with you the existence of the drawings."

"Ah. It is nothing. I am glad I could help at last. If you have further ideas or needs in the light of the new complexion of the case, please give me a call. I shall try to help as best I can. Good day, gentlemen." He walked out past Harry with a dark look on his face.

CHAPTER SIXTEEN

Harry left Pierre and Nate to work on the warrant, and went back to his office. He inserted a demand in a settlement package Bridget had worked up. She had two other files ready except for the updated medical bills and medical reports she had ordered.

Harry told her that he was going out to run an errand, and he set out for Dunn's Guns to pick up his parcels. They were ready as promised. To Harry's surprise, no confirmation was received from the State that he was cleared for a gun purchase. But it was a negative option system. If you don't hear otherwise, go ahead and sell. Harry wondered how many guns were sold to nut cases when the phones were busy, or the office got backed up with processing papers. Harry bought a couple of boxes of ammunition for each gun and packed all the stuff into his trunk.

Later that afternoon, Nate, Pierre, Veronica Atkins, and Dornan from E.S.U. made their way into Rick Hansen's apartment building, chatting like people on a double date. Their guns and the warrant were hidden under their jackets.

Hansen was at the Hall under surveillance, so Pierre was free to use his lock picks on the door. In thirty seconds, they were in. They pulled on rubber gloves, and Dornan checked that there were no bugs or hidden cameras. Nate snapped Polaroids of the entire place so that anything that was moved could be put back exactly as it was. They divided up the apartment and began to search.

In ten minutes they were done, and reported their findings to Pierre. Nate had found books on construction, electrical engineering, clocks, surveying, Shakespeare, computers, local history, politics, including radical politics, martial arts, and weapons of all kinds. He also photographed Hansen's exotic dagger collection. There were flame daggers, Nazi stilettos and bayonets, balanced throwing knives, and even a saw-toothed dagger that could inflict a nasty, jagged cut, or grip an opponent's knife blade in a fight.

Ronnie had checked the computer and recorded the internet sites Hansen had book marked, including, *Urban Warrior Handbook*, *Fantasy Mercenary's Quest*, *Deadly Diets*, and *Sherlock's Cyber Puzzlers*.

Dornan had a productive foray into the bedroom. In the top dresser drawer she found a driver's license in Hansen's name. In the photo Hansen was made up to look African-American. She also found makeup, false mustaches, eyebrow pencils and women's clothing in Hansen's sizes.

Nate searched for hidden compartments and for signs of abduction supplies like duct tape, handcuffs, guns, and torture instruments. He found nothing.

"Either we've got the wrong guy," said Pierre, "or he's hidden all the incriminating stuff somewhere else. Time to clear out. I'll do the once over. Give me the reference photos. I'll be out in ten. Be sure and take your gloves with you."

The three left, and Pierre put everything back the way it had been. Then he swept the carpet with a broom to remove their foot prints. When he was done, he joined them downstairs.

After Dornan and Ronnie left in another vehicle, Pierre and Nate sat and talked in Pierre's car. "A burglar with more imagination than most, in my book," Nate said.

"Not quite. The books show a wide range of technical topics that would all be of interest to the Hellhound, and the license shows more than just imagination. Also, he's got dozens of disguises with various kinds of makeup. He could go unrecognized most anywhere—black, white, male, female, Catholic priest, or Hindu. Did you see the turban cloth in the bedroom?"

"All of which makes it easy for him to loiter and case a place without being recognized. So what's our next move? Round the clock tail?" Nate asked.

"I don't think so. It probably wouldn't do any good. If Hansen is the one, he'd spot a tail right away. If we've found our man after all these years, I don't want to spook him. I think a more thorough background check is our next step."

"What about Alquiza? We're not kicking him out as a suspect, are we?" Nate asked.

"Not yet. We still have to see those psych records before we know for sure."

Nate shook his head. "Well, if Alquiza is the guy, God only knows what he'll do with all the extra free time you just gave him. I hope medical records and the Hall's court files will establish his whereabouts at the time of the crimes. That might exclude him or confirm his probability."

"I don't think tracing a suspect's whereabouts will clear or nail anyone now. You're forgetting the stooge. One could have a perfect alibi while the other one is out killing someone."

♦

Harry left Dunn's Guns, picked up some pizza, and went home. There he unpacked his pistols, loaded them, and laid them on the couch. He ate in front of the TV and watched for a few minutes before bed. He was drowsy and drifting when the phone rang. It was Dr. Paschov.

"I am sorry to disturb you at home. I would not call if it were not important."

Harry was suddenly wide awake.

"Sorry about the static at Homicide, doctor."

"Think nothing of it Mr. Maxwell. I was calling for your benefit, not to complain."

"How's that?"

"Are you a man of hunches, Mr. Maxwell?"

"Often. I always say that the gut is usually right. If you have a strong feeling, believe in it."

"That has been my philosophy as well. I agree wholeheartedly with Inspector La Croix's bringing a civilian into the case. The files I read suggest that someone with police expertise may be the perpetrator or perpetrators. I called you because you are the only one I feel completely safe about."

"Thank you, but he didn't bring me in. I blundered into it. What is your hunch?"

"That I think you need to watch your back."

"That's nothing new, Doctor. We have other police officers on our primary suspect list, besides the one you saw on TV."

"Yes. Yes. I know. I just want to point out that if your partners don't know everything you do, then compromised police communications will not defeat your efforts. Keep an edge that you don't share with anyone."

"Doctor, are you suggesting that it might be Nate or Pierre?"

"I have suggested no such thing, but police have rigid procedures that are predictable. How often does evidence disappear from their property room? I myself have been involved in three cases over the years where that has happened. You told me that you thought the Hellhound might be someone you know, didn't you?"

"Yes."

"Then, not knowing who it is, wouldn't it be wise to assume that no one is above suspicion?"

"Including you?" Harry asked with a smile.

"Of course," Paschov answered. "I'm somebody, aren't I? Watch out for everyone, Harry. Everyone." The voice now came through the phone softly and almost childlike in its gentleness. "Suspicion is the thing that might keep you alive, Harry."

For a few long moments the only sounds of which Harry was aware were the soft rustling of his ear on the receiver and his own breathing. The tightness in his throat made it hard to talk, so he gently put the handset back in the cradle without saying another word.

The doctor's words bounced around in his head, and he thought again of Alissa and Yvonne. He was not the only one who might pay if he screwed up. Again.

Harry sat and worried his lip between thumb and forefinger. Trust no one? Prudent advice, no doubt. Nate was on the list, and so was Nate's boss, Tiny Ratto. So was his own investigator Tyrone. Even his brother-in-law Rico was on the list. What about Pierre? He's big. Why couldn't such a top detective find this guy in eight years?

Alquiza had a grudge against Harry apart from the Hellhound investigation. If he were the Hellhound, he was surely marked for a particularly uncomfortable interview. Any police officer might be the stooge, or his shoe shine man. Now Harry's thoughts drifted to Osmund. He seemed to have a network of information that would be the envy of any cop.

Harry's thoughts whirled in a swamp of doubt. He shook his head to clear it. Too many suspects. How could he solve the crime alone, without trusting anyone? He wanted to withdraw and go back to his own little law practice. Could he, he wondered? Maybe the chat room insults were nothing but amusing to him alone. Then Harry remembered Audrey Langley and the personal note the Hellhound left him: "Thank you, Ishmael."

He undressed and got ready for bed, feeling that he was treading in neck-deep water. He set his alarm and pulled down the covers, then realized instantly that he had forgotten to check the bobby pin when he came home. The Hangman was there below his pillow staring up at him. It had nine elements done, and only two to go. His knees went weak.

"Goddamn you lock-picking son of a bitch," he whispered. "Don't you ever sleep?"

CHAPTER SEVENTEEN

The Hellhound was humming the tune to "Knick-Knack Paddy-Whack" as he glanced left and right out the smoky windows of the moving van. The rumbling of the engine kept the rhythm of the song as it idled at the light. The light turned green, and the Hellhound slipped   into first gear. A low growling of gears diffused into the night air. His watch showed 3:30 a.m. He was perfectly on schedule and continued his advance toward the Hall of Justice. Bryant was a one-way street, so he pulled all the way left next to the parked cars. He came to a stop about 200 feet from the entrance to the Hall's Northern Police Station. The thick coating of cigarette smoke on the windows made it impossible to see clearly into the cab, so he calmly checked his mirrors. No traffic or pedestrians were about, so he adjusted his stocking mask and got out.

In seconds he was at the back roll-up door, not much slowed by his dragging left foot. He raised the door up only about a foot and reached in to fish out the end of the rope. He craned his neck to look up, and swung the lead diver's weight on the end of the rope. His practiced hands sent it straight up to the street lamp. The weight went over the cross bar on the first try and raced back down to him. In five more seconds he raced around the car parked next to the lamp post, making a large loop around its wheels. He tied it off, leaving the rope lassoed around the car.

He got back into the driver's seat and quietly shut the door, loosening a few flakes of chalky, olive green paint from the metal. His mirror showed one old Honda Civic chugging up Bryant a block behind him, but it turned right. The street was otherwise clear, and no one was showing any sign of entering or leaving the Hall. He started off and drove toward the next lamp post, which was only twenty feet short of the Hall's glass doors. As he covered the distance, more rope came reeling out of the back of the truck. A low thud sounded when the rope yanked the body out of the van and it hit the pavement behind him.

"Bumpsy Daisy," the lips whispered through the nylon mesh.

An eighteen-year-old redhead, who should have known better than to open her door to a stranger, was strung to the middle of the rope by a hangman's noose.

When he reached the next lamp post, the Hellhound jumped out of the truck. He yanked many lengths of slack rope from the back of the truck, seized the other weighted end of the rope, and threw it over the cross bar. This end of the rope was forked. One fork was made into a second hangman's noose and the other had a much longer trailing end. He snugged the noose quickly onto the truck's towing hitch.

He drove forward slowly, and the truck took up the slack. When the rope from the truck up to the lamp post and from lamp post down to the girl was tight, the engine began laboring to take up the weight of the body. The ropes groaned resonantly, and then the corpse was hoisted steadily into the air. The stocking-masked head leaned out the window. When the Hellhound saw the dead girl, clad only in panties, strung high up between the two lamp posts, he set the brake.

The faint smell of the girl's perfume, *Clinique* "Happy," was still in the air at the loading door. He took the free end of the rope and threw it under the nearest car, then tossed it back over the roof. Then he pulled up the slack and tied it off onto itself. Satisfied, he flicked open his knife and cut the hangman's noose off at the truck hitch, freeing the rope from the truck. The body lurched downward as the remaining slack was taken up. The two arms rose up as she plunged the short distance, and then petulantly slapped down against her thighs when the rope held. There she remained suspended like a ghastly long john on a hellish clothesline high overhead. The body stopped bouncing and began to sway quietly back and forth, like a child on a swing.

The Hellhound closed his knife, threw the severed noose into the truck, and rolled the door down. He looked up once more and smiled. Now humming "Swing Low, Sweet Chariot," he limped unhurriedly to the cab and got into the truck. He released the brake, pulled the silenced pistol out of his jacket, and laid it on the seat in case anyone approached as he was pulling away. No one did. Gun oil permeated the air in the cab, and he looked toward the police station doors again. Still clear. It wasn't necessary to cap any cops emerging from the station. The entire operation from start to finish had taken a minute and a half.

As the truck rumbled unhurriedly past the Northern Police Station entrance, the Hellhound turned left and smartly saluted. Then he continued on his way down the still, peaceful street, obeying all traffic laws.

♦

At 5:00 a.m. Nate and Pierre were roused from their sleep by a visit from uniformed officers urgently summoning them to the Mayor's mansion. There the Mayor's personal police bodyguard met them at the front entrance and motioned them inside without speaking. He didn't have to. His funereal expression said paragraphs. Inside the opulent foyer a butler showed them stiffly to the library. Already seated at the conference table was Police Chief Pete Tanaka. Nate looked at him inquiringly. "We weren't told why we're here, just to come. What's up?"

"I asked that, and Her Honor didn't tell me," said Tanaka. "But I think it's to do with the Hellhound. That's why I had you two called here. I can guarantee you it's bad. The Mayor was not a happy camper when she called me."

"She called you personally?" Pierre asked.

"Uh-huh."

The three men all jerked their heads toward the door, which stood ajar. They responded in unison to the sharp and rapid click-clicking of high heels on the marble steps which led down from the sleeping quarters above. What was surprising about the noise was that someone was flying down those stairs in high heels at break neck speed as if fleeing from a fire. Or going to one.

The door burst open with a slam, and the Honorable Wendy Cathcart marched into the room. She was meticulously dressed in a silk suit and flowing scarf at the neck. Swooping over the table, she flung a stack of 8 1/2" x 11" photos onto the table and sat down at the head chair. She had obviously wanted nothing to soften the moment or to give them any chance to prepare any defense. The photos were picked at and spread around the table top amid curses, groans, and cries of disgust. The desecrated body of the poor redheaded girl was clearly framed in front of the Hall of Justice. In the unlikely event that anyone could miss the significance of the location of the crime, the entrance to the Northern Station was visible at the right edge of the photo.

"Gentlemen, this will not DO!" said the mayor in a clipped and angry voice, looking around the table at all of them. Chief Tanaka was flushed and silent while Nate broke into a sweat. Pierre's Adam's apple bobbed as he squeezed his lips between the fingers of his right hand.

The Chief spoke first, "Uh, when were these taken, Your Honor?"

"About an hour and a quarter ago," she snapped as if the question were either stupid or impertinent. "Would somebody PLEASE tell me how the hell this is even possible?"

"I...I, I'm damned if I know," stammered Tanaka. "Mayor, even at 3:00 a.m. that station is properly staffed. Officers bring arrestees into the lobby of the Hall of Justice all night long. They come and go by this door twenty-four hours a day. How some psycho can set up this horror is beyond my comprehension. In God's name, Mayor," he said painfully, "to look at this photo you would think the entire graveyard shift had taken the night off, but they were there. Any noise outside their doors would have been investigated. You can't possibly think that my officers would arrive at the Hall, walk past this awful thing, and just go right on inside for coffee and donuts?"

The Mayor glared at him. "The newspapers already have this. The TV cameras were there even before the police photographers. It'll be out on the wire services by dawn. I want three things. I want to know who the hell did this sick, monstrous thing. I want a plan of attack to give the press in one hour. And I want my City back! Nobody does this in my City and gets away with it. *Nobody!*" she nearly shouted.

"There is no doubt in my mind who did this, your Honor. The Hellhound."

"Of *course* it's him," she shouted, thumping the walnut table top. "Do you take me for an idiot? What I'm saying is that I want to know *who he is*, once and for all."

Pierre jumped in. "Absolutely, Your Honor. It's something only he could have pulled off. Look at the ropes here," he said, leaning forward and gesturing at the pictures. "He got the lengths just right. He had to have calculated it all out mathematically and done practice runs so that it could be pulled off in seconds."

"Seconds?" the Mayor asked. "Are you suggesting that one man could have done all this in a matter of seconds?"

All eyes studied Pierre. After a moment he shrugged. "Had to. Like the Chief said, day and night all year long, people go in and come out. The station never closes. The act was done. We see the proof. Only way it is possible is if it happened so fast that a car didn't have time to go three blocks from start to finish. If someone knows the routine at the Hall, he'd have a good idea when the foot traffic is lightest. And if he was monitoring the police dispatch communications, he could know when any cars were bringing in prisoners. The Hellhound studies his moves very carefully. My guess is that he worked it out so that the whole abomination was done in a couple of minutes."

"What about my second question?" she snapped.

The Chief spoke up. "Your Honor, I'll meet the press and outline a 'no limits' investigation that will include door-to-door questioning, DNA testing of all the equipment he used, and extensive canvassing of informants. The headline will be 'City declares WAR on Hellhound.'"

"OK," said the Mayor, "but I also want to see you shaking the noose on camera vowing a swift end to this horror. Now tell me, when *are* we going to see this case closed?" She looked around the table at the three faces. Silence met her question. "Well?" she pressed.

"Your Honor," Pierre began, "the part about the DNA? That's fine to reassure the public, but we've tried DNA sampling in every crime this guy has committed. He never leaves a trace of anything usable. If we don't turn up an eyewitness who will talk, well…"

"Not good enough," she cut him off, "*not good enough*. Up until now this guy was just our worst murderer of history. Now he's into terrorism. He's made San Francisco an object of world-wide disgust. Tourism will suffer. It's a different ball game now. This Hellhound has made himself my administration's number one priority. You *will* catch him. I'm insisting on it."

"Yes, your Honor," responded the Chief. "We'll get him. I just can't promise the exact day."

"No? Then I'll promise *you* something. In thirty days, if the Hellhound isn't dead or in custody, I'll have a new Chief of Police." Her words were still in the air as she spun on her high heels and strode out of the room.

♦

On Monday morning Harry parked in his lot and wavered between going to his office and the Hall. He needed to settle some cases, but it was Monday. Bridge did not come in today, and the office would be lonely. His feet found their way to the Hall.

Oz was on duty today, with a broad smile for Harry as always. Word had it that Tiny Ratto and a number of his ranking friends were out to get Pierre and "that shit friend of his Maxwell." No news there. Harry ponied up as usual and then clapped Oz on the shoulder. Oz pumped Harry's hand.

♦

Harry waltzed into Homicide and found Ronnie at work. He asked if she had any results yet. "Almost, Harry. I'm merging and tabulating now. Let's meet early this afternoon to go over some of the results."

Nate walked in. "Harry, glad you're here. I just paged Pierre and was about to call you. There's something at the Wharf that I think might interest us. Want to come?"

"Sure, but wait a second." He took Pierre's pistol out of his briefcase and gave it to Nate, who locked it in Pierre's desk.

It was just past noon when they got into Nate's Trans Am. Harry cringed, contemplating the traffic tedium that would obstruct their way to Fishermen's Wharf, more than thirty hilly blocks away. "What's up, Nate?"

"Some fishermen at the wharf were working down at the water line on their boat. They spotted a duffle bag stowed under the pier with some stuff in it that might interest us."

Harry looked down and reassured himself that his seat belt was fastened. They were climbing Taylor Street. It was a straight shot almost all the way to the wharf, albeit a steep run. Nate was using his siren, so progress was snappy. Harry got a good hold on the door handle, braced his other arm to the dash, and found that his teeth were clenched in spite of himself. Stores flew by, shoppers on the sidewalk stopped and stared, and Harry's stomach surged and plummeted at each intersection.

Nate parked close to the pier. They walked past throngs of buzzing tourists who flocked around giant steaming crab pots cooking up fresh Dungeness crab. The day was sunny, and, as always, the Wharf carried the party atmosphere of people on vacation.

Neither Nate nor Harry were surprised to see Pierre's Chevelle already there when they arrived. The yellow police tape was already up. Pierre walked with them to the edge of the pier. A couple of sea lions were cruising the surface, looking for handouts.

A ladder led down to a tied-up rowboat. A young fisherman with a blonde beard was already aboard when they unsteadily embarked. The boatman introduced himself as Alex and paddled them a short distance under the pier. Soon he stood up and pointed to an orange strap drooping below the joists supporting the pier's floor.

"I found it just like it is now," he said, "except that I opened the zipper to see what it was, and something fell into the water, maybe a knife."

"I've called for a police diver," Pierre said. "He should be here soon."

Alex positioned them under the bag and then looped a line around the piling next to them. He drew the line tightly so that the boat hugged the piling, and Pierre boosted Nate up so he could reach the bag. It was held only by some nylon twine fastened to a couple of nails driven into the joist. Nate untied the twine and lowered the bag gently into the boat. They brought the bag up onto the pier and opened it as Nate swore quietly about the creosote on his hands and slacks. He donned rubber gloves and prodded the contents of the bag, but did not remove them. Immediately visible were makeup containers, wigs, clothing, tools, and pantyhose.

While they were discussing the find, the diver arrived and began to suit up. She already had her swim suit on and began to pull on her tight-fitting "Farmer John" blue and orange wetsuit pants. She helped it slip on more easily by taking the air hose from her tank regulator and flashing a jet of compressed air down the arms and legs as she pulled it on. Then she slipped her arms into the straps of the air tank back pack and fastened the straps.

Alex got back into the row boat and returned to the spot where the object had fallen. The diver jumped off the pier with legs spread wide and a hand holding her mask in place. Alex pointed her to the spot where the bag had been tied, and she dove straight down. She was down for only a minute and resurfaced with a dagger in her hand, holding it between her thumb and fingers by the blade.

"That's all I found, Pierre," she said. Pierre thanked her, and she packed up her gear. Nate threw all the evidence into his trunk, and they arranged to meet back at Homicide.

♦

Half an hour later, the three men congregated around a long table in the large conference room. On the table was a plastic tarp, and on it lay the duffle bag. All three wore rubber gloves. Harry manned the camera and snapped each item as it emerged. First came wigs and clothing. There were two pairs of men's pants, both with long inseams, plus a large-size dress, pantyhose, shirts, blouses, sunglasses, and items of ostentatious costume jewelry. From the bottom layer Nate began to pull out tools, including slip joint pliers, a set of screw drivers, a razor knife, a glass cutter, a battery-powered drill with titanium and carbide bits, a long metal tube with a mirror mounted on the end, a propane mini-torch, and a roll of duct tape. More sinister than these were the scalpel, a speculum, a bottle of chloral hydrate, a metal coat hanger, a slim jim, and an eighteen-inch piece of flexible steel conduit with a taped handle at one end, suitable for flogging. In a plastic bag beside the duffle bag was the dagger that had fallen under the pier. It was a middle eastern flame dagger, so called because its blade had a curved, undulating shape.

Harry asked, "So what is this? Why would the Hellhound or anyone else stash this stuff there? If he wanted to get rid of the evidence, a mile offshore in 200 feet of water would be better."

"It's simple, Harry," replied Nate. "First of all, he doesn't want this incriminating stuff at his home in case he's ever searched. Second, this guy plans in advance for emergencies. He assumes every kind of screw-up and disaster, and plans what he'll do then. Am I right, Pierre?"

"Exactly. He'd have been caught long ago otherwise."

"So I think he stashes emergency supplies like this all over the city," Nate said. "If he's on the run, he might need a key to a storeroom to hide in, or a quick change of clothing if he's bloody. Or he might need to disguise himself as a woman to walk out of an area that's being cordoned off by police and searched."

"Sounds far-fetched to me," Harry said. "He'd only draw attention to himself trying to pass as a 6'2" woman."

"Would he?" Nate asked with a laugh. "In Iowa, maybe. Harry, when was the last time you turned your head and stared at a man in women's clothing in San Francisco?"

Harry raised his eyebrows and nodded. "So, could the dagger still have any prints after its dunking?"

"Maybe," Pierre said. "As long as it was not wiped or smeared during recovery from the mud, the skin oils that make up the prints are not easily water soluble without soap. If the prints sit on metal long enough, and the sweat and oil are acidic enough, the print can even etch into the metal. We'll see."

They all looked at each other for several seconds, until Nate said, "Well, minus the lamps and the TV, we're looking at Rick Hansen's apartment in miniature."

"Nate, would you get Forensics here ASAP to dust this stuff?"

"It's done," Nate called over his shoulder on his way out.

"If we're really lucky, that flogging cable will have blood traces on it. If it matches Audrey Langley's blood, we'll know it's his stash," remarked Harry to Pierre.

"I didn't see any residue, and that would be really careless of him, wouldn't it?"

"Well, he *is* getting more reckless and outrageous, isn't he, just like Dr. Paschov said?"

Nate returned with Matt Thomas, the fingerprint technician, and explained their request. "Call us when you're done," Nate told him. Turning to Pierre and Harry, he said, "Let's see what Ronnie has for us on the victim database."

The three found Ronnie sipping a cup of coffee. She began without prologue. "What came up positive in one hundred per cent of the victims' backgrounds was what was good about them or was innocuous. They all ate at pizzerias, but there was no consistency as to where, and what teenager doesn't eat pizza? About the only thing I found that you wouldn't statistically expect to see, was that they were all straight-A students."

"And that's it?" Nate asked.

"I'm afraid so, until you guys tell me what other questions to ask the database. It's cheap and easy to just pull up one hundred percent correlations, but beyond that I have to know what to look for. Maybe you want to know how many of the kids participated in any sport? Or how many had a family member with a cosmetology license? I can get creative, but you have to tell me what to do."

"Thanks, Ronnie. Good work."

"Well, we have two questions to work on with the grades issue," Pierre said. "Why would he care, and how did he know? Ideas?"

Nate spoke first. "Maybe the grades issue ties in with wanting the innocent type; you know, too wholesome and studious to be hanging out on the street."

"That makes sense," Harry said. "But more helpful would be how he knew." Suddenly his face lit up with an idea, and he grinned. "Could the bastard be hacking into school computers?"

"Sure," Pierre said. "How else could he have all the personal data and grades?" Suddenly Nate stiffened and shouted, "I'll tell you how else. Scholarships. It's scholarships. They put racial data, grades, and addresses into each application. Family. Income. Employment. It's all in there. A bonanza of information for the dedicated hacker. Ronnie, find us scholarship info, please."

"Hey," Harry said, "I don't think I asked that in the survey."

Nate pulled out the victim list and divided up the families. Each of them began making calls. In a half hour they knew that all twelve had made application by direct internet filing to the F.A.F.S.A., Free Application for Federal Student Aid.

"All right, so he broke the encryption and hacked into these applications. He could hack into the website from anywhere, including from a portable laptop with a stolen identity. So this one's a dead end."

"Still, are you going to warn the public to watch out for scholarship website hacking?" Harry asked.

Pierre sighed. "Not much point, Harry. Anyway, why warn him that we know? We've issued public service warnings many times advising people not to open their doors to strangers. They still do it. If we warned about the scholarship scam in particular, he'd just use a new one that's even better."

"Yeah, like Alquiza's scam with the fake star."

"Harry, you have a single track mind," said Pierre.

"We haven't cleared him."

"Well then, relax. I received the psych records today," Pierre replied. "They show a psych hospitalization six years ago that lasted for six weeks. He was without question inside an institution in San Diego during the time that one of the victims was murdered here in San Francisco. Nurse's observation notes are present five times a day over the entire hospitalization."

"I thought we agreed he might be working in tandem with someone else. How does that clear him?" Harry asked.

"Well then get this, and then forget forever that you heard it, Harry. Ten years ago he was on vacation with his wife at Lake Shasta. He was water skiing. She was operating the boat, and she was drunk. He was waiting for her to take up the slack in his tow line, and she put it into reverse by mistake. The prop tore into his thighs and groin before she realized her error.

"They put out the word it was a heart attack, and he was off work for three months. But believe me, Harry, he's no rapist. However, it destroyed their marriage, made him a very bitter man, and finally led to her suicide. He's been so screwed up with anger and guilt over her death since then, that it's affected his relationship with his daughters. If he weren't already torqued out of shape enough, they blame him for their mother's death."

"But what about him posing as a cop, and taking girls away for handcuff and lube work?" Harry asked.

"Harry, the poor guy gets them to perform, and he just watches. Get it? He can't do anything, so he watches. Now let it lie, will you?"

"Okay," Harry said. "I actually feel sorry for Alquiza. But I still don't understand how this clears him. If the Hellhound was actually a team, who more than Alquiza would have need of a partner to debase his victims? And who could have more of a motive?"

Pierre sighed, shook his head, and said, "It's 4:00 p.m. already. I think we're done."

"Fine," said Harry. "I've got some work to do on my own cases."

◆

He walked slowly across the street to his office, doing his customary surveillance of parked cars, windows, and doorways. He went up, popped a diet soda, and checked his e-mail. Several mass e-mailings offered untold riches. *Delete, delete, delete.* He hit the *News* button to catch the headlines and saw "Urban Terrorism: Is Anyone Safe?"

The room was eerily quiet. Only the computer's cooling fan broke the silence, pushing a gentle curtain of air toward his face. His fingers were cold. Suddenly he was filled with an empty feeling, as if he were standing in a chilly auditorium listening to echoes.

His mind raced. Daily he was bouncing between terror, exhilaration, worry, excitement, desperation, and other feelings he couldn't name. One feeling he couldn't shake was that his life was changing, and there was no going back. What perplexed him was that, in these worst days of his life, he was not sure he wanted to.

CHAPTER EIGHTEEN

A stack of Harry's files were queued up clamoring for some attention, so he set to work. When he next checked his watch, it was 8:15 p.m. already and dark. He had missed lunch and dinner. His attention span had crashed, so he locked up the office and went to his car. "Shut up," he said aloud to his stomach. Holding down his shoulder holster, he latched his seat belt.

Less than a block from his office, Harry looked in his mirror. A sedan's lights went on at the right curb just after he passed by. The car pulled into his lane and followed behind him. He continued east on Bryant Street in the far right lane, and then moved one lane over to the left. He watched the following car do the same. He speeded up a bit, and it did the same, keeping about seventy feet behind him. Harry stopped at a red light, and now he could see it in his lane about twenty-five feet back. It was a Caddy. He could not see into the car, but at least nothing protruded out of the windows. Harry watched closely to see that nothing did.

When the light changed, Harry took off abruptly, and his tail did too, matching his own pace. When he was 100 feet away from a left turn, he swerved left into the next lane and made ready to hang the left turn squealing. He checked his mirror, and the car lurched into his lane again. Harry opened his side window and slowed down to let the car close the gap on him.

When the car was only twenty feet behind him, he whipped the wheel to the right and slammed on the brakes. He quickly pulled out his .357 out and slipped off the safety. As his car slid to the right and suddenly stopped, the other car drew up beside him on the left. Harry began to raise the pistol and then froze. Next to him in the other vehicle was an elderly woman who looked both lost and scared.

The passenger side window of the Caddy came down, and she blurted out to Harry, "I'm so sorry, sir. I almost hit you. I'm lost, and I couldn't figure out the map. I was trying to follow someone to get back to the main part of town."

Harry relaxed, his loud heartbeat slowing. He smiled and slowly clicked the safety back on below the window level. He shoved the pistol back in its holster and said as pleasantly as he could, "You can follow me. Market Street good?"

She smiled back. "Oh yes, that would be wonderful. I'm staying at the Hyatt. Thank you."

Harry's breathing evened out. He drove carefully over to Market and led the woman past her hotel. Then he drove home and began the nightly ritual of cruising for a parking space.

◆

Atop the Mark Hopkins Hotel at the peak of Nob Hill, some of the city's most wealthy and influential families were attending a political fundraiser. The guests at the Top of the Mark were enjoying the spectacular view of the city that had thrilled people since its opening in 1939. Women in designer gowns and grape-sized diamonds sat enjoying the fine crystal, mahogany walls, and history. The air was filled with the sounds of happy chatter and soft footfalls on thick carpeting, and the odors of expensive perfumes and delicious food.

Mrs. Winifred Belford stopped to look at the World War II photograph of sailors on shore leave sitting at the bar with their laughing girlfriends. Beside that one was a photo of a fighter plane with "Top of the Mark" painted on its nose, and another of a nubile female lounging in a giant cocktail glass. Winifred made her way back to her small table next to a large picture window, where she rejoined her husband Winston, whose considerable money derived from a very successful Silicon Valley software start-up.

The elegance of the evening was suddenly punctured when a well-lubricated patron shifted his foot to the aisle without looking, and a waiter bearing a silver tray with a crème de menthe parfait tripped. The dessert with its luminous green syrup went flying, and then eased sluggishly down the front of Winifred's Paris original. The maitre d' delivered his profuse apologies along with offers of immediate free dry cleaning. Win and Winnie Belford opted instead to return home so Mrs. Belford could change.

Although Mr. Belford could afford a chauffeur, he preferred to do his own driving of his vintage Silver Cloud Rolls Royce. He pointed it toward his home at the northern tip of the City, the Marina. The Belfords' home faced the Marina Green and the yacht harbor. Tonight the salty sea air of the Marina was thickened with fog.

♦

As Winston Belford approached his house, he saw dimly through the fog that on the left side of his driveway was parked a black Triumph motorcycle. As he pulled into his driveway beside it, he could hear the throaty, rhythmic thrum-thrumming of the idling engine. No apparent owner was in sight. Even if their seventeen-year-old daughter, Tracy, had disobeyed and invited an unknown friend over in their absence, that still did not explain why the bike was left running.

Winston hit the remote garage door opener so they could walk up from the basement entrance. As Winston entered the door to the interior, he heard running footsteps, the slam of an interior door, and then three gunshots accompanied by loud clanging noises. Next, he heard more hurried footsteps running downstairs and out of the house. Then the motorcycle exploded into life, with the loud clunk of hastily meshed gears clashing into place. Winston called out for his daughter, and heard Tracy screaming from above, "Help meeeeeee…"

He bounded up the basement stairs two at a time, to enter the living room just as his daughter was staggering downstairs. She collapsed onto the living room floor, holding her head. There was blood on her forehead, and more on her torn white blouse, which hung open to reveal scratches on her breast.

Her father ran to her and took her into his arms to turn her over. She had only one cut on her forehead over her left eye, but she was nearly hysterical. Examining his daughter's face, he heard his wife outside screaming, "Police, police! He's wearing a mask."

Within seconds she came up the stairs and entered the living room too, going pale when she saw her daughter.

"Dial 911, Winnie!" shouted her husband. "Get the police and an ambulance here. Tell them the guy is on a black Triumph and which way he went."

She had the phone in her hand, but she was looking at her daughter. "Call. *Call!*" he shouted at her. She called and reported a man in a stocking mask and a yellow jacket on a black motorcycle, who limped as he ran out of the house. In response to a question she added that he was last seen on Marina Boulevard racing his motorcycle toward Doyle Drive and the Golden Gate Bridge.

Winston looked at his wife and heard her say hoarsely into the phone, "Rape and attempted murder." Mrs. Belford went to Tracy's room to get a robe to cover her daughter. She sat down with her on the couch to hold and rock her while the girl cried hysterically. Winston stood helplessly and watched the tears streaming down both faces. Winnie said nothing more but only stroked and smoothed Tracy's long blonde hair.

In seconds they began to hear the sound of sirens. First one police car, then another, and then several more. The sirens seemed to be converging from many directions until they all seemed to merge into one great wail.

◆

When the motorcycle left the Belford driveway, the driver had raced west on Marina Boulevard. Three blocks away the vehicle merged onto Doyle Drive, which traveled over and through the Presidio, a decommissioned military reservation. Doyle Drive fed directly onto State Highway 101, which crossed the Golden Gate Bridge north to Marin County. Margie Hellman, the emergency police dispatcher this night, tried to get the approach to the bridge closed off before the suspect could make it across. She also notified the Marin County Sheriff's Department to wait on the northern end of the bridge to intercept him. It would take several minutes to cross the bridge, especially in the fog, so she set about tightening the noose. At Margie's direction, two marked units sped down Marina Boulevard toward the Belford mansion and the bridge. Two other units were approaching from the south on Park Presidio Boulevard, which also merged onto Doyle Drive, in case the suspect reversed direction to escape. Several other units were directed to station themselves in the Presidio in case he got off Doyle Drive and tried to hide in the grounds. Two other cars were headed for the southern observation point for the bridge and at Fort Point, a 19th-century military emplacement just below the bridge supports at water's edge. With luck, they would all be in place within minutes.

The motorcyclist did not waste time. When he took off on Marina at high speed, he slowed only enough at the end of the street to swing up and to his left onto Doyle Drive. A car coming from the opposition direction was starting to turn into the same on-ramp, but the cyclist jerked his accelerator, raising his front wheel off the ground to jump the curb. The motorcycle then cut in front of the car, pitching into a slide to make the sharp corner. He gunned the cycle past the last exit before the bridge, the scenic overlook. Then he pushed a button on a box in his pocket, and a loud explosion was followed by another and then yet another.

In a moment the night sky was lit up with flames which rose above the tree tops and turned the fog into yellow soup. A trash container had just exploded at the intersection of Lake Street and Park Presidio, the last intersection before Park Presidio became freeway. Inside the trash container was a ten-gallon barrel of gasoline, and the surging flames closed off the entire approach to the bridge from the south.

"Three-X-23, what was that explosion I heard?" Margie asked on the air.

"Dispatch, the whole friggin' intersection of Lake and Park Presidio just exploded. I can't get through. I have to stop and help motorists trapped in the flames. Request fire department assistance."

"5-Hotel-217, what is your position?"

"God damn it, Margie! I can't enter Doyle Drive from Marina; the whole on-ramp is in flames. It was a bomb of some kind. A BMW is burning. Am going to assist."

"7-Foxtrot-445, can you enter Doyle Drive?"

"Negative, dispatch. WATCH IT, SALLY. BACK UP, BACK UP! PUNCH IT! Dispatch, send me backup and a fire truck. Am in flames. Repeat, 7-Foxtrot-445 is burning. Officer needs assistance. Cannot reach Doyle Drive. No passage until flames abate. STOP, SO I CAN SPRAY THE HOOD, SALLY."

"Dispatch to Golden Gate Bridge Police, request your assistance," Margie broadcast. "Murder rape suspect escaping on black Triumph north on Park Presidio toward Golden Gate Bridge. Cannot send units to intercept. Can you pursue? Over."

"Bridge Police to SF dispatch. Rodriguez here. Negative. The road is closed by flames. Our door is blocked by fire, too."

"Isn't there any way you can get out?"

"Negative, dispatch. Even if I climbed out the window, I can't reach our parking lot for a pursuit vehicle."

"Find a way," Margie said. "Most urgent that you follow and apprehend. Suspect extremely dangerous."

♦

Sergeant Luis Rodriguez, twenty-six years old and with the Golden Gate Bridge District Police Force for two years, threw the microphone down and jumped up on his desk. From his window he saw the Triumph go past, not on the roadway but on the northbound sidewalk. He kicked out the window, knocked the loose glass from the frame, and jumped to the sidewalk. "Jamie!" he called back up to the office, "Jamie, call for officer airlift by chopper. Have them meet me on the span. I'm going after him."

Rodriguez ran down the southbound sidewalk. He could feel the flames hot on his back, and the smell of oily smoke was in his nose. He glanced back over his shoulder and saw that the entire front of his station was in flames, along with dozens of civilian cars. Beyond, he saw the sky glowing rosy pink with other fires burning off the fog. Over all of it, he heard the snapping of the flames and the screams of scared people.

Fifty yards up the road, a blue-jeaned Honda cyclist stood trapped in the stopped traffic. Rodriguez ran to the bike and shouted, "Police officer. Get off the bike!" At the same moment he drew his pistol and yanked back the slide. The cyclist jumped off the bike without a word, and Rodriguez got on. He gunned the Honda and tore along the center line of the roadway. Far ahead of him was the Triumph, but he could go faster on the road than the Triumph on the sidewalk.

Rodriguez held the pistol in his left hand, and twisted the throttle with his right. The speedometer read eighty as he thundered north on the bridge. Abruptly, the Triumph came to a stop, and

Rodriguez shot a short distance beyond him. He saw the suspect in his mask and yellow mountaineering jacket run to the rail with a limp.

Rodriguez slammed on the brakes and put the bike into a skid. He saw the suspect aim at him, so he laid the bike down, sliding with it a short distance just underneath a fusillade of bullets. Bent at the waist, he ran to the rail near the suspect, who was now standing looking over the edge. Rodriguez took cover behind the rear fender of a nearby sedan and shouted, "Surrender! The bridge is sealed off. Throw down your weapon or I'll shoot."

The suspect's only response was to fire three more shots at him and to quickly change magazines. Rodriguez fired back twice, but he could not get a clear shot. When he next poked his head up, he did not see the gunman at all, but from his right he heard the sound of another motorcycle roaring toward him. He looked to see Jamie O'Malley screaming "Drop it!" and drawing a bead on the masked figure. "Jamie, take cover," shouted Rodriguez.

Rodriguez looked again at the Hellhound and saw him crouch and fire. He heard Jamie's revolver firing back rapidly, and then Rodriguez also stood and returned fire. The Hellhound wheeled and fired at Rodriguez. At the same moment Jamie's cycle began to wobble and veer to the right. Rodriguez stole a quick look and saw Jamie's gun clattering across the roadway toward him, followed immediately by the motorcycle crashing into the hood of a car in the left southbound lane.

At that instant the Hellhound fired again from behind another car's hood, hitting Rodriguez in the right shoulder. The gun flew out of his hand, and he went down. As if in slow motion, he saw Jamie's cycle stopped dead on the southbound car's grille, while Jamie flew over the roof of the car, tumbled in mid-air, and crashed into the windshield of the next car northbound.

Panting and groaning, Rodriguez dragged himself to where his gun lay and took cover behind the car whose shattered windshield cradled the unmoving Jamie O'Malley. The driver opened his door, crawled out at pavement level, and ran north on the bridge.

Rodriguez retrieved his pistol and saw the Hellhound standing on the railing with fog swirling around him. Facing the roadway, he turned his head as if looking straight at Rodriguez. Then he threw his gun over his shoulder and off the bridge. He bent his knees slightly and jumped backwards a step, dropping off the railing. Rodriguez's mouth opened wide as the suspect's torso and then his head disappeared. The face, as best he could see through its mask, seemed to be smiling as it vanished into the fog below. Seconds later, Rodriguez got up and walked unsteadily over to the guard rail. He leaned heavily on the railing and peered over it, seeing only black night and impenetrable fog.

After a few seconds he walked to where Jamie lay. Gradually, the silence imposed by his single-minded concentration on the pursuit was replaced by the infernal noise of fire crackling, horns blaring, people screaming, children crying, and the distant sound of gas tanks exploding. When he reached Jamie, he turned his friend's face toward him and saw the bullet hole in his temple.

He stood and cast his eyes right to left and saw the starry Marin sky to the north and a glowing red and yellow sky toward the City. He could see bright headlights around him, but only through a haze. He sank to his knees and the glare of the headlights blurred. He fell to his elbow and lay there below Jamie O'Malley. Only then was he aware of how cold he was. Then all was darkness.

◆

When Luis Rodriguez regained his senses, he was being tended by a man in a camel hair blazer. "Don't move. I'm a doctor. You're going to be all right. I've called for help on my cell phone. No, don't move. You'll start the bleeding again." Luis looked down and saw the doctor's hand pressing firmly against his wound with a white cloth.

Soon other bridge police officers arrived. Some came running on foot. Others were rappelling down ropes from a helicopter. He briefed them on what had happened. His Lieutenant radioed for boats to begin searching for the suspect. It would be a tossup whether his body would be recovered or whether it would be swept out the Golden Gate to become part of the undersea food chain.

"He was smiling," Luis said in a soft voice.

"What?" the lieutenant asked.

"When he jumped off the railing, he was smiling. I could see it through the mask."

"Just lay back, Luis, buddy. The chopper will have you at the hospital soon."

"How many dead?" Luis asked them.

"Don't know yet. Could be ten or twenty. Most of them burned to death in their cars. Sick son of a bitch."

◆

At 10:00 p.m. Nate's pager went off, just before he was ready to go to bed. "Inspector Hutchinson, we think we've had a Hellhound incident."

"When and where?"

"About two hours ago in the Marina."

"What? You wait two hours to tell me?"

"We've kind of had our hands full. You'll see."

He sent a voice mail message to Pierre and then he called Harry as well to tell him to meet them at Homicide. Harry arrived at 10:25 p.m., and Pierre and Nate were already there.

"I heard the radio broadcasts about the bridge," Harry said, "But that's all I know."

Nate briefed them on what they knew.

"It's gotta be a trick," Pierre said. "I just don't know how he could risk it. Any jump is against all odds of surviving, for even the most expert diver."

"And obviously he wants us to think that he's dead. We must be making him nervous," Harry said.

"Well, take what comfort you can from that, boys, because it cost us eighteen civilians' lives and one cop so far, and still counting."

"I can only think of two ways he could survive," Pierre said. "Either he grabbed onto something on the bridge structure and hid underneath, or he had a parachute on under his clothes."

"If it's the former," Harry said, "he might still be there. Shouldn't we have it searched now?"

"Agreed," Pierre said, and made the call.

"If it was a parachute, where would he go when he hit the water?" Nate asked. "Any boat or jet ski would be too conspicuous. If he swam away, he'd be dead meat. It had to be underwater."

"Of course," Harry said. "The chat room. He used a diver's metaphor about reserve tanks, remember? He'd be long gone by now."

"Depends where he went," Nate said. "Would he risk beaching near the bridge with all of San Francisco on high alert? How about Oakland?"

"IxNay," said Harry. "No way could he go all the way to Oakland under water. He'd have to swim a lot of it on the surface. That would be too risky."

"How do you know, Harry?" Nate asked him.

"Scuba is a hobby of mine. An experienced diver can make a mile underwater in fifteen to twenty minutes if he doesn't go deep and keeps a steady pace. He could cover six miles under water in two hours if he had a double tank."

"Well, doesn't that limit him to San Francisco then?" Nate asked.

"Let's look at a map," said Harry. "I've got an idea but I need to measure it."

"Yeah, here's one," Pierre said, laying out a Bay Area map on the desk. The finger-shaped San Francisco peninsula jutted north in white against the blue ocean and bay. To the east were a few islands and Oakland on the mainland.

"Well, what about Treasure Island? It's only halfway to Oakland. If he had a car stashed there in a lot, he could be on I-80 immediately. Let's see, what's the distance? Three inches on the map and the scale is a half inch to the mile. He could have been dried off and back home in the City a few hours after his plunge off the bridge. We're too late."

"Let's notify all Coast Guard units just to be sure," said Pierre. "And have the radio stations advise people to report any unusual beachings. Proceed with high caution, do not approach, and such. Include all of San Francisco, Angel Island, Alcatraz, and Treasure Island. Nate, get the night investigations unit to make the calls."

"What happened to the girl?" Harry asked.

"She's at home, unconscious. Unfortunately, the doctor sedated her first thing," Pierre said. "The mother saw him fleeing, but from the back only. I told them to call me as soon as she's awake. This could be a break if she heard his voice and saw him up close."

♦

"I've been thinking about our scholarship theory, guys," Harry said. "If he showed up on a girl's doorstep with a stocking mask on, she'd never let him in, right? If he didn't have it on, and something prevented his carrying through, he'd risk being identified."

"Uh, fine Harry, but that can wait," said Pierre. "We have time constraints here."

"I'm not sure it can wait, Pierre," Harry insisted.

"Why?" Pierre asked.

"In the Wildman incident, there was a small lobby in the building. He could enter from the street dressed normally and use the hall to put on the mask before he knocked."

"That would protect him against anyone on the street spotting him in the mask," Nate said. "So what?"

"Well, those Marina mansions are single family dwellings with entrances that front on a busy boulevard. He couldn't possibly have a place to put on a mask, which means that when she answered the door, she probably saw his face."

"I hope you're right, Harry," Nate said.

"I don't," Harry said. "If his information networks are as good as we think, he'll know she's alive."

Pierre's expression shifted to one of alarm. "God!" he cried. "What the hell were we thinking? He's *got* to go back." Pierre got the home phone number from dispatch and called them.

"This is Inspector La Croix. The perpetrator may return to finish the girl off. Where is she?"

"Here with us. I have four guards outside and two in her room, Inspector La Croix. Not to worry. Will you be coming out?"

"Affirmative. Good work…It's Sergeant Packard, isn't it?"

"Yes, sir."

"I knew your dad. Helluva cop. Call for additional security, and post them inside and out. Nobody without picture ID gets in. Be on high alert until I get there."

"Acknowledged. Out."

"Nate, wait here and co-ordinate with any results of shore searches and forensics. I'll see to the girl," Pierre said. "Harry, you can take off, unless Nate needs you."

♦

Pierre arrived at the Belford mansion and was challenged by three officers with drawn weapons. They made him show his ID before he was allowed to enter. The officer in charge was Sergeant Betty Packard, and he found her sitting guard in the kitchen.

"Is the girl conscious yet?" Pierre asked.

"No sir, she's completely out."

"Can I talk to you in private, Sgt. Packard?"

"Certainly," she said, leading him into the living room.

"Are you aware that this is probably a Hellhound incident?"

"Yes, I was told that. We're on full alert. When her parents came home unexpectedly, she apparently used the distraction to run and lock herself in the upstairs bathroom. He fired through the door to try and kill her, but she was smart enough to dive into the tub. The parents heard the shots and the tub ringing like a church bell. You can see the bullet damage to the porcelain on the tub exterior. He tried to break down the door, but it's an old solid one, and the lock held. I'm surprised he didn't just take his time and kill all three," she added.

"He could certainly do that, or kill thirty if need be, but he's very organized. Maybe he was just on a very strict timetable and didn't want to vary from it."

"Judging from the bridge reports, I wouldn't be surprised."

"Listen, Sergeant, I want you to move her as soon as you can arrange it. She probably saw his face, and he'll have to return to take her out. Call dispatch and have them scare up Laughlin. He'll have access to some safe houses you can borrow. Make the arrangements, but don't use the radio. Move her ASAP."

"Yes, Sir."

"Have the statements of the parents and the injured bridge officer on my desk first thing in the morning, and notify me when she's awake. Here's my pager number."

"Will do."

"If you don't mind, I'll take a once around the premises to see that everything is buttoned down tight."

"Mind?" she asked with a laugh. "I'm glad to get the great La Croix's help."

"You're very kind." At that, Pierre began his tour.

Although in San Francisco peaked roofs were unnecessary to shed snow, this house had one anyway, with the resultant attic. In the attic were two smallish guest rooms. Pierre checked them and opened the windows. There were no ledges or roof surfaces to allow entry this way. He closed and locked the windows. On the second floor he entered each bedroom and made the same check. One had a sloping roof right under the window, so he warned Sgt. Packard to station an officer outside in view of that window at all times. He rechecked Tracy's bedroom, including under her bed and in the closet. He found nothing amiss. He revisited the main floor and found it very insecure, but several officers were inside moving around and fully alert.

He checked the basement next and found there were no windows at all, and it afforded few hiding places. It was quiet and uncluttered, and there were no unusual sounds or smells. Pierre sat down and studied the room. Then he got up and searched the entire basement, checking under the stairs, inside containers, and shining his flashlight up among the rafters. Finding that all was well, he tramped slowly upstairs.

"Don't let your guard down," he warned Packard. "This guy is a master of getting in and out of places. Expect anything. Good luck."

Leaving the house, Pierre began to drive away. Only fifty feet down the street, his car was rocked by an explosion that slammed him sideways into a fire hydrant. He threw open his door and jumped out to look back at the house. The first floor was gutted, the second floor and attic were virtually gone, and flaming debris showered down.

A neighbor of the Belfords two houses down looked out her window when she heard the explosion. Though she could not see the house, she could see a man wearing a beret pounding on the roof of his car in the street and screaming something she could not hear. Burning debris fell around him and bounced off the roof of his car, but he neither flinched nor took cover.

♦

It was 11:30 p.m., and back at Homicide Harry and Nate continued anchoring the investigation. When Harry remembered that the matter of the wharf duffle bag was unresolved, he checked phone messages and played them back. Among them was:

Nate or Pierre, It's Matt Thomas in forensics. I finished that job. It took me until 9:00 p.m. No blood or DNA samples that I could find, but the dagger had clear fingerprints on it. They came back to Richard Hansen. I think you know the gentleman. He's the Hall of Justice Shoe Shine guy. Hope this helps, because I gave up symphony tickets to do it.

Nate groaned.

"What's the problem, Nate? Sounded like favorable news to me."

"At this hour it won't be easy to get a warrant," Nate said. "I can't imagine the duty judge being excited about getting woken up to issue a warrant for a guy who left a duffle bag unattended, can you? We have no evidence linking him to either the Hellhound or this bridge thing."

"Who cares? We don't need any. Can't you just pop him for possession of burglar's tools? Your average building contractor doesn't hide his drills and carbide bits under a wharf, right? If you're afraid he'll run, arrest him right now."

"Works for me. Want to come?"

"Count on it," nodded Harry.

"All right, but first I have to get night investigations to field my calls and reach me with any new developments."

That done, they left to see if Hansen was looking particularly damp this evening.

It was 11:00 p.m. when they arrived at his apartment and knocked. There was no answer. They returned to Nate's car and waited. In an hour and a quarter, Hansen showed up and parked on the street. He walked toward his apartment in no particular hurry.

Harry took his magnum out of its holster and put it in his pocket with his finger on the trigger and his thumb ready on the safety. They detained him at the front door, and Nate showed his ID. "Mr. Hansen, can we have a word with you?"

"Sure, what's up?"

"First the preliminaries. Stand up against the wall, hands up, feet out. Turn those toes out." Nate proceeded to frisk him while Harry slipped the safety off and watched over the proceedings carefully. Nate found no weapons.

"Where have you been tonight?"

"I was with a girl."

"Named?"

"Sherry."

"Last name?"

"I don't know."

"You're with a girlfriend and you don't know her name?"

"I didn't say she was my girlfriend. She's a hooker, okay? We went to a motel."

"During what time period?"

"Seven to nine, thereabouts. What's this about?"

"Anyone else see you for those two hours?"

"No, I'm not into threesomes."

"Don't get smart ass with me, punk," Nate said.

"What the hell? Look, I don't have a clue what this is about. If you won't tell me what's going on, I'm not answering any more questions."

"Okay, Mr. Lawyer. Here's the thing. You wouldn't by any chance know anything about a duffle bag stashed under the pier at Fisherman's Wharf, would you?"

"No. Why? Should I?"

"You missing any knives lately, Hansen?"

"I don't like the sound of this. I don't know what you're trying to pin on me, but I want a lawyer."

"No problem, Rick. You'll have one appointed, but it just might go easier if you cooperate."

"Oh sure it will. That's what they told me on every damn one of my drug cases. And it did go easier, *for you guys*. Talk to my lawyer. I'm not saying any more."

"Fine. Put your hands behind you." Nate cuffed Hansen's hands behind his back. "You're under arrest for possession of burglar's tools." As Nate prodded him into the back seat of his car, he stopped and put his nose right up against Hansen's scalp and sniffed. He did not smell sea salt. In fact, Hansen smelled entirely too clean.

"What the…" Hansen said, and then fell silent. They took him to the jail and turned him over to booking.

"What's the bail?" Harry asked.

"Scheduled bail is only $10,000, but that can't be helped. I'll ask the DA to ask for a higher bail at arraignment in two days, but it's really the booking photo I'm after. We'll have more than enough time to get the Belford girl to ID the photo. I guarantee you he won't make bail then."

Harry focused on the radio chatter behind the booking desk. The air traffic was heavy with reports on the obliteration of the Belford mansion.

◆

Tuesday was an even blacker day for the S.F.P.D. Nine police officers had died in the explosion at the Belford house, and more were wounded. At one o'clock Harry found himself standing in a pew in St. Mary's Catholic Cathedral at the top of the hill on Gough Street. Beneath the huge dome of the Cathedral stood a large congregation. Next to him were Nate and Pierre. Arrayed ahead of them were hundreds of police officers in their dress blues, families, friends, and strangers, all staring at the coffins lined up in a row. Beyond them were the Archbishop of the Diocese and five priests to assist at the requiem mass.

The Archbishop, who was presiding over the requiem, needed no microphone. Harry could hear his every word amplified by the great dome. He could also hear the sobs and whispers of the bereaved. But St. Mary's pipe organ, the largest in the country, stood silent. The Archbishop raised his hands, and the entire Cathedral grew hushed. Without warning, from the rear of the church the stillness was broken by a deafening blast that raised the neck hairs of everyone present. Seven bagpipes shrieked the opening bars of "Amazing Grace" while shivers coursed up and down the spines of all present. The pipers were dressed in full County Kerry green and gold regimental kilts. They marched solemnly to the front of the church as their shrieking pipes voiced community grief. Harry wept. Nate wept too, as did others, but Pierre La Croix did not. His jaw was set as tightly as a steel clamp.

When the pipers had finished, a soprano stood and sang the first verse of the same haunting tune *a capella*. Her soulful voice glided high and swooped low, while her words told of a triumph that gave comfort to the mourners. In the first row stood Luis Rodriguez listening quietly. This was a send-off that his friend Jamie O'Malley would have loved.

As Harry listened to the clergy's words of comfort and of faith, his mind drifted to consider a jigsaw puzzle that seemed composed of pieces of swirling mist. The pieces never assumed any concrete shape, and when one seemed to do so, it changed again. None of what was happening made much sense. Suddenly the ultra-careful Hellhound had turned into a reckless show-off, taking needless risks and carrying out unnecessarily spectacular escapes. He was striking too often now and seemed so anxious to show off his cleverness that he had even left a DNA sample.

The last thing the Hellhound should want would be to make it a personal goal of every San Francisco police officer to catch him. But what else could he have thought would follow this wrenching requiem mass? One thing Harry knew for certain as he stood there. It was going to get worse.

CHAPTER NINETEEN

After the funeral Pierre faded into the departing crowd without a word. Harry and Nate went straight to Homicide. Nate retrieved a fax and scanned it quickly.

"It's a report from Treasure Island. A double scuba tank backpack was found by the water's edge. No prints, of course. You were dead right, Harry."

"Could the gate guard identify him?" Harry asked.

"No. They were having a wedding reception for the daughter of a retired Navy admiral, and hundreds of cars were coming and going. We have zero description."

"Anything on the search of the bridge?"

"Yeah, some. There was a perch below the jump point where the dust and rust were disturbed. Something had been tied up there, maybe a parachute. The forensics team also found remnants of twine tied to the steel at roadbed height. It would have to have been a rope or trapeze of some sort, to allow him to swing up to the parachute."

"Damn, that's a tough climb up there with full dive gear to stash," Harry said.

"I don't think he had to. Divers found a carabineer clipped to the rebar under water under the jump point. When he hit the water, he must have free dived to some scuba gear, and then he swam to Treasure Island."

"Why would anyone go to all that trouble and risk? He's disappeared quietly lots of times. It's his specialty."

"Well, if you want my guess, it was for the fun of it. He's showing off now, earning his place in the history books." Nate rubbed his chin, and then looked at Harry. "Hey, how's Pierre doing? He didn't look too steady at the funeral mass."

"He's not. He's barely said a word since last night. I know he's blaming himself for the police officers' deaths, and add to that the girl and her family."

"How could it happen, Harry? Either the Hellhound always plants a bomb in a home and removes it on the way out if it goes well, or the alternative is awful."

"Yeah, I know. To have the brass and the ability to just walk into a house full of cops and plant a bomb is beyond belief, but I wouldn't put it beyond him."

"How? They were on high alert. Even if a cop showed up in full uniform, he'd never get in without someone knowing him, would he?"

"I wouldn't have thought so, but I'm not sure of anything anymore. If you told me he used a magic spell to transport the bomb there, I'd consider it."

"Something else," Nate said. "If the Hellhound is trying to break Pierre, he may be succeeding. I got a report from a bomb squad investigator that a neighbor saw Pierre standing next to his car while burning pieces of the house were crashing all around him, and he never even moved. Maybe he wants to die."

Harry blew out a long breath between pursed lips. "What do we do? Should he be relieved?"

"I've been thinking about exactly that, but I'm going to give it a day and see if he evens out. He's been through a lot, and he's not sleeping." Harry recalled his own state of mind after he learned of the horrible consequences of his own game playing on the Web.

"Uh, Nate. Nasty thought. This disaster makes Pierre look really bad. Who has a grudge against Pierre, and also has the ability to pass through any police line?"

"Oh, shit. Tiny. Our esteemed Captain Ratto. I'll find out if he has an alibi, and if he was seen at the Belford home." Nate paused a moment and then continued. "Don't take this personally, Harry, but it's strange how the whole game changes the week you poke into it. I really hate coincidences."

"You mean you think that if I pull out he'll settle down again?"

"I'm not sure I want him to. The guy can't keep on taking chances like this and still stay safe. No, I just meant that there is something connecting you to the Hellhound, and I wish I knew what."

"No more than I do, but I'm afraid that the more we push him, the more people he will kill," Harry said.

"So what should we do, back off because he's on a killing spree? That's the reason we're chasing him. I say it just means we're having an impact on him, and we should push harder. Keep digging. Nip at his heels. You ever play hoops? You give a guy some elbow in the teeth on a rebound and he's a little slow on the next jump. Intimidation. Discouragement. It's an old game. Gee, you cops better stop chasing me or no more Mr. Nice guy. Bullshit."

"I have an idea, Nate. I've been mulling over Hansen's stash at Fisherman's Wharf. If he sets up stashes like that and rigged the bridge for an escape, then he's probably been doing that kind of preparation all along. If we go back and reinvestigate the prior crimes to see if he was doing similar stuff, maybe we'd get a profile of some of his other skills beyond scuba diving, or maybe even a direct link to him."

Nate's face took on a weary aspect. "Harry, first of all, don't grab too fast at it being Hansen. It's just a bit too easy, you know? And second, do you have a few thousand hours to go back over all those files? I sure don't.

"I was thinking of being a little more selective than that. I want to review the cases where he made the strange escapes and see if it gives me any ideas."

"So give it a try."

"Right. See you later," he said. Harry walked over to his office building. Oz greeted him as he passed, but Harry did not hear or notice him.

◆

He stared at the wall across from his desk. He saw his daughter's photo, the one when she was four and he had carried her giggling on his shoulders at the beach. Suddenly he missed her terribly. He had pushed thoughts of her out of his mind for too long, and she would not stay out any more unless he did something about it. He thought about a sneak visit, but the Hellhound's recent unpredictability dissuaded him. A call to the house was just as dangerous if a listener was out there. He tried to convince himself that the precautions were foolish, since the Hellhound could easily find his ex and daughter if he wanted to, but a corner of his brain nagged him never to let Alissa's name out anywhere a crazy man might find it.

Finally he pinched a sheet of paper out of his laser printer and hand wrote a note:

Dear Lissa Punkin:

It seems so long since I last saw you. I miss you a whole bunch. Hugs for you. (((((((((((((((((Lissa)))))))))))))))). Please don't be mad at me for not coming to see you. I just don't think it is safe yet. I got new shoe laces to replace the broken and knotted ones like you told me. Please remember all the safety precautions we talked about, okay? Sweetie, I know I don't say this nearly as often as I should, but you know you are the best thing that ever happened to me since the day I was born. I'm so proud of you.

Love, Dad

He stamped the envelope and took it directly to the corner mail box. Then he resumed going over the files in his "IN" box. Two were cases that Bridge had worked up for settlement. He jingled the clients to obtain authorization, then filled in the demand amounts, and finally sent the letters out. After a few letters and a couple of demands for discovery, he returned to the Hellhound dead files.

How long had it been since that awful day he had chatted with the Hellhound, and his life of calm control had become one of constant fear? It seemed like years rather than weeks, and in those few weeks the twelve unsolved crime reports spanning eight years had become fifteen. The fresh reports on Claudia Wildman and Audrey Langley sat on top of the piles. Soon Tracy Belford, her family, nine cops, and all the unlucky burned motorists would join them. Harry quickly scanned the files to find those in which some escapes had occurred.

One in particular interested him, the Paula Prescott killing. Harry called Nate at the Homicide office. "Do you remember the Paula Prescott homicide?"

"Yeah, that's the one where he killed the girl and then disappeared in a blind alley."

"Right. I'd like to play 'If I had known then what I know now' with that case. What do you think?"

"Okay. Give me the name of the cop who followed him into the alley."

"Peter Corrigan."

"Yeah, I know him. He works days now in sex crimes. I'll check and see if we can borrow him. I'll call you back."

"Thanks," Harry said.

It was only two or three minutes later when Nate rang back. "Corrigan has court duty and can't break free. Are you available at 3:00 p.m. tomorrow?"

"Yeah."

"Okay, then meet us here, and Corrigan will lay it out for us."

"Great. See you then. Thanks."

Harry immersed himself further in the files. When he next checked his watch, it was after seven o'clock. Another dinner missed. He dumped his unopened mail into his briefcase. As he walked to the parking lot, he noted the street traffic had thinned out. Everyone else had gone home, even Oz. He unlocked his car, plopped into the seat, and shut the door. Within seconds he was startled by a loud rap on his window. He looked up and saw Tyrone Washington's smiling face. Harry rolled down the window and waited for the whiskey breath to assault him. Instead there came a fruity sweet smell, a vaguely familiar scent that he couldn't place, but certainly not one a man ought to wear.

"Shit, man, you surprised me," Harry said.

"I been waiting for you. You had a chance to look over the stuff on my deuce case?"

"Yeah. There might be a constitutional violation that I can work. If I didn't say it, Tyrone, you did a great job on that murder case for me."

"You know I love the heavy cases, Harry. That cloak and dagger stuff takes me back to my Army days."

"Geez, I can't believe you said that, Tyrone. I was just thinking of my Army days too."

"Yeah? How come?"

"I don't know," Harry said, puzzled. "Something about that pansy-ass cologne you're wearing," he said with a broad smile.

"I ain't wearin' any damn cologne."

"Yeah, right. It's so fruity, it smells like that C-4 crap we used in military demolition before Semtex…Oh fuck!"

Harry threw the door open, grabbing his briefcase with his right hand. Tyrone had already grabbed the collar of Harry's jacket and was hauling him bodily out of the driver's seat. Hanging onto his arm, Tyrone dragged Harry toward the opposite curb. Harry was now at a full run, and Tyrone let go. Each of them made for separate spaces between the bumpers of parked cars. Harry reached his first. Tyrone was just entering shelter when the explosion lifted Harry's car six feet off the ground and ever so gracefully flipped it over, letting it down again on its roof.

The concussion of the explosion threw Tyrone into the trunk of the parked car next to him, and he skidded up the back window and rolled off the far side. His body slammed to rest at the edge of the sidewalk against a low stone planter box. As soon as the debris had finished falling, Harry ran over to his companion and turned him over. Tyrone's head was bloody, and he was eerily still. Harry lifted one hand and took his pulse at the wrist, but felt no heartbeat. Harry lowered his head and said a prayer for his friend. He was concentrating on words dimly recalled, when he heard a hoarse voice say, "Shit, and you wonder why I drink so much."

Harry and Tyrone's eyes locked on one another for a moment, and then Harry said, "You had me scared for a while there, fella."

"Yeah, well, that's another thing we got in common."

"I *knew* that smell was familiar," said Harry. "Basic training. The drill instructor threw a ball of C-4 plastic explosive into the crowd of trainees just as we were smelling and touching samples of it. They set off an explosion outside at exactly the moment that the ball of C4 landed. That is a smell I thought I would never forget."

Tyrone groaned. "Yeah, well amuse me with your army stories another time," he said, looking at the blood on his hands. "This a thank you from another satisfied client, Harry?"

"No. The Hellhound has a personal grudge against me."

"Harry, in the future, if you piss off some heavy dude like him, don't you think you could warn your friends to stay the hell away from you?"

"Hmm. I'll keep that in mind the next time I have a homicidal psychotic irked at me. Here, let me help you up."

Tyrone stood and tried out his limbs and found them functional. "Where's your car?" Harry asked him.

"Yeah, right. You think I'd get in it now, before the bomb squad checks it out? Let's walk. I want to put a few blocks between us and here." They walked quickly up the alley right next to the Hall, and crossed to Harrison Street. There they caught a taxi to Civic Center and went into a modest sandwich shop on Market Street. Tyrone used napkins to clean up the blood on his head.

"Tyrone, shouldn't we have gone to the hospital?"

"You don't learn, do you, Harry? Isn't that just where the dude would figure we'd go? So do the opposite of what he figures you'll do."

"Okay. I'll make a note to be unpredictable."

"We gotta talk right now. Nobody who wants to kill you sets a bomb to go off five minutes after you open the door. You never put your key in the ignition, did you?"

"No."

"So what made the bomb go off?"

"I don't know."

"What's the point of having the bomb go off after you've been driving for five minutes?"

"None I can think of."

"Right. If you was taking a four-minute trip, he'd miss you. And a timer is more trouble than a straight electrical switch wired to the door latch or ignition. And then, your bomb goes off as soon as we get to the other side of the street. Seems like someone waited to set it off once we was clear. Oh excuse me…once *you* was clear." He dabbed at his bleeding head.

"And why would he do that? If I'm a pest to him, he's hardly been timid about playing exterminator."

"You got a list of suspects for the Hellhound case, right?"

"Yeah."

"You know any of them?"

"Everyone I *know* is a suspect, even you," Harry let slip.

"Well fuck you very much. That's it. I'm outta here." He stalked outside and began walking up Market Street.

"No wait, please," Harry said, pursuing him. "I'm sorry, Tyrone. I know it's not you."

"Do you? Are you sure?"

"Yeah, I'm sure Tyrone. I trust you. In fact, at this point you're about the only person I do trust."

"Well, here's a tip for you, Harry. The dude don't want you dead. He wants you out.

He's just asking politely this time. He's saying 'Don't make me get nasty.'"

"No more Mr. Nice Guy, huh?"

"Exactamundo."

"What should I do, Tyrone?"

"I can't tell you that, Harry. It's your life."

"What would you do?"

"I don't have any family. I can go to any city in the country and make the same living as now. You got family, a California attorney license, a law practice. It's not the same. But I will tell you something. Stop being so damn passive and predictable. You dudes are just reacting to him, while he sets the pace. You let him lead the dance, and you all follow."

Harry's mind turned over Tyrone's words: "too passive." Was he talking about his reaction to the Hellhound threat, or about his life?

"Play his game on him. Take the damn lead, and you might live out the year. And Harry?" Tyrone gestured into a dark doorway and whispered to Harry, "Come here." When Harry and he were huddled in the darkened doorway, Tyrone held Harry gently by the right shoulder with his left hand. He placed his right palm on Harry's chest and whispered, "You got to go back to not trusting anyone."

Tyrone suddenly reached into Harry's shoulder holster and drew out his magnum, slipped off the safety without hesitation, and put the muzzle up against Harry's nose. He stared into Harry's eyes and pushed sideways on the pistol, until Harry's nose pointed at his ear.

Then Tyrone put his finger on the trigger. Harry's eyes crossed looking at the trigger, and he deferred breathing for a little while.

"You see, Harry? Two lessons for the price of one. The unpredictable one wins every time, and trusting people gets you dead." Tyrone put the safety back on and slipped the pistol into the holster. Then he took off at a brisk stride and waved goodbye over his shoulder without looking back. Harry stood rooted to the spot with his heart beating rapidly. He was less upset by the charming safety lesson than by the fact that Tyrone did not say a proper goodbye when he left. He was left with the feeling that Tyrone considered him already dead.

Harry patted his weapon, and a bizarre thought forced itself into his mind. What if he just went ahead and killed Hansen? They had the prints on the dagger, and the stash of implements at his place almost screamed "Hellhound." He fit the profile, and he was one of only two people to overhear that Harry had been the person chatting with the Hellhound. His supposed alibi for the Tracy Belford murders was thin. On the other hand, his job at the Hall was also a good way to gather information on good places to burglarize. Things such as security, guards, alarms, and payrolls were frequently discussed at the Hall. Harry also remembered that nothing in the duffle bag was a direct linked to any Hellhound crime. He also had to admit to himself that he could not pull the trigger of a gun in cold blood. He took out his cell phone and dialed Nate.

"Nate, I forgot to mention to you that I got another hangman drawing. Now I only have one to go. Weren't you already at one piece to go?"

"Yeah."

"You haven't gotten a new one in the last couple of days?"

"No."

"Nate, I think it'll be soon."

"You okay, Harry?"

"Yeah. That bomb you heard? It was my car."

"I'm glad you weren't in it."

"I was. I got out just in time. Hansen still your top candidate?"

"Best we got."

"Uh-huh."

"You sure you're okay, Harry? Where are you?"

"Not a scratch, Nate," he said, ignoring the second question. "See you tomorrow at 3:00 p.m.?"

"Uh, yeah. 3:00 p.m. Can you come to Homicide a little early and do some paperwork on the bomb, Harry?"

"Oh, yeah. Sure will. Bye."

◆

Harry dialed ETOH Beverages and placed an order for delivery of a case of Stolichnaya vodka to a Mr. Tyrone Washington. He gave the address and his credit card number and asked them to put a note on it saying, 'Tyrone, Thanks. Harry'. Harry disconnected and mumbled to himself, "Heck, if he's going to drink himself to death, might as well be something good that won't show on his breath."

As he headed up Market Street, a wrinkled man with straight short grey hair and sooty face peered out from under his red knit cap at Harry, much like a dog warily checks out a stranger who invades his territory. He hailed a cab and told him the address for home. A block later he told him, "I changed my mind. Make that Lombard Street where all the motels are. Stop at the first one whose name begins with the letter C," he said, hoping to enhance his unpredictability. The hack turned all the way around, smiled politely, and said "May I see your money first, sir?" Harry showed it and sulked the rest of the way.

Harry checked in using cash and a false name. Then he used his cell phone to call the bomb squad. He left a message on their machine, asking them to clear it with Nate and to go over Harry's apartment and office, and Tyrone's car. He asked them to do it as soon as possible, and to page him when it was safe. By now they should know why it was necessary.

Almost immediately he drifted off and dreamed of being chased down the dark streets. It was hard to move his arms and legs, but finally he was back at his apartment. He was dead tired and turned down his bed covers, where he found that his pillow had two eyes. They suddenly opened and glared at him. He woke with a gasp, wet with sweat. He got up and went to the bathroom and then checked the time. It was 2:00 a.m. He took a lined pad from his briefcase, scrawled "Survival Plan" on the top, and began to write. At 5:00 a.m. he crawled back into bed and slept.

He was blasted awake by a loud rat-a-tat sound that assaulted his face. He looked and saw his pager vibrating its way across the night stand toward the clock. It was 11:00 a.m. already.

He checked his voice mail messages and learned that the bomb squad had already cleared him and Tyrone. He checked out, went home, showered and changed. He put a fresh battery in his phone and took a taxi to a used car lot. There he bought an aged Chevy Nova–they were agile; fit small parking spaces; and got good gas mileage. This one had 87,000 miles on it and was cheap. The name also suited his sense of humor. "Nova" was a Spanish language joke. *No va* in Spanish meant "it doesn't go." Presumably the person in charge of naming that car was not bilingual.

It was close to lunch time, but first Harry had to check in with Bridge and sign papers and answer some questions. That done, he wolfed a light lunch and worked files for a while before his 3:00 p.m. appointment. At 2:30 p.m. Harry broke off and went across the street, remembering that he had to do a report on his car bombing.

♦

The afternoon was clear and sunny, but Oz was not at his post, a rare event. Harry waited at the elevators. When the next one arrived, his narc brother in law, Rico Benedetti, got off and said, "Hey Harry. So you're re-opening the Paula Prescott case?"

"How the hell did you hear about that?" Harry asked.

"Gina, Captain Ralston's secretary heard about it when Pete Corrigan asked him for permission to go with you."

"And Gina told you?"

"No. Gina goes shopping with Pat's cousin, who told Pat, and your sister told me." Harry just shook his head and went on his way.

When he arrived at Homicide, Pierre gave him an incredulous stare. "What is it, Harry? You don't bother reporting a car bomb? Too boring for you?"

Harry rubbed some of his almost healed cuts and bruises from the first bomb and replied, "Well, you know, Pierre, unless a bomb gives me a good twenty-foot loft, I just feel kind of short-changed. Hardly worth mentioning."

Pierre smiled weakly and handed Harry a form to fill out to report the property damage. "Your insurance company will want this anyway. Take five minutes to complete it, okay? It's only 2:40

p.m." Harry filled out the form and gave it to Pierre, just as Pete Corrigan walked in. Pierre made the introductions.

"Where's Nate?" Harry asked.

"He had to do a field interview with a witness in another case. Relax; it's a routine barroom murder. It'll just be the three of us on this trip."

Harry asked Corrigan, "Did you mention this outing to anyone today?"

"Just a few buddies. Shouldn't I have?"

Pierre shrugged and asked, "Ready?"

"I have another appointment after this one," Pete said," so I'll drive my own car and meet you there."

Pierre drove Harry to the scene and parked on the sidewalk. Pete identified the points of reference on the chase through the backyards and alleys, and the end point in the blind alley they were looking at. When he was done, Harry and Pierre entered the alley and began to study it, with Pete answering their questions.

"That it for me?" Pete asked them a little while later.

"Fine for me," Pierre said. "You have any more questions, Harry?"

"Nope. Thanks, Pete."

Harry scratched his chin and rolled his eyes upward to take in the alley from top to bottom. It was a short, unremarkable alley defined by two red brick apartment buildings, one of which was L-shaped, forming the dead end of the alley. They strolled to the end without much hope that there was evidence that could yet be found. Pierre's heels spun smoothly on the manhole cover that Corrigan had mentioned, as he quickly took in the entire 360-degree view.

Harry took a short pry bar out of his coat and tried to lift the manhole cover. It was too heavy to lift, but when he shifted it a bit, it made an enormous noise. Harry went back out of the alley and told Pierre to do it again. The noise echoed, even in the racket of mid-afternoon.

The apartment windows were easily eight feet off the ground, leaving sheer brick faces on three sides of the blind alley, with the exception of a small outcropping of brick that rose about waist high, on which Harry steadied his weary backside.

"What's that?" asked Pierre, pointing.

"My butt," Harry replied.

"No, clown, what you're sitting on."

Harry was leaning rather than sitting on the brick outcropping, as the top edge was slanted down at an angle. It was about four feet wide and two feet deep.

"I don't know. I'm not an architect. Maybe it's earthquake reinforcement?"

"Maybe," Pierre said. "Since the 1989 Loma Prieta quake, a lot of buildings have been retrofitted with earthquake reinforcements, but I've never seen anything like that."

"Well, it's similar to the old medieval Romanesque church buttresses," Harry said, "but it's too low to support this wall. It barely reaches a fifth of the way to the top. There are no fittings on it for gas, electricity or water. I can't see any purpose it could possibly serve."

Pierre examined the stubby buttress, running his fingers around the edges, and Harry joined him in studying it. The brick structure was not actually incorporated into the wall, but was somehow fastened to it. Where there should have been a solid mortar joint between the buttress and the wall, they found a gap all around, though it was caulked. Pierre could not budge it with the edge of a key, nor pull it with his fingers. Harry kicked the structure with his toe and heard a hollow sound. He gestured for Pierre to stand back and positioned himself in front of the box, reasoning that if there were a catch, it might yield to gentle persuasion like a TV or car trunk. Pierre stepped back and watched.

Harry clenched his fists and stood facing the box. He began breathing in a measured rhythm. His body swayed slightly in a twisting motion, and then he pivoted on the ball of his left foot, spinning to his left until he was facing away from the box. His upper torso swung down horizontally while his right foot shot out behind him and slammed into the box with the sound of metal striking metal. He did not lose his balance, but returned to a standing position facing Pierre. "Not bad, huh? Didn't know I studied karate, did you?" he said. But Pierre wasn't hearing him. He was staring over Harry's shoulder. His mouth was hanging open, and then it managed four words, "Here we go again." Harry heard what sounded like a rusty hinge in an echo chamber, and he turned around.

The brick box had swung partly open on a hinge concealed at the right side. Sticking out of the left edge was a hand. The two men looked into each other's eyes, and then both approached the brick-faced locker slowly, as if not wanting to disturb its tenant. Harry reached out and gently pulled the edge of the locker toward him. It crept forward like a ponderous vault door at first, and then rapidly swung outward.

Suddenly the locker spilled its contents on their feet. It was a man. Specifically, it was Osmund. He would not beg for change today. His dead body now lay face up on the concrete with arms splayed, looking into the sun with unflinching eyes. But Pierre's attention was drawn to something else. A seven-inch carpenter's gutter spike was sticking out of his chest right over his heart, but the spike was merely the push pin in this bulletin board. It was the memo posted there that held Pierre's riveted attention. It was a photograph. The glossy color photo showed a little girl about eight years of age. She was blonde, cute, and seemed to be dancing. Her arms were swinging out, and one leg was thrown out to the side as she balanced on one foot and smiled toward the camera.

The spike pierced her photo directly through the throat. Pierre's rapt attention was distracted only by the sound of Harry vomiting, an unsurprising reaction that even rookie officers experienced until they got used to death and blood. He looked at Harry kneeling on the pavement. Harry tried to speak, but his stomach commandeered his mouth as he was stiffened by another spasm. Finally he raised his head and looked miserably into Pierre's face with tears in his eyes.

Between gasps Harry said in a quivering groan, "My God, Pierre. It's my daughter."

CHAPTER TWENTY

Harry's eyes were drawn once more to the body, but then something else drew his attention. He crawled over the pavement to Osmund's corpse and reached under the thigh. He pulled out a white slip of paper and held it out to Pierre. On it was a hangman, and it was complete. Underneath the scaffold were three dashes with letters filled in over them: AIM.

"AIM?" Pierre said. "Whose hangman is this? Was Osmund on the list too?"

"No, Pierre. It's my hangman," Harry said between wracking breaths. "AIM is Alissa Ina Maxwell. What time is it?"

"3:18 p.m."

"Come on. We have to run," Harry called as he ran to Pierre's car. "Lissa gets out of school in twelve minutes."

Pierre caught up to him with keys in hand and then looked back at Osmund. "Harry, I can't just leave a corpse lying here. We have to secure the crime scene and wait for backup." Harry stared at him. Through his brain flashed fragments of thoughts: Do as you're told; years of law school; following rules; punishment from Dad. In a fraction of a second Harry's eyes widened.

"*You* have to wait," he said, as he snatched the keys from Pierre's hand. Harry jumped into the driver's seat and started the engine. He slapped the transmission into reverse, and the car screeched backwards. When he slammed on the brake, the driver's door pounded closed. He put the car in drive just as Pierre shouted after him, "What school? I'll send backup." Pierre reached for the radio clipped to his belt. Harry floored the Chevelle, and the tires screamed black tracks over the asphalt. He yelled out the open window, "Peabody Elementary." Pierre yelled after him "Harry, wait for backup." but Harry was rapidly pulling away, so he screamed after him. "Harry, if he's there, DON'T HESITATE."

Pierre called for three units to cover the school and to be on the lookout for an adult male, possibly with a limp, trying to molest an eight-year-old blonde girl. He declared the suspect "armed and dangerous" and warned them to watch for the girl's father, describing Harry. He also summoned the coroner and two patrol cars to his own location.

The first car arrived at Pierre's location in only forty-five seconds. Pierre ran to them with his gold star held high and yelled to them, "Homicide Inspector La Croix. Establish a crime scene here, seal off the area and wait for the coroner. Get photos and fingerprints on the body and the brick locker. Give me your keys."

The startled driver was a young guy who seemed reluctant to hand over his squad car to a strange man with a badge at a murder scene, but his older partner shouted, "Get out of the car. *Move.*" The keys were in the ignition, and Pierre did a power turn. The officers could hear the engine racing as Pierre slammed on the brakes and put the unit into a powered sideways skid. When the rear end had slid all the way around, Pierre took his foot off the brake and the car raced off with the siren blaring.

As Harry had raced away from the alley and Pierre, he buckled up and found a custom toggle switch on the dash. He flipped it up, and the siren went on. He stole a quick look to the back seat and saw Pierre's cherry unit, a portable magnetic red flasher. He could not reach it, so he unbuckled as the car raced past a green light at sixty-five miles per hour. His head hit the roof as he hit a chuck hole. He stood up on the accelerator and could reach the cherry light with his arm extended backwards. He turned the switch at the base, and it began to flash. He stuck it on the roof and rebuckled his seat belt. The buckle had just locked into place when he hit the sudden uphill grade at the far side of an intersection. The Chevelle scraped a gouge in the street, but he continued on without pause. Checking his watch, he saw that he had five minutes left. The next traffic light did not cooperate and was red when he approached it, so he had to come to a complete stop at the cross walk. As soon as he had jerked his neck left and right with his feet on the accelerator and brake simultaneously, he released the brake and the car shot ahead through the intersection.

Harry checked out the next three intersections on the uphill grade and could see the first one changing to green while the next two were still red. He knew they would change to green by the time he reached them, so he floored it and reached eighty-five miles per hour. The second light turned green as he raced through the first one. Six seconds later the third one changed as well. He did not slow down.

At the second intersection, on the other side of the road divider, a middle-aged woman in a yellow Honda had begun a left turn. She had already blocked the first lane and was halfway across Harry's lane when she heard and saw Harry coming. Eyes wide with fear, she braked and stopped, blocking the entire intersection. Harry swerved all the way to the left, his left tires climbing the curb of the median with his right front fender clearing her bumper by two inches. Mounting the curb at that speed lofted the Chevelle into the air, but he came down with his foot on the gas, and the positraction rear wheels kept him going straight. Now out of danger, the woman in the Civic suddenly accelerated with squealing tires to get out of the way. Harry sighed and continued the last five blocks at high speed. At last the school rose into sight on the left.

Harry spied the exit Alissa used near her home room at the left rear area of the school campus. He slowed down suddenly at the school zone, because the children were already streaming out. Just short of the school, he swerved across the street and into the driveway of a small teachers' lot. He blocked the driveway and jumped out. As Harry slammed his door, he saw a black and white marked car approaching at high speed from the opposite direction. He did not wait, but immediately ran across the soccer field toward Alissa's exit. As he went, he scanned the parked cars for watchers, but saw none. Lissa was always one of the first out, but today she was nowhere to be seen.

From far behind him at the street, Harry heard Pierre's voice. He was screaming something Harry could not make out. He turned and saw Pierre pointing diagonally across the soccer field far to Harry's left and ahead of him. It was Lissa crossing the soccer field toward the side street flanking the soccer field, and she was not alone. A tall man with hunched over shoulders was leading her by the hand. Harry began to run flat out toward them, pumping his long legs as hard as he could. Now he could see that Lissa was tugging at the man's hand and grimacing.

When Harry got close enough to see their faces clearly, he could also hear Lissa shouting what sounded like "Daddy." No, Harry realized when he heard it again; it was "dagger." She was challenging him with the password. He knew that meant that he had told her that Harry or Yvonne had sent him. From behind him Harry heard Pierre shout "Halt, Police," but just as Harry turned to look, he saw Pierre's foot catch a gopher hole, and he went down hard on his face. Harry ran as he had never run, ignoring his laboring lungs.

When he was about 175 feet from Lissa he saw the man's face clearly. It was Rick Hansen. Harry pulled out his weapon and took the safety off. He continued running, screaming, "I'll kill you, you son of a bitch. Let her go!" From behind him Harry could hear the unmistakable high pitch of Yvonne's voice shrieking her daughter's name. Hansen had stopped, but Lissa continued trying to free herself, and now she was screaming "Daddy, Daddy," as she saw him coming. Hansen screamed "You back-stabbing prick!" as his hand went inside his jacket pocket.

In one fraction of a second, Harry saw the tears on his daughter's face glinting in the sun; heard Yvonne scream "Oh my God, *Save her, Harry*"; saw Hansen's right hand begin to withdraw something shiny from his pocket; and heard Pierre shout, "He's got a gun, Harry!"

Harry did not slow or stop. He did not think. Still about 130 feet distant from Hansen, he flung himself to the ground in mid-stride with breath held, his stomach and chest hitting hard on the turf. He brought the pistol up with his right hand and slapped the butt into the palm of his left hand to steady it. He sighted along the barrel just as Alissa broke free of the man's grasp, and Harry squeezed off a shot, then another and another. Hansen's left hand went to his mid-section, and his body turned as his right knee buckled.

Harry could now clearly see the pistol in Hansen's hand rotating toward Alissa. Harry knew by the knot in his throat that he had only one more try. He sighted and fired again, aiming at the top center of Hansen's chest. Immediately he could see a flash of red spraying from Hansen's head, and he flew backwards and down like a cement sack. He did not move again.

Harry jumped to his feet and ran to Alissa, with Pierre hobbling not far behind him. Sirens howled and slowed as they came to a stop at the street. Yvonne was running across the soccer field as Harry reached Alissa where she lay on the ground covering her face with her hands. He glanced over and could see the top of Hansen's skull blown off by the magnum load. He gently pulled Lissa's hands away from her eyes and said, "It's over, Sweetie." Her arms flew around his neck, and she bestowed a strangle hold on his throat. He did not mind.

As Yvonne came up beside them, Alissa raised her face and said, "Oh Mommy, I didn't go with him. I didn't. He didn't know the password, 'finger.' It was his finger that Daddy cut with the dagger. I didn't go with him, Mommy. He dragged me."

Yvonne took her in her arms then and said in a whisper, "You did just fine, baby. You did great."

The Maxwells all developed the same tear duct disorder at that moment, just as Pierre limped up to them and holstered his own pistol. He put his hand on Harry's shoulder and said, "You did great too, buddy. And it *is* finally over." Pierre gripped Harry's arm tightly, and it felt good. Uniformed police officers were swarming over the soccer field now, and Pierre shouted, "It's under control. Call an ambulance, but no hurry. This one's dead." Pierre used his pen to lift Hansen's pistol from the grass and placed it into his coat pocket. Then he bent low over the body, inspected it closely, and went through his pockets.

"Come on, honey," Yvonne said to Alissa. "Time to go home." She held out her hand, but Alissa shook her head and jumped into Harry's arms again. He picked her up, and they began walking toward the street.

"Watch out for gopher holes, Pierre," Harry said.

"Uh-huh," Pierre said, as he limped along.

Alissa had buried her face into Harry's shoulder and seemed to feel most secure there for now. "So, Pierre, as the case of the century seems to be over, will you finally take a vacation? How about Cabo San Lucas?"

"Dunno," he said. "Maybe I will, but if you damaged my ride, you better find somewhere farther than Cabo to hide. Don't suppose you locked it?"

Yvonne walked close beside Harry, very close. The sun was warm on Harry's face, and now he could feel the pain in his bruised ribs. Life slowed down to normal speed again, and Harry did not scan the parked cars as usual. At the curb, one paramedic was unfolding a body bag, while the other was unfolding a gurney.

♦

Pierre went to his car and began looking it over. Yvonne smiled at Harry and put her finger to her lips and pointed at their daughter. Harry cocked his head and could just barely see her face. Almost asleep. He smiled back at Yvonne and handed their daughter off to her. "I've never seen that side of you before, Harry," she said.

"No one ever tried to steal my treasure before."

"Do you think Alissa might get over this better if you came and stayed with us for a while?"

Harry pondered that offer and all its unstated implications. "I have to go and get grilled for a few hours until all the paper gods are appeased, but I'll stop in later to check on her. Maybe stay for dinner?"

"Yes, that'll be good. Uh, she'll appreciate it. She's missed you so much."

Harry ran his hand through Alissa's hair one last time. For a moment he looked at her and tried to imagine her as a teen, awash with hormones and frantically bungee jumping between surly and berserk. *Nah*, he thought. Never happen.

♦

Pierre and Harry got under way in Pierre's car, and a couple of minutes later Pierre said, "I still don't know how he could have known that you were going to go to that alley to find Osmund, or why he wanted to warn you, for that matter."

"Well, the first part is easy," Harry said. "That visit was all over the hall, thanks to Corrigan, but it doesn't make a lot of sense for him to send us scurrying to the school right on time, does it? Do you think he just wanted to cut it close and have us kick ourselves in the ass for being two minutes late, but he timed it wrong? That would have fed his ego if he had pulled it off, just like the thing at the Golden Gate Bridge."

"I hate to bring this up," speculated Pierre, "but what if Dr. Paschov is right and there are two? Could the brain have just served up his stooge, to tie up a loose end?"

"To quote a friend of mine," Harry told him, "Let it go. We don't know that there were two of them, and maybe the guy is just psychotic enough that he has different goals and styles for different murders. Maybe he just evolved into a breakdown and engineered his own end. It's not a new concept with these guys. They want an end too, right?"

"It does happen," Pierre conceded.

"Well, this guy fits that pattern. All the recent high-risk capers? The sudden hunger for notoriety and spectacular stunts? Look, he left a hangman on Osmund, so he's authentic, right? Then he grabbed Alissa and drew on me. He's the guy, Pierre. There is no other explanation."

"I don't know."

"I think you've forgotten how to live without this slime. Like you said yourself a whole fifteen minutes ago Pierre, it's *over*." Pierre let himself think on the idea and laughed. Then he slapped the dash board and laughed again. Then he punched Harry's shoulder and laughed even harder. Harry began to relax for the first time in a long time.

CHAPTER TWENTY ONE

Harry waved a couple of fingers at Pierre and headed for his Nova which, in fact, did go. It was way past five o'clock, so he went directly to Yvonne's. He pulled into the driveway in his old spot at the too roomy four-bedroom bi-level. As he shut the car door, he could hear his daughter's voice trilling within. Alissa yanked the door open and hugged him around the waist. Then she led him inside and Harry noticed her little girlfriend Luanne was in evidence as well.

He greeted Yvonne cordially and made the obligatory remarks of interest in the savory aromas. When he retrieved the vodka in the bar cabinet, he noticed that the cabinet door sagged from loose hinge screws. Harry dropped ice into his Stoli martini and found olives. After taking a sip, he secured a screwdriver and a razor knife, both of which were exactly where he had left them. Then he shaved some splinters of wood off a piece of scrap, and forced them, wet with glue, into the overlarge screw holes. Yvonne briefed him on Alissa's violin accomplishments, her soccer, academics, and other details he had missed during the forced sabbatical.

Yvonne had prepared beef goulash, Harry's favorite. This did not surprise him any more than the new bottle of Stolichnaya vodka or the new jar of olives. He continued screwing the hinge on tight, and she repeated how she had never before seen him like that. He thought about it but said nothing, as his daughter watched him work. Yvonne told Alissa that she had rented the movie the girls had wanted to see, and the little girls ran to pop it into the TV.

Harry and Yvonne looked at each other a long moment while Harry washed his hands.

"It's good to visit after the long absence. Goulash, fresh martini makings, a friend to occupy Alissa," said Harry carefully. "Something on your mind?"

She pressed her lips together but did not answer. The slinky fit of her new dress did not escape Harry's notice, as it emphasized the graceful contours of her well-rounded breasts and curved hips. "It's easy to look good when there's a crisis, and I arrived in the proverbial nick of time, but soon enough I'll seem just as annoying as I did before. My predominant traits will again be my childish sense of humor and messiness. Can you see what I'm trying to say?"

"Yes."

"The divorce wasn't my idea."

"You don't have to remind me."

"I don't want to reopen old wounds, try again, and then have it happen all over again. It hurt too much the first time."

"Maybe I've gone through some changes, Harry."

"I expect so. I certainly have."

"So how have you been doing, Harry? Really."

"I've been lonely. Really."

"Haven't found anyone else yet? It's been two years."

"Uh, no. Not yet. Can we talk about something else?"

"Sure. Whatever you like." Then the conversation began to dwindle like an icicle hanging in the sun. The talk got smaller as the minutes and hours passed. During dinner Harry enthused with Alissa over each of her snippets of news, and he enjoyed the giggle fits that were inevitable when little girls flocked together even in small numbers. Harry helped clean up the table and the kitchen, and the evening ended amicably.

When Harry went home to his apartment, he did not set the bobby pin into the carpet. He slept without dreams.

♦

Thursday morning he went to the office late. Bridget was there. He brought her up to date on what had occurred, and she listened wide-eyed. She told him there were hearings to attend this week that had been postponed from last week, and then she handed him a stack of telephone messages from news reporters.

"It seems you're a popular item today, Oaf."

"Yeah, great. The reporters will be in a feeding frenzy."

"Perhaps not, luv. I told them that you went out of town to escape the media attention until it had blown over."

Harry smiled broadly, and then continued the ruse by returning some of the calls from "out of town", being careful to block caller ID. Now they could file their stories without haunting him. The flames of celebrity could settle to embers, he mused. He looked out his window, and the memory of Osmund stabbed at him. That clap on the shoulder had undoubtedly cost him his life. Hansen had no doubt observed it.

Friday morning Harry did not wear his guns. He made two court appearances at the Hall, but was met by only three reporters who had had the initiative to check the court schedules for his court dates. He answered their questions and was photographed, but the resultant stories were less ballyhooed than the initial reports of the death of the Hellhound. The reporters would not be hanging around Yvonne's to photograph Alissa anymore, and the Hellhound coverage could wane.

Afterwards Harry stopped off at Homicide to see Nate, whom he had not seen since Hansen's death.

"It's kind of quiet right now," Harry told him. "Maybe Hansen was the whole show. But you're following up to find evidence that links him to the other Hellhound cases, aren't you?"

"Sure am, Harry. Problem is, no one seems to know what he ever did after hours, always a problem with loners."

"Keep me posted on what you turn up?"

"Absolutely."

"Okay. Until I hear to the contrary, I'm going to relax for a change."

Harry went back to his office. Since it was Friday, he was alone. He worked on preparations for an upcoming trial until the phone interrupted him. It was Dr. Paschov, offering both sympathy and congratulations. But what he had to say otherwise was less consoling.

"Mr. Maxwell, I am sorry to tell you that I do not see any similarities in the conduct of the man at the schoolyard and the man whose exploits I have studied in detail in the Hellhound files."

"Well, he's either one of the two as we discussed, or he was the only one, Dr. Paschov," said Harry with a trace of annoyance.

"Remember the 'calling card' that we mentioned? Hansen left one nailed to a corpse with my daughter's picture staked to it. That's what led us to rush to the schoolyard and what ended in my killing him."

"The newspapers hinted as much, but I do not think that Hansen is the man you have been seeking. And I think you should maintain high caution."

"Wait a second, Doctor. *The* man? You were the one who said there were two."

"Obviously I am not perfect. You gentlemen hampered my efforts by not trusting me with the "calling card" evidence from the outset. As it was, I had to come up with a theory quickly. Not an optimum method for analysis, as I am sure you will agree."

"Are you suggesting that not only is there only one man, but that I killed the wrong one?"

Paschov was silent for several seconds. He cleared his throat and then replied, "I am suggesting no blame whatever, Mr. Maxwell. Indeed, from all that I have heard, you had no choice but to kill the man."

"Well, then, what is this about?"

"I doubt that Mr. Hansen left the last 'calling card' or any of the earlier ones. After this newest incident I have restudied all the materials in the light of the 'calling card' issue and in the light of the schoolyard experience. We have all agreed that the Hellhound meticulously plans his crimes many steps ahead. He habitually foresees possible problems and provides escapes. Correct?"

"Yes."

"And yet you and Inspectors Hutchinson and La Croix are satisfied to accept the fact that he left you that brutal clue that he was about to kidnap your daughter, and then allowed you to get there to rescue her in time?"

Harry interjected, "It's a fact that he's been getting more reckless and taking more chances. He could have done that. Maybe he didn't know we'd leave ten minutes early for the search of that alley. You told me yourself that serial killers get more elaborate and more frequent in their crimes as time goes on. Wouldn't that result in more mistakes?"

"So how did Hansen know you would search that alley at all?"

"It was all over the police department and outside of it too, unfortunately."

"Be that as it may, it reinforces my impression that the Hellhound must be a police officer, a suspicion that I have had for some time. Now please be candid with me. How many police officers besides Captain Ratto are on your list of suspects?"

"Well, a few, but none who are really serious suspects."

"How many of them do you know personally, Harry?"

"Besides Tiny Ratto, two: my brother-in-law, Rico Benedetti, and Nate Hutchinson. Try to remember, Doctor, that even the coroner was on the list due to his height and his office being at the Hall."

"Surely you're joking. Nate Hutchinson is on the list, and he's been, so to speak, investigating himself?"

Harry sighed and once again explained the distinction between a suspect list and a list of people who have not been excluded. "In other words, we don't suspect someone just because he's tall and works at the Hall of Justice. We just eliminated those who were not. You see?"

"Yes, but apparently Inspector Hutchinson assisted you in deciding that he would not be among those who became real suspects."

"Doctor, with all due respect, we never intended for you to help in deciding who should be a suspect. We only asked you to do the psych profile."

"True enough, but to do so I have to have some confidence in the data I'm provided. And how smart would I be if I were not concerned with this conflict of interest?"

"For the last time, Nate was never a suspect."

"Ask yourself this: why did Hansen make no contingency plans whatever to escape from the schoolyard? He allowed you to intercept him, and we are supposed to believe that he was the one who sent you to do so? Don't you see, Harry? The Hellhound's level of planning for the Golden Gate Bridge episode is totally inconsistent with the lack of planning at the school. Those events were close in time, so how much could he have changed in the interim?"

"Then please explain to me how Hansen got to know about the calling card?"

"Simple. He did not. The real Hellhound planted the corpse, the calling card, and the photo, so that you would kill Hansen."

"That occurred to us, of course," said Harry. "And it fits in with your team theory. We considered that maybe the true brains of the team gave up the stooge to satisfy us and take us off the track. Although I'm not so convinced of that either."

"Perhaps you gentlemen so desperately want this investigation to be over, that you'll accept even this kind of evidence. But think. Where was Hansen's bullet-proof vest? Why did he not simply pick up your daughter physically and use her as a shield? Then he could have killed both you and Inspector La Croix, with you helpless to return his fire. No. He was a dupe. There is only one Hellhound, I am convinced."

"Well, excuse me for not believing you. Do all the crimes now bear the marks of only one man, contrary to what you insisted last time?"

"No, Harry. Please believe me. You are in great peril. There is only one man, but he has several personalities. I now believe that the man has a multiple personality disorder. One persona may well not even know what another has done, or even that it exists. That would explain why there are different M.O.'s in the attacks and murders."

"What do you mean?"

"When one personality is in control, you could see behavior that would be totally out of character for the other personalities."

"Plural?"

"Oh yes. There could be several, each different. One who is into S&M, and one is a misogynist. You see?"

"And is one of these personalities a carnival hypnotist?" blurted Harry incredulously. "So he just put Hansen into a trance and made him kidnap my daughter and try and shoot me dead?"

"Please, Mr. Maxwell, don't turn your fear into anger at me. You have need of all your faculties. I don't know how he might have arranged that. With your criminal expertise you might better tell *me* how anyone could trick Hansen into doing it."

"Well, I have no idea."

"Obviously he wanted to fake his own death. That would not work for long, but it might take the pressure off him for a while. I think he had a second goal. By having the person you love most in jeopardy, you might decide to stay clear of the investigation."

"So I'm the greatest threat to him as a criminal investigator? I don't think so."

"Perhaps not, but if he wishes to avoid killing you for some reason, he might want to drive you off the investigation. Use your own logic. Why would he want to avoid killing you, when he randomly killed dozens of innocent bystanders on the bridge?"

"Because he wants to play with me? Oh God. Or because he's a friend of mine?"

"Your guess here is as good as mine."

"Isn't this crap ever going to end?"

"It will, but I am hoping that you yourself will not be a casualty before it does. Good luck, Harry."

"Thanks. Bye." Harry hung up the phone feeling sick.

◆

In a moment, by the return of that familiar knot in his stomach, he knew the doctor was right. He hurried out to the nearest public phone and called Yvonne. "Yvonne, do you still have the key to Teri's house next door? Please go there right now, and wait for me to call you."

"I thought we were done with this."

"Yvonne, just do it. Now. And take Lissa with you."

Two minutes later, Harry called the number, and Yvonne answered on the first ring. "Yvonne, I just got off the phone with the police psychiatrist. He believes that Hansen was set up to appear to be the Hellhound and to be killed. And after listening to him, I think he's right."

"No, Harry, please don't tell me that. We're just getting over this horror and living like normal people again."

"There is no choice, Yvonne. His theory makes more and more sense. If the bastard tried for Alissa once, he might do it again. I'm going to be there in ten minutes. Go back home and pack one suitcase each. Don't answer the phone or the door. We're leaving town as soon as I arrive, whether you're done packing or not."

"But Harry, she'll miss a whole semester and..."

"Yvonne, there's nothing to discuss. You stay there and her death is your doing." Harry knew that was cruel and unfair, but the two minutes he spent arguing with her might be the wrong two minutes to gamble with. "Just get ready."

He ran to his car and raced over to the house. As he pulled into the driveway and began to get out, Yvonne and Alissa came rushing out the front door. As soon as they were in the car, he started off.

His daughter said tremulously, "Daddy, he's dead. You killed him."

"I'm sorry honey, but it was a trick. The really bad man set that whole thing up so that we'd think he was dead and stop looking for him. The man I killed wasn't him. Now you and Mommy have to hide so you'll be safe. You're getting a vacation from school for a while."

"But Harry, if he knows so much about you, won't he know all of our relatives and friends?" asked Yvonne.

"Yes, that's why you have to go somewhere you've never been and have no connection to."

"Where, Daddy?"

"I won't say it out loud, and neither should you. You'll see soon enough." As Harry drove, he thought of the awkwardness when they arrived. He had not even taken the risk to call them. He watched behind him carefully. The street was clear. He turned a corner and pulled immediately to the curb. No other cars followed for a full minute, and then an elderly man dawdled by. He pulled back out onto the street and drove another two blocks to a house with an iron gate. In a moment the three were standing on the porch while Harry knocked.

Ila Cobb answered the door. "Can we come in, please?" asked Harry. Without hesitation she stepped back and swung the door open, though with surprise on her face. She called to her husband, and he came into the hallway. Yvonne shifted her weight uneasily as Harry murmured his thanks for letting them in. Amos showed them into the living room and had them sit down.

"Mr. Maxwell," he began, "it's good seeing you again. This visit seems to be urgent, so please just tell me what you need."

Harry spoke rapidly. "Mr. Cobb, I am in desperate need of help, and I have nowhere else to turn. I have no right to do this, because I am bringing you into danger, but I have no choice."

"Tell us, what do you need?" Ila said softly.

"You know of my involvement in the Hellhound case?"

"The whole country knows," said Amos.

"Well, we thought he was dead, but it now appears that he tricked us into thinking so. The real Hellhound is still out there, and I am afraid he will try to catch Alissa again, or Yvonne." Harry suddenly realized that he had not introduced them. "Oh, this is my wife Yvonne and my daughter Alissa. Mr. Cobb was once a client of mine, and Amos and Ila Cobb are also friends of mine." They all nodded to each other, but Yvonne's face was still showing signs of confusion.

Ila spoke to Alissa. "Your daddy saved my Amos, honey. A horrible woman accused him of a terrible crime, and your daddy proved his innocence. We'll never forget that."

"I can't send them anywhere to stay with family or friends," Harry went on, "because it turns out the Hellhound is probably someone I know. And I can't send them out of state or out of the country, because he may well be a cop and would have access to any computers used to book passages. Yvonne won't even be able to use any credit cards. Mr. and Mrs. Cobb, if you'll do this for me, what I would like is for them to stay here and never even go outdoors. Can you help?"

"Of course, Mr. Maxwell," answered Ila. "We would be honored to host your family."

Harry looked at her and at Amos. "You do realize that this is dangerous? If he found them here, he could kill all of you to get to her."

"Are you sure you were not followed here, Mr. Maxwell?" Amos asked.

"I'm sure I wasn't. And I never told anybody or wrote down where I was taking them. This monster may be a cop, and he certainly has extensive resources. As long as none of you mentions this to anyone nor makes any phone calls to friends or family, you should be safe enough."

"We will keep them safe here, Mr. Maxwell," Amos pledged.

"Thank you," Harry whispered.

He gave the Cobbs cash for groceries and went to the front door to peek out through the glass panel at the top. No unusual cars or watchers appeared to be out front, so he opened the door.

He looked back once and saw Ila in the living room with her hand on Alissa's shoulder and Amos at the side of Yvonne. Harry started his car and again carefully scanned the street and sidewalks. There was nothing to be seen, so he drove back to his office.

♦

Harry opened his mail. It included a check on a settlement that Bridge had worked up for him, and other cases were now in the pipeline, so the money picture did not look so bad for a change. He picked up the phone and punched in the number for Rico Benedetti in the narcotics squad office. Rico was glad to grant the favor Harry asked of him and agree to see him at home tomorrow, Saturday. Harry hung up the phone mulling over Tyrone's words about unpredictability.

CHAPTER TWENTY TWO

The next morning Harry drove to the home of his sister Pat. From inside he heard the sound of a loudly whining power tool. The noise stopped, and tall Rico came to the door in his work clothes and tool belt. His dark curly hair was flecked with sawdust. He greeted Harry with an easy smile, and they chatted a few minutes until Pat came out too. Her laugh lines crinkled as she wiped her hands on her apron. Harry leaned down and kissed her proffered cheek.

"Hi, sis. This bum messing up your house again?"

Rico smiled and then excused himself. He soon returned and handed Harry a folded up brown paper bag.

"Thanks Rico. I'll probably only need it for a few weeks."

"Take your time. Keep it as long as you need to." Pat was looking on in a way that Harry was sure meant she had no idea what was transpiring, and he meant to leave it that way. Thinking again of Nate, Harry mused that it must be a cop thing not to tell wives anything.

"Well, I'll let you guys get back to work."

"I'll walk you to your car, Harry," Rico said. They went out to Harry's Nova and Rico spoke in a low voice. "Harry, is there anything else I can do to help?"

"If I think of anything, I'll let you know, but right now, no." Harry opened his door and then paused, exhaling between his teeth. "There is something. I don't want to draw you into this, but I need for at least a couple of people to know in case something happens to me. Will you promise me that you won't let anyone know what I told you, and especially no one in the P.D.?"

"Harry, you know I don't like open promises. If you're going to confess that you're the Hellhound, I'll break my promise," said Rico with a smile.

"No, but I'm on the list of potentials. Hell, so are you. So is my investigator Tyrone Washington, and Tiny Ratto, and the Medical Examiner Dr. Barstoff. And on and on."

"You've gotta be kidding me, Harry. How did you and I become suspects?"

"We're not." Harry sighed, and recited his litany about the elimination list. "What I need is for someone who's not involved to know that I suspect that the Hellhound might be either Nate Hutchinson or Pierre La Croix."

This time it was Rico whose eyes went wide. "Unbelievable," he said, shaking his head. "How long have you thought this?"

"I don't know. It's just a feeling that's been festering in the pit of my stomach. If I'm right and I disappear, I don't want my suspicions to die with me."

"The biggest serial rape and murder investigation in the history of the city, and the two detectives in charge of the case are both suspects? Incredible." Something about Rico's tone of voice told Harry that he knew more than he was saying.

"I don't blame you for not believing me, Rico. Don't think I don't spend a lot of time calling myself paranoid. And they are not officially suspects. It's just me, riding the periphery of the investigation, thinking it. But I'll be honest with you. I don't know what to believe anymore, and I don't trust my own judgment either. If I went to the Chief with this, you know he'd dismiss me as a nut. Then I'd have to tell him that I'm on the list, and you. Where would that lead? And I'd really rather neither of them knew I even had these thoughts."

"Why do you suspect Nate and Pierre?"

"The short answer is that the Hellhound must know me. He knew immediately that it was me who matched wits with him in the chat room. He's a regular at the Hall, has access to secure areas, and above all he knows everything that happens in the investigation. Lastly, he's taken some pains to avoid killing me, while trying to scare me off the case. He's not squeamish about killing people who are in his way, so it's hard to explain why he hasn't taken me out, unless we're friends. Believe me, I have antagonized him."

"Then pull out and leave it to the Department."

"Yeah, to Pierre and Nate? Anyway, I'm not sure that walking away is an option anymore, as many times as he's gone after me."

"But if all he wants is to get you out of the investigation, then get out and he'll stop, right?"

"That's a maybe. What's certain is that I had to fire a .357 magnum at a man who was standing three feet from my daughter. I'm not taking the chance that he's going off the deep end, or that my guess about his being a friend is wrong. I want to find him."

"Don't, Harry. Stay out of it. Tend to your own business."

"Protecting my daughter *is* my business," Harry said, raising his voice. At that point Rico turned to look toward the house. He stepped quickly around to the passenger side of the car and got in, then motioned to Harry to get in and close the door.

Rico spoke quietly, "I know you're scared, Harry, but it's just because you're scared that you're dangerous. Back off."

"Why do you keep telling me to…" Harry trailed off, but Rico saw suspicion in his eyes.

"Oh, you *are* paranoid. That's it. Pierre made me promise not to share this with anyone, but I'm damned if I'll let this come between us. Pierre recovered a key from Hansen's pocket that belongs to a storage locker at the airport. Pierre and I went this morning and opened it together. We went through it in a security office at the airport so that no one at the Hall would know."

"Why did Pierre go to you for that? Is it a departmental reg now that only people on the short list of possible suspects can work on this case?"

Rico chuckled. "I would guess it's because I'm not in homicide, and because we worked together years ago, and he trusts me."

"What did you find?"

"More keys, maps with marked locations of homes of past Hellhound victims, plans for the Golden Gate Bridge, underwear souvenirs of old kills, a gun, rope, burglar's tools, rubber gloves, a ski mask, more disguises. The usual."

"Keys? To what?"

"And well you might ask. Other lockers, houses not identified yet, padlock keys to who knows what sheds. We opened up two other lockers and found more of the same."

"So it was Hansen all along?"

"Not quite, Harry. Nate's fingerprints were all over the stuff. We're busy trying to account for his time during each of the killings. We're assuming for the moment that Hansen was his accomplice, and that he was sacrificed to derail the investigation."

"But every survivor insisted he was white."

"We also found Caucasian wigs, mustaches, and skin makeup."

"I don't know," Harry said. "Hellhound likes to throw red herrings across the path."

"I discreetly asked Nate's wife if she thought he was working too hard. She assured me he was. Comes home at all hours, misses dinner more often than not, and never accounts for where he's been." Harry suddenly remembered his talk with Selma and recalled his own perplexity with that inconsistency. Nate had been in a perfect position to detonate the lab bomb with a pocket radio controller. His own minor injuries would even throw suspicion off Nate.

Rico frowned, and his eyes tightened. "Harry, I know you're under a lot of stress, but you don't really suspect me, do you?"

"I trust you. I trust you because you're standing here with sawdust in your hair, home with your family. I'm looking for the guy who's got no family or is gone all the time. He spends all his free time setting up bizarre schemes and escapes. He doesn't have time to cut wood."

Rico laughed. "I really don't either, but it's got to get done."

"So are you going to arrest Nate?"

"Can't yet. As you said, the Hellhound is fond of leaving false trails. We need more evidence. That's why we're checking out his whereabouts for the times of the murders. There is one very interesting tidbit we learned, though. Nate was in the Navy Seals."

Harry looked surprised. "Wow. You won't find a better bunch of divers, commandos, and demolition experts."

"Harry, promise me you won't breathe a word of any of this."

"Of course." They shook hands, and Rico got out of the car. Harry drove off.

As he pulled into the street, he did not look back. His mind was too tangled. If it were Nate, why was he the one who had allowed Harry access to the laptop to talk to the accomplice? That was what brought Harry into the investigation. And then why would he cut the explosion so close? They were both nearly killed. Another tenth of a second and they would both have been blown through a wall instead of down the hall. And Nate was not so close a friend that he was certain that Nate would not consider him expendable.

A car to Harry's right blew his horn loud and long to warn Harry back into his own lane. Harry thought of Pierre. He was a close friend, but he was a loner otherwise. Pierre had also come within seconds of being blown up on the Marina Green, and had not even taken cover from the rain of debris. Why would the Hellhound kill a dozen people on the bridge to cover his tracks and then court suicide later? Harry knew that Pierre cared about the victims. He had even cried for them. He could not be the killer, nor would he risk Harry's daughter's life.

Nate had lied to Selma about working late. What did he do with all those hours? Why did he get so angry when Harry suggested that he warn his wife of the danger? Did he know she was *not* in danger? And if it were him, why would he have stayed so clear of the Hellhound investigation for so long, when the only reason he would have come to San Francisco's Homicide Department would be to keep an eye on his own case? Still, it was Pierre who was dead set against Harry's getting involved. But so was Tiny Ratto. Harry's mind swam with endless circles and dead ends.

Out of all the cops in the city, why would Pierre pick someone on the short list to accompany him to the locker? Because Harry trusted him? Hell, who was not a potential suspect? Harry wiped his sleeve across his forehead and rubbed his cheek.

How could it be either Pierre or Nate? Claudia Wildman had seen both of them in her home after her attack and had not reacted at all. Her attacker would never have risked facing her again, especially so soon. Or would he? Whether he would have to face her or not, clearly the Hellhound was getting off on the risk of leaving her alive. He could think of no other reason to do so. Harry's head swirled as he blundered across the center line, and an oncoming car swerved and honked a long angry note at him.

"Dammit!" Harry shouted out loud to his dashboard, as he slammed on the brakes and pulled to the curb. "He's screwing with my head and leading me in circles." He sat in thought a few minutes. "Yeah, *leading* me," he repeated out loud.

He turned around and drove to the Hall. He went up to Homicide to see if Pierre might be in. He walked in and saw a light on. There was no receptionist on Saturday, but when he entered the inner room he found Nate at his desk. "Hi, Nate," he said cheerfully, walking up to him quickly. Nate promptly covered up what he was working on.

"What are you working on, bud?"

"Oh, just another murder. It's nothing to do with the Hellhound case, Harry. I spend so much time on that maniac that I need the weekends to catch up."

"I can imagine. I wanted to talk to you about the investigation, though. Have you done any new work that you need to brief me on?"

"Well, not too much. Tiny Ratto was not at the Belford house that night. But when the first units began arriving, the perimeter was not very tightly buttoned. We have no assurance that unidentified uniforms were not wandering around. Also, we have nothing new on Hansen's background, except that one man who knew him from the neighborhood had heard that he had been in a mental institution for a year or two. That's about it."

Harry nodded and smiled. Then he reached out and lifted the corner of the file in front of Nate, who suddenly slapped his hands down on it. "I just want to see what you're working on."

"Well, just because you're assisting in the investigation doesn't mean you get to see everything in the case, Harry. Some things are still confidential."

"I thought you said it wasn't about the Hellhound case?"

Nate placed his palms down on the desk and gave Harry a stern look. "Harry? Out."

"Fine," Harry said. I'm gone." He had a satisfied feeling as he jogged down the stairs.

He had managed to see one word on the tab of the file before it was covered up, "Carmen." It meant nothing to him when he read it, but as he walked out, the name rattled around inside his head. Carmen. Carmen. *Carmen was right. Right about you.* Tiny Ratto.

Harry hurried outside and dialed the S.F.P.D. office at Juvenile Hall on his cell phone. After being passed around, he learned that Captain Ratto was in. "Would you like to be connected?" the voice asked.

"On second thought, no. Thank you anyway." Harry hung up.

He drove straight to Juvenile Hall, where he marched up to Ratto's office and handed the receptionist a business card. He asked the woman to ask Captain Ratto a specific question for him "word for word." When he had laid out the question, she stared at him as if sighting a loon.

Harry said again, "Just say, 'Would you talk to Harry Maxwell if doing so would screw La Croix?'" Harry urged her, "Please. Just ask him exactly that."

She got on the phone and in a whisper repeated the question, with a look of distaste on her face. Soon a uniformed sergeant with the name tag "Martin" came in and showed Harry to Ratto's office. The captain did not rise from his chair, nor did he shake Harry's hand. The sergeant stayed in the room with folded arms.

"This is personal," Harry said.

"You have no idea how fucking personal, counselor. The officer stays. I don't talk to you or anyone about this without witnesses. You don't like it, get out."

"I know you don't like my being in on the Hellhound investigation. If I had it to do over, I'd have done as you wanted and kept out, but now it's too late."

Ratto smiled slightly. Sergeant Martin was overage for his rank. Harry knew the type. He would kiss ass for twenty years, but his career would never go any further. Harry went on. "There have been leaks in this investigation for a long time, and the Hellhound seems to know everything that happens."

"No shit. If I'd had that case, it would have been solved years ago," Tiny said, rattling his chin wattles.

"Let's just say at this point I'd like to know a little more about my friend Pierre. I remember the last time I saw you, you said something like 'Carmen was right about you.' I'm wondering who Carmen is and what she said about him."

"His auntie, I think. She's as crazy as he is."

"Did you ever meet her?"

"What's this to do with me, and how does this 'screw Pierre'?"

"Did you ever meet her?"

"No, and fuck you. You answer my question or I don't tell you shit."

"You say Pierre is crazy. I'm trying to find out if that's true, and if so, just how crazy he might be. You want to help or not?"

"I never met her and I don't want to. She called up for 'her boy' a couple of times. This was years back. Once or twice. She's flaky. Pierre told her not to call anymore. I think she must be in some institution. I haven't heard from her in a long time."

"Do you have any idea where she lives?"

"No, but I think it's Texas. Yeah. I remember seeing the phone record from when he called her. Unusual to see calls to Texas, so I remember it."

"Do you remember what city by any chance?"

"No. No. It was…something with two words. Was a song about it."

"El Paso?"

"That's it. El Paso."

"Does her kind of craziness seem similar in any way to Pierre's, as you see it?"

"No. On the phone she bitched and whined about him not calling. 'He's such a bad boy' kinda shit. 'He doan' never call me,'" he mimicked in a croaking whine. "La Croix is vicious. He doesn't know friend from enemy. Like some damn rattlesnake."

"I don't get it," said Harry. "You were really mad when you said that to him. From what you've told me, this Carmen thing is nothing. I would have thought you'd needle him about not catching the Hellhound for eight years."

"It's a mystery to me too. All I know is that it always set him off anytime someone talked about Carmen, so I use it when I need to. It gets him where he lives. I don't forget things like that," Ratto said with a throaty chuckle.

"One last question, please. You ever know Pierre by any other name than La Croix?"

"No. An alias? I'd love that. Tell you what. I'm definitely gonna look into his history. If I find something good, I might let you know. Might not." Harry gave no reaction to this, but wondered if he had just destroyed a long friendship for nothing.

Ratto turned to say something to his lackey. That seemed to be the end of the audience, so Harry took his leave. As he was passing out the door, Ratto called, "Wait, I just remembered something. That Carmen woman. The first time she called, I didn't know who she was talking about, because she called him Pedro, not Pierre."

"Well, Pedro and Carmen are both Hispanic names, so that kind of makes sense. Pierre and Pedro both mean Peter," Harry said. Ratto shrugged.

◆

Harry stopped at the pay phone in the lobby to call Bridget at home.

"Hi, Bridge. Still alive here."

"That's good to know. Anything wrong?"

"I've never asked this before, but I wonder if you could work for me tomorrow."

"Sunday?"

"Aahh, yes. If you could."

"Well, it must be important then, aye?"

"I think so. I need you to spend most of a day on the phone to Texas trying to find a woman named Carmen, but I'm not sure what her last name is."

"You're joking, aren't you?"

"No. We're pretty sure the city is El Paso."

"Oh well, that should cut it down to a mere 10,000, I should think. And if I should pull this proverbial rabbit out of the hat, do you win a really big case?"

Harry told the truth. "Maybe my family and I stay alive."

"I see. Well, wouldn't it do as well if I did it right now?"

"That would do nicely, Bridge, but I'd rather you did it from home and I reimbursed you for the long distance charges, so we'll know no one's listening."

"Give me what you have, luv. Ready."

"Her name is Carmen. Her nephew's name is Pierre La Croix, maybe known then as Pedro." Harry heard the sudden intake of air on the other end. "She is supposed to be Pierre's auntie, but we don't know if it's paternal or maternal."

"Harry, if the name was La Croix, it might not be hard to trace, but what if it's a maternal aunt?"

"I know it's not much, but twenty-eight years ago, El Paso was a small town. Maybe a tall, smart kid like Pierre would be remembered by old timers, by whatever name. If you connect with Carmen, you'll know. Her voice is shrill and whiney. She sounds like this." Harry did his best imitation of her voice as portrayed by Ratto, saying, "He such a bad boy. He doan' call never."

"And if I find her, what do I do?"

"Get her address. See if she can confirm that Pierre is Pedro. If she seems talkative, ask her what kind of boy he was. Did he get in trouble? Strange behavior? Hobbies? If you can pull it off, tell her she shouldn't call him at work again. It gets him in trouble. Last thing I want is her calling him and reporting our inquiry. Don't use my name. Be a reporter or something."

"Sounds more investigative than secretarial. Have I gotten another promotion?"

Harry laughed. "Write your own ticket."

"It's not that. I'm curious why you don't just use a P.I. for this."

"Because you're smarter and more sensitive than any of them, and can charm a snake out of his shoulders."

"Flattery will get you everywhere."

"Be careful, Bridge. Block your calls so there's no trace back to you."

"I thought you just said I was smart, Oaf."

"Bridge? Thanks." His voice wavered slightly on the last word. Harry wondered to himself if she had ever given any thought to going to law school.

Harry picked up a pizza and went home. He fetched a bottle of cranberry juice and picked at his pizza while he researched Pierre La Croix and Nate Hutchinson on the internet. He found official records about Pierre, but nothing he did not already know. He logged off and napped until the phone rang. It was Bridge.

"Sorry, luv. I didn't find anything in the directories under Carmen La Croix. Not surprising, that. It's not very West Texas, is it? I called the El Paso Police Department. At least some of those fellows have to draw duty on Saturday, with all those thirsty Texans in their Stetsons mucking about."

"Absolutely. Good thinking."

"I said I was a journalist researching 'Our Heroes, The Police,' and I needed some local history on constables and ruffians. I followed a string of referrals until I found one Sam Twillum, a retired officer who sounded every bit of seventy-five. We had such fun discussing his heroic exploits, and eventually we got around to desperados he had 'collared.' I casually inquired, by the bye, whether he knew a Pierre La Croix, a tall, bright rascal, who would have been a teenager some twenty-five to thirty years ago. He didn't, so I suggested that he might have gone by the name Pedro then."

"And that name meant something to him, I'll bet."

"Indeed. He asked if this person had an aunt named Carmen. I confirmed that, and his disgust was immediately evident. He volunteered that he had little use for any of the Cruz clan. Cruz, I asked him? Yes, that would be Pedro Cruz and his crazy aunt Carmen. Couldn't be two families like them, he was quite clear. Harry, you realize that Pierre La Croix is French for Peter Cross, and Pedro Cruz is Spanish for the same name?"

"Yeah Bridge, I did notice that."

"He said he couldn't count the times he'd gotten called out there by neighbors who heard the kid screaming. They'd find she had whipped him and was still scolding him. In those days there was hardly any protection for homeless kids, so he stayed with her."

"Parents?" Harry asked her.

"None," she said. "Both dead. Carmen was his only living kin, and she was always drunk. She'd go on to the police about his laziness or how he would fake illness or injury to get out of his chores."

"Sounds like old Pierre was an intractable teenager," Harry said.

"Teen? Oh. I see. Harry, this is from when he was only eight."

"Good God," was all Harry could say.

"Pedro became a problem for the police in his own right long before he became a teen. Fire setting, bullying, truancy, running away, theft, vandalism. Over time, it got worse."

"Not surprising," Harry said.

"But this is, Harry. By the time he reached thirteen, he didn't get into trouble anymore, or at least he never got caught. Mr. Twillum suspected Pedro in many unsolved crimes in the next four years, but could never catch him again. From age twelve, Pedro seldom went to school."

"So he got expelled?"

"Well, that's where this gets really strange. No, indeed. When he was not burning or damaging something, he was a voracious reader. Sometimes even his school books. He'd show up for his tests at school and get top grades. Then he'd disappear for a week and not be seen in school. They didn't want to expel him because his work was so good. Twillum knew his English teacher, and she would rave about his essays."

"Did he graduate?"

"He did. Ten days after his eighteenth birthday he graduated first in his class. Eleven days after his eighteenth birthday he was arrested for his first adult offense, a tavern brawl. He was in jail for three days for that and was sentenced to time served."

"Then we can match Pedro's prints to Pierre's."

"I'm afraid not. The morning they released him, they had a fire at the jail. Fingerprint cards awaiting processing for distribution to state and federal agencies were lost."

"How convenient."

"Quite, luv. Then he walked out of the jail and was never seen in El Paso again. According to the demented aunt, he didn't even go back home to pick up his clothes."

"Well, Bridge, you've scored ninety-nine percent so far. Did you get the address?"

"Yes indeed. 6942 Bandero Way, El Paso."

"You're great, Bridge. It's everything I could have hoped for. Thank you for doing this."

"Watch your back, luv. I know I will."

So, was that it, he asked himself? If this was Pierre's childhood, he was suckled in hell, but a lot of people overcame such beginnings. If you took the toughest kids from any high school and looked them up fifteen years later, half would be criminals and half cops.

As he slipped into sleep, a question nagged at Harry's fading consciousness: Did Pierre become the cop? Or both?

CHAPTER TWENTY THREE

Monday morning Harry was boxing closed case files in his office. He was stooping to lift a box of files when he heard the voice behind him. "Hi, Harry." He froze. It was Nate. "I wanted to talk to you in private."

Harry stood up and turned around, knowing he could not reach his gun in time if he needed it. He sat at his desk and gestured to Nate to take a seat.

"I'm in a very awkward situation, Harry."

No shit, Harry thought.

"I think I was wrong not to share this with you before. If the Hellhound makes good on his threat to kill me, I don't want my evidence to die with me." Harry certainly understood that thinking. "And you just can't go after some people alone. If it's my word against his, likely as not the Chief would back him."

"Who are we talking about, Nate?"

"Pierre. I'm nearly certain that it's him."

"The Hellhound?"

"Yes."

"There are hundreds of cops to share this with. Why me?"

"Because you're not a cop. Pierre's got strong support in the department. Some cops would never believe any degree of evidence. Also, there's this epidemic of leaks in the police department. I don't know who's trustworthy."

"Including me. I was on the list too, remember?"

"I know. But part of the time the crimes have been happening you were married. I talked to Yvonne, and she says you were always home right after work. You couldn't possibly be the guy."

Unlike some people, Harry thought.

"Harry, what I was looking at when you came into my office was part of my file on Pierre. I've been checking sign-in sheets, arrest reports, and computer files to find out where Pierre was during the Hellhound crimes."

"And what did they show?"

"He could have been at the scene of each of the crimes."

"As could a hundred other people, but you're forgetting the Langley murder in the chat room. Pierre was with us."

"You're forgetting, Harry. When Gene Behrens first ran in, the Hellhound's ID was logged into the chat room, but he wasn't talking, right? He didn't start talking again until after Pierre left. How do we know he didn't log into the chat room while 'at lunch' and leave it running when he came back and sat at his desk? As soon as he left us, he could have resumed the chat."

"Opportunity alone is poor proof of murder."

"I know. I need more, but I'm here to warn you. You're Pierre's best friend, maybe his only friend, but I'm not sure even that will protect you anymore. He's got to be feeling a lot of pressure now, and if he considers you a threat, maybe now you're as expendable as I am."

"These are slim grounds to accuse Pierre," Harry said. Whatever his own suspicions, he felt it was wise to share little or nothing with Nate.

"There is a lot of evidence that points to him. He was there to plant the bomb at the Belford mansion. Once again, the explosion was a close call, just beyond lethal distance. That's happened three times, and all three times Pierre was within fifty yards to control the timing.

"And what about his lack of progress in eight years? He never tried a database elimination. He never methodically surveyed the victims to look for commonality. He never secured a single hair for a DNA check and never secured a written psych profile. Harry, how do you rape a dozen women and never leave a single pubic hair on the victim? Or was it just that he was careful never to collect one of his own?"

"I'm not believing this," said Harry, looking under his brows up at Nate.

"Well, who has had complete control over what evidence is seized at crime scenes? He is the perfect suspect for the lab bomb. And with his hours, he could work at midnight in complete privacy."

And so could you, Harry thought. "What do you want of me, Nate?" he said. "Did you come to me because he's my friend, and if I turn against him, you'll have some credibility? Well, get evidence if you need credibility for your theory."

"I knew this would be hard for you. I just don't want him to take you out before I can get the rest of the proof. I'm close, Harry. I'll have the rest soon, very soon. Don't disappear on me before I get it."

"I'll try not to. Who's Carmen?"

"His aunt, I think. I'm trying to find her. Maybe she can fill us in on Pierre's childhood. How about Alissa? Is she safe? Where did you put her?"

"Where no one will find her."

Nate frowned, then nodded, and rose to leave. "Good. I'll be back in touch when I've got more. Take care, Harry."

"You too, Nate."

It was now 1:30 p.m., and Harry had to attend the afternoon settlement conference calendar. He made his way to the Hall, and felt a twinge of remorse at seeing Osmund's empty spot.

CHAPTER TWENTY FOUR

Harry drove straight to the airport and locked his court files and guns in the trunk. He hustled his overnight bag into the terminal and found his flight already boarding.

The aisle was full, but he found his seat and leaned over to stow his bag. Suddenly he was face-to-face with a smiling Tiny Ratto. Harry sank down and asked, "Are you following me now?"

"Nah, too hard. I got the major airlines to watch for ticketing. Funny how the action always seems to follow you in this case, so I thought I'd do the same."

"Besides tailing me, anything else on your agenda?"

"I thought I'd see what Carmen can tell me about 'Bad Boy's' history, particularly whether he's ever been committed."

"At least we agree about that."

"You know, I gave La Croix free rein on this case, because I know he's good. Then he lets you get involved, and a civilian gets tortured and murdered. This might surprise you, Mr. Pierre's friend, but that offends me. I start asking Pierre for reports on what he's doing, and next thing I know I'm on the six o'clock news."

"Listen Tiny…"

"You don't call me that, okay? You can call me Cliff or Captain Ratto. You pick."

"Sorry, Cliff. I know how much you hate Pierre, but it looks more like Nate to me. Pierre and Rico went to the airport and opened some lockers with a key he found in Hansen's pocket. It was full of incriminating stuff like disguises, skin makeup, and possibly victims' underwear. Nate's fingerprints were all over the stash. They're working on trying to establish Nate's whereabouts for each crime to see if it could be him."

"Yeah, that sounds bad, but isn't laying false trails a part of this guy's M.O. too?"

"Yeah, it is."

The drink cart arrived, and Ratto ordered a scotch. Harry grabbed a magazine and read for the rest of the trip. When the plane touched down, Ratto retrieved his gun at baggage claim, and then they picked up Ratto's rental Ford. "We've got to check in with the local P.D. first, Harry. Protocol."

In fifteen minutes, Ratto pulled into the parking lot of the El Paso P.D. At the desk Ratto showed his ID and then explained his mission to the duty sergeant.

Sergeant Akins asked Ratto if there was anything he needed.

"Well, as a matter of fact this rental car's ignition is dicey, and I don't want to waste the time going back to the airport. Don't suppose you got an extra squad car you could spare for a few hours?"

"No problem. Jimmy Bob, give the captain here car 18 Delta, would ya? Fine. Anything else? Well, happy hunting. Anything else come up, y'all just give a holler."

"Thank you, Sergeant. Much obliged for your hospitality."

Outside, Harry asked "What's that about? There's nothing wrong with the car."

"No. It just encourages cooperation to see a local squad car. Otherwise, we're just civilian looking guys with no clout."

Ratto checked out the car, and they were on their way. Carmen lived about a fifteen minute drive away, judging from the map. Harry checked his watch and asked, "Cliff, it's late. You figure to wake her at this hour?"

"Nah, I'm gonna get some sleep and see her first thing in the morning. That suit you?"

"Well, I don't feature sleeping for six hours sitting up in this car. How about checking into the first motel we see on the highway?"

"Suits me."

They found a small motel one mile down the highway. Ratto laid his pistol on the night table and went straight to bed. The room was very dark once the lights were out, thanks to some heavy black out curtains. Harry climbed out of bed and grabbed his toiletry kit from his open suitcase. "I forgot to brush my teeth." He disappeared into the bathroom, then came out and checked the door before getting into bed.

◆

Harry was awakened by a loud clinking noise. He saw a fully dressed Ratto backlit by the open door, with the door knob still in his hand. Harry's shaving cream can, aspirin bottle, and the motel's drinking glass, which Harry had stacked in front of the door, were scattered on the carpet. Harry checked his watch. It was 5:30 a.m. in the morning.

"Just taking a walk, counselor," said Ratto.

"No, you're not," Harry corrected him. "I have Carmen's number. You leave without me, and I call her."

Ratto closed the door, took off his pants, and went back to bed, but neither slept after that. At 6:30 a.m. they both rose and caught some breakfast. Then Ratto drove to Carmen's place.

By the time they arrived at the 6900 block of Bandero Way, the ambiance of the passing neighborhoods had progressed from benign neglect to seedy and threatening. As Ratto pulled to the curb, they were looking at a shack with one window in front and a roof of corrugated rust. In the front yard sat the wheel rims of a car and the cancerous hulk of a washing machine.

Neither movement nor light came from within. Harry rolled down his window and could not hear any sound coming from the house.

"Why did you try to ditch me?" said Harry.

"Maybe I wanted to keep an eye on you, but I'm already flush with constitutional lawyers looking over my shoulder."

"Fair enough, but it's funny. Since I got sucked into this quagmire, I've grown kinda indifferent to the Hellhound's constitutional rights."

"Gets that way when it's your ass in the line of fire, don't it, counselor?"

They went up to the front door, and Harry was struck by the absolute silence. They stood on the door stoop, and Cliff patted his shoulder holster. Harry sniffed to see if he could detect coffee brewing, or any other odor, for that matter.

Ratto raised his fist to rap on the door. As he cocked his forearm back, Harry's hand caught his wrist tightly, preventing his hand from pounding on the door. Ratto turned and saw him holding a finger to his lips. Harry sniffed the air three times and looked at Ratto, who also began to sniff. Harry watched Ratto's brow furrow. Then the captain suddenly pushed Harry off the stoop, pulled his pistol, and with one powerful kick splintered the door inward.

The strong smell of blood and putrification surrounded them as it rushed out the front door. The door crashed against the interior wall and swung back. Harry remounted the stoop and placed his right foot at the base of the door. Both men wrinkled their noses at the second wave of stench. "Not good," Harry said, as they rushed inside.

Ratto began panning the small front room with his extended pistol. The room was empty except for an ancient, ragged stuffed armchair and a worn, stained end table. The entire house was dark and dingy, despite the morning light. The kitchen was to their left, and a short hallway lay ahead of them. Harry could see that the kitchen wall sported two fist-sized holes. He could also see a doorway down the hall that he judged to be open from a swarm of flies circling in the hall, whose flight paths seemed to take them beyond the doorway.

Ratto motioned for Harry to stay where he was, and cleared the kitchen area first. Harry edged to his left slightly, where he could see a dirty white sink and dish drainer next to it. Scattered on the floor were crushed soda cans, napkins, and spirals of accumulated dust.

Ratto came back out and turned down the hall, with Harry following. The smell of rot got stronger. Ratto crouched frozen in the doorway of the bedroom for several moments. before Harry heard his throaty whisper, "*Mother McCree.*" Then his bulky figure disappeared into the room. Muted carpet footsteps became the louder clicks of shoes on tile.

Harry followed him and stood in the bedroom doorway. Ratto was standing in a bathroom doorway, holstering his pistol. The two men silently surveyed a ghastly scene, keeping their mouths closed to avoid inhaling any of the flies. The floor was a caked mess of clotted blood, garbage, and dust. A rumpled double bed had dried blood on the pillows and an unself-conscious rat grazing on bedspread clots. Spider webs covered the corners of the room, exposed rafters, and window recess.

Then there was the ceiling. Driven into the rafters at various locations were ten-penny nails. To these were tied pieces of twine of varying lengths. From one piece was hung a human leg, from calf to foot. Another suspended an arm with bulging blue veins, gnarly knuckles, and garish nail polish. From another dangled what appeared to be a flabby thigh. Farther away hung the head of an old woman with very pale skin and tangled white hair. The twine suspending the head was threaded through holes in the cheeks, stretching out the cheeks and lips and revealing rotted teeth. Dangling from one eye socket was the handle of a cat-o-nine-tails. The spiders had crafted a web between the whip and the matted hair. The other rafters displayed remaining body parts.

Harry crossed the sticky floor to the bathroom. The tub enclosure was also stained dark purple with dried blood, and streaks of it pointed the way to the drain. The walls and floor of the bathroom were also speckled with body fluids. Near the light switch on the wall were the bloody imprints of three finger tips. Harry, looking closely, saw that the prints were smooth, the fingers evidently covered with rubber gloves.

Ratto re-entered the bedroom, holding his handkerchief over his mouth. Harry pulled his jacket lapel up over his mouth. Out in the hallway, Harry spoke first.

"We won't be able to get any prints here," he said.

"No, but if he showered to remove the blood, he can't have missed leaving dead skin cells and hair in the drain."

"This makes no sense," Harry said, coughing. "He's a crackerjack bomb maker. He could easily have obliterated this shack and not left any evidence. Why this?"

Ratto looked disgusted. "He's *proud* of this work."

"I guess so. He sure went to a lot of trouble to impress whoever came through that door, but why would he wear gloves if he's going to leave us DNA?"

"Because finger prints are immediate, but DNA takes weeks."

"So it's just a stall? He doesn't care if we know who he is, but he needs some time to make his get away?"

"That's my take on it."

Harry considered his next move, and then told Ratto what he knew. "I had my investigator speak with a local cop who knew these people. Carmen used to whip Pedro something awful."

"I know. I've inquired too. That might explain the whip handle shoved into the eye. Judging from the amount of blood down the shaft of the whip, she was alive when he did it. And he had plenty of rage left over after she was dead."

"Good Lord. So it *is* Pierre?"

"Much as that would please me, I don't like it. It's too pat. If Pierre didn't kill her in the last thirty-five years, why would he pick now, just to point suspicion to himself? And the whip? Might as well sign his work. Maybe this is a little too convenient, coming hot on the heels of all the evidence pointing to Nate. We could be looking at more disinformation here."

Harry wavered for a moment and then told him he had paid Homicide a visit and talked to Nate, who quickly covered up the file he was working on. "But before he did, I saw the word on the cover, 'Carmen'. He said he was looking for her. We'd better get back to San Francisco in a hurry. If the Hellhound is shutting down, as you put it, he could be gone already, or liquidating other people."

"Same thing occurred to me." Ratto radioed Sergeant Akins and filled him in. The local homicide detectives arrived within fifteen minutes. Harry listened as Ratto explained the need for their prompt departure back to San Francisco. Detective Larabee understood and was anxious for them to go back and "corral" the maniac. He made a call and arranged for the airline to bump two passengers to allow them to make an emergency departure on the next flight out.

♦

On the plane, Harry debated himself. Was it Pierre shutting Carmen's mouth, or was Nate pointing a bloody finger at Pierre? Or even someone else? Harry ransacked his memory. He had told nobody of his plans to go to El Paso. He had been careful to make his reservations on his cell phone. So who knew he was coming? Ratto, of course, but if he was the murderer, why did Harry walk out of Carmen's place alive? Someone else must know.

Harry nudged Ratto. "Cliff? Any precautions taken at your office against electronic bugging?"

"Never saw a need," he said.

"Homicide has. Where is the telephone junction box in your building? Basement?"

"Yeah, that's right."

"So he sneaks into the building at night, goes to the basement, and splices into your line. He could set a recorder or transmit by radio. You'd never know. Who was that kiss-ass lackey I met at your office?"

"Martin. Why?"

"Is he the kind of lackey you can send out on a special job, and he'll thank you for the privilege?" Ratto snorted and nodded.

"Well, how about calling him on this airline phone and having him go check out the basement and dust the junction box? He should look for a wire that's been stripped on only one side. There will be a splice, or a small alligator clip."

Ratto called Martin at home and caught him. "Here's what I want you to do." Harry listened to him give the instructions and then tell him to get it done within seventy-five minutes, then to go back home and wait for Ratto's next call. He also told him not to disturb any tap he might find but to look for prints and report back. Harry set his watch alarm for seventy-five minutes later.

Harry awoke to the beep-beep-beep of his watch, and so did Ratto. He called again, and Martin had already returned as instructed. After they talked for a few minutes, Ratto hung up and relayed the news. "Okay, Harry, you were right. The phone junction box was tapped, and the suspect used an alligator clip just like you said. Martin called in a friend who does ID work. He put in a bypass splice and removed the alligator clip. Its head was wide enough that they think they might get a partial print from it."

"When will we hear?" Harry asked.

"Before we land."

"As it stands now, Cliff, what do you do when we land?"

"That's between me and the Chief. I assume you know not to compromise the investigation by blabbing to anyone about being there or seeing anything?"

"Yeah, I know."

Ratto fixed his eyes on Harry. "Not to mention that it could be hazardous to your health."

"Figured that too," Harry said in one heavy exhalation.

Later, Ratto called his lackey. "Any results yet?" and then he just listened. Then he muttered into the phone, "Okay, thanks. Just keep it quiet."

After he hung up, he said nothing for a long moment. "You gonna tell me?" Harry asked.

"There was a latent partial print found on the clip. The forensic examiner identified six points of similarity to a known index finger, right hand. Nate Hutchinson."

"Now what?"

"Now I'm gonna get an arrest warrant and see if that throws a crimp in his style."

"That will be a problem," Harry said. "Look at it. Nate's still on the investigation, and you're a suspect. How do you know that the tap wasn't authorized by warrant?"

"I don't."

"You can't get an arrest warrant if you don't know the tap was illegal. You could even be going to the judge who issued the warrant for Nate's tap. If that happened, he'd refuse to issue your warrant, and then call Nate as soon as you were out of his office. That could be hazardous to your health. If you try to arrest Nate without a warrant, it will only reopen suspicion against you."

"I don't care. I've got enough to move on him, and I'm going to. After what I saw today, I'll take the chance that I'm wrong."

"It's your life, but if the Chief backs Nate because he had the warrant, then our boy may bolt and we'll never catch him. Vancouver or Sydney will inherit a talented serial murderer."

"I got no choice. I'm not letting him stay loose with what I got."

"I have a choice. Give me the phone." Harry checked a number in his wallet and punched it into the air phone. "Becki? I need a big favor on the Hellhound deal. We might have a major break in the case, but it's complicated by the possibility that the Hellhound is a cop. I need to know if any judge in San Francisco has issued a warrant to wiretap Captain Cliff Ratto. Yeah, you remember that. It was in the papers. No. The guy I'm worried about is the one who would have gotten the warrant issued."

Ratto watched as Harry listened. Then Harry said rapidly, "Can you? Listen, I'm on a plane. When can I call you back? Great. Thanks."

After twenty minutes had passed, Harry called again and spent most of the conversation listening. After thanking his informant, he hung up and turned to Cliff. "No warrant."

"Thank you, Mr. Maxwell," Ratto said now in his official tone of voice. "But from here on you got to stay out of this. This is definitely gonna be dangerous. No offense, but I'll use my own people."

They arrived at SFO at around 1:15 p.m. Cliff went to baggage claim, and Harry headed for his car. There he retrieved his guns and drove to his office to wait for word.

CHAPTER TWENTY FIVE

Fitting his key into the lock, Harry pushed his office door open. He waited a moment and heard nothing, so he snapped on the light and briefly looked around. All was as he had left it. He sat and tapped at the desk top with a pencil. Then he stabbed at his auto dialer to check messages. There were two messages from clients who needed to speak with Harry, and two from new clients wanting a consultation. The next message began with a moment of silence, and then Nate's voice came on. The words hit Harry like a slap in the face. "Harry, I have Alissa."

There was no more to the message. He called the Cobbs' home and let the phone ring. There was no answer. He took the stairs two at a time out without closing any doors, leaped into his car, and sped desperately to the Cobbs' address.

There were no unusual cars out front, and nothing seemed out of the ordinary. He knocked and got no response, then rang the bell with like results. He peered through the windows at curtain's edge and saw nothing. He walked to the side of the house and made his way to the back, stepping quietly to the rear entrance. The door stood an inch short of being closed. He drew his S&W, mounted the stoop, and entered the kitchen. He thought back to the way Ratto had cleared Carmen's home and did likewise. He worked his way to the front of the house and found no one. He checked the bathroom, living room, and bedrooms. None of the furniture was disturbed; nothing was broken or upturned. In the den he found their computer on. A document was on the screen. It read "Bring company if you like attending funerals, Harry. Pier 27, Embarcadero." He swallowed hard and ran to his car.

He parked the Nova one pier down and across the street from the designated address. It did not seem to be an active pier, and he saw no lights on. The building was greater in size than a football field and was built out over the water. In bygone days ships had been directly off loaded here. The roof was high, to allow for cargo to be staged and stacked twenty-five feet to the ceiling.

This building had been partly converted into offices, and the right front corner had a window and a paneled entrance door. To the left were the original huge twin doors where trucks used to enter and load up. Another small door had been set into one of these. The front window was blocked with boxes, so Harry chanced walking on the opposite side of the street past the building so that he could see the side of the building too. He paused at a bus shelter and saw a man pressed into another doorway on that side of the warehouse, but he could not see who it was. He walked farther past the building until he had a clear view. It was Pierre.

At that moment Pierre saw him, put his finger to his lips, and motioned Harry to join him. Harry crossed over and whispered, "How did you know they were at the Cobbs to even see the note on the computer?"

Pierre squinted and shook his head. "I don't know about any note. He's been moving boxes and files, and his car has his clothing in it, so I put a satellite tracking transmitter on his car. I didn't have to tail him. I got here five minutes after he did."

"He's got Alissa, and maybe Yvonne too. He left a message on my voice mail and a note at the house where I put them, giving this location. I don't know what the game is, but I'm afraid he'll kill them if I don't show up alone."

"I think maybe you've just been too big a thorn in his side, Harry." Pierre looked intently at Harry. "You don't want me to leave. Do you think you could take him alone?"

"I don't guess so. What do we do?"

"The front right of the building is a subdivide with storage. We could enter that room without being heard and then get into the main building." He looked at Harry's chest. "Make sure there's a shot in the chamber and the safety is off, partner."

Harry drew his pistol, filled the chamber, and took the safety off. Pierre used his lock picks on the door and it opened without a sound.

It was pitch dark inside, but as the afternoon sunlight washed quickly past the door, Harry could see that the room was perhaps sixty feet long and only twenty feet wide, taking up only one third of the width of the building. Harry followed Pierre and softly pulled the door closed. It was very quiet inside, and dark as a cave. Pierre pulled his pistol and forged ahead.

They moved slowly through the darkness. The ceiling was low, only eight feet, and the room was of rough construction. Stacked all around this room were crates and boxes. The smell of ancient dust filled Harry's nose, while spider webs brushed over his forehead. Pierre picked his way along a narrow passage between the outer wall and the row of crates. The single, blocked window admitted scant light.

Pierre whispered to Harry to be alert to any noises behind them, so that no one could enter without their knowing it. They moved quietly down the dark alley of crates and cut left at the end of the room. Harry kept one hand on Pierre's back to stay with him, because it was again too dark to see him. Suddenly Pierre stopped and turned to put his hand gently on Harry's shoulder. "Shhh, did you hear a movement?" he whispered.

"No," Harry whispered back.

They stood in silence for a full minute. Harry heard nothing. Pierre began to move forward again, but after a short distance stopped. "I heard something," he said. "Didn't you?"

"No."

"It came from behind you, Harry," he whispered with some intensity. "I'm going back to check. You stay here and don't make a sound."

Pierre squeezed past him and disappeared back the way they had come. Harry waited in the darkness alone. The air was still and suffocating. Standing completely still in the deathly quiet, Harry could taste the dusty air. In two minutes Pierre returned. "What was it?" Harry
asked.

"The door wasn't fully closed. It was shifting a little in the breeze. Go on."

Harry moved forward with his pistol leveled, Pierre right behind him. Harry began to have thoughts of SWAT teams and wondered if that wouldn't have been a better idea. Rick Hansen suddenly appeared in his mind, as he inched through the dusty tunnel of crates. Hansen's last words came back to him: "You double crossing..." Why double crossing? Harry had never wronged him at all, much less betrayed him. But Hansen had been talking to him, Harry recalled, unless...unless he had been talking to someone else behind...

A strange sound rose in the darkness. The soft footfalls behind him had changed. One of the two feet seemed to be dragging, and the scraping noise echoed in Harry's mind like the closing of a granite tomb. The hairs jumped at the back of his neck, and in an instant he knew who was behind him. His mouth suddenly went bone dry, and he sucked air in and out through burning nostrils.

Harry held his gun in his right hand and slipped his left hand slowly into his coat pocket. He turned to his right, to face Pierre. In a flash, those large hands shot out toward him. His magnum was effortlessly stripped from his hand. Harry felt himself spun around and thrown face first into the wall. Pierre's forearm pressed him powerfully forward while a pistol was pushed into his kidney. Pierre stooped down, and in a moment had relieved Harry of his ankle gun as well. "Did you think I didn't know about that one, Harry?"

"Pierre, don't do this. I'm your friend."

"I'm not Pierre," he said, "and don't ever call me that. Pierre is a weakling and a coward. I'm Bumper, and no one fucks with me." The voice was angry and whining.

"What have you done with Yvonne and Alissa?"

"Oddly enough, nothing. You know that tracking transmitter I mentioned? It wasn't on Nate's car. It was on yours. I had the satellite fix on your next stop right after you picked them up at Yvonne's house. When I went to collect them, they were gone. Wary old buzzard, your rapist friend. Take another two steps forward," he said, pushing Harry with a powerful hand. "Okay, stop. You should be right next to the door. Can you feel it?"

"Yes."

"Open it very slowly, if you want to live a little longer, and don't move until I tell you." Harry turned the knob and pushed the door open. A broad shaft of light flooded the room around him.

"Take that hand out of your pocket, and step through the door."

Harry slowly turned to his right to face Bumper, but did not take his hand out of his pocket. "No, I don't think I will."

"Then I guess you want me to kill you," Bumper said, raising the pistol in his left hand to chest level. *Pierre might be right-handed*, Harry thought, *but Bumper was not.*

Harry never flinched, but Bumper's facial expression instantly reacted to the metallic click that came from Harry's left coat pocket. "A third gun? I'm proud of you, Harry. Surprised, but proud."

"I remember what a great detective once told me when he popped Judge Alquiza, 'He might have a gun in his pocket and get me, but I'd damn sure have him before I hit the ground.'"

Bumper smiled. "Tell you what, Harry, instead of killing each other right now, how about we go into the next room? I've got a surprise for you."

Harry nodded, his throat tight.

"Okay, follow me."

Harry backed through the doorway and then stepped to the right, keeping his eyes on Bumper. Bumper followed and flipped a bank of switches, and the immense building blossomed to life. In rapid glances, Harry took in the room. Off to the right were pallets of cartons stacked on large steel racks. To his left, farther out the pier, were racks holding hundreds of blue fifty-five gallon drums stored on their sides.

As Harry backed up, he angled toward the front of the warehouse. To his left and behind him, some peripheral movement caught his eye. He did not turn his head, but moved his body so that whatever was there could come more within his field of vision. At that moment rose a loud muffled sound. As Harry backed up, Bumper stayed close to him.

Now Harry could make out the source of movement. One blue drum stood on end near the racks of drums. Nate was standing on top of it, and there was a noose around his neck.

The barrel was stenciled "Acetone," and Harry recognized the distinctive smell of that volatile solvent.

Still keeping Bumper in view, his eyes followed the rope up to the rafters, where it was fastened high above them. Nate's hands were apparently tied behind his back. He was gagged, but was trying urgently to say something. Harry supposed that Nate wanted to warn him that Pierre was the Hellhound.

"I know, Nate. I know who he is," Harry said aloud, keeping his eyes on Bumper. The loud noises continued, more urgently than ever. Harry looked at Bumper, who was now grinning as if he were relishing an immense private joke.

"How long has he been up there like that?" Harry asked.

"Oh, just since yesterday, but I don't think he's trying to convey his...how shall we put it, weariness? No, I fear my colleague is peeved at me." Nate's head rolled from side to side as he continued trying to shout something through his gag. "I didn't want him to be bored, so at lunchtime today I came and poured some of that stuff down the front of his shirt. Sort of a practical joke, you see."

Harry looked over at the floor where Bumper's hand had pointed and saw a plastic bottle of liquid drain cleaner. Drops of water began to course down Harry's temples. He didn't have to worry about the safety on Rico's .38 Derringer. There was none.

Harry side-stepped closer to Nate, and Bumper followed. "Does Pierre even know you exist, Bumper?"

"Not a clue. Imagine how nuts it must drive him, wondering how I always know what he's up to? I know everything he does, but he knows nothing about me. I mean, it's so rich. Who could ever investigate a crime, and then conclude, 'Oh, it must be me?'"

"Listen, Pierre—"

"Call me that again, and I'll cut your tongue out and shove it in the hole where your eye used to be."

"Okay, Bumper. Okay." Remembering Carmen, Harry did not take this for a figure of speech. "Sure, Bumper," he repeated, to etch the name into his mind. "I saw Carmen. I know how she treated you. I understand why you hate women so much, but that's not Nate or me. Everyone knows who you are now. Tiny is on to you, and he's running you down right now. A judge and two other people know it's either you or Nate. I've left a letter to be opened in the event of...well, you know the drill. You have nothing to gain by killing us."

"Well, you're right. You two are a little out of my area of specialization, but I just hate loose ends. Don't you? And you do so insist on making yourself a nuisance, Harry, don't you?"

Harry moved close enough to see the front of Nate's shirt clearly. The fabric was soaked and bloody, beginning to fall apart in pieces. There was the chemical smell and also the smell of blood and feces. Harry guessed that Nate had not been force fed any of the caustic chemical; otherwise he'd be dead. He chanced a glance up to Nate's face and quickly lowered his gaze to Bumper again. Nate seemed to be losing alertness.

"Would you tell me something, Bumper?" Harry asked him. "It's obvious why you hated Carmen. I can even understand your hating older women in general, but why teenaged girls?"

"No. No, of course. You wouldn't know about that, would you? When old Carmen used to torture me, she sometimes let her sweet daughter Rita watch. Call her a bitch in training. You know how some images in your life just stay indelibly vivid? I have all those fond memories of being chained spread-eagled on the bed. Meanwhile, Carmen poured generous splashes of boiling water from her kettle on my balls, while sweet Rita giggled."

"I'm sorry. If I had been there, I would have stopped it."

Bumper screamed, "*No one* ever stopped her. And they *KNEW*. When I was twelve, I finally put a stop to it."

"How?"

"Carmen's precious Rita had a bad accident," Bumper said with a smile growing on his face. "She was apparently trying to start a trash fire with some gasoline, and the can exploded in her face, or so the police concluded. For some reason, old Carmen lost her taste for torture after that. I'd keep a cigarette lighter in my pocket, and if she'd get that look in her face, I'd just take it out, light it and smile. That would stop her. For some reason, crazy Carmen thought I had something to do with Rita's death."

"And after all that, Carmen still called you up to see how 'her boy' was doing?" Harry asked.

"Hey, family is family," Bumper said with a one-sided smirk, then continued his story. "For the next six years we went our separate ways, and I used the time to read up on useful topics. Ways to make people leave me alone. Ways to fix people who screwed with me. Chemistry, explosives, electricity, poison, weapons, booby traps, toxic chemicals, battlefield strategy, famous escapes, magicians' illusions, and above all, police investigative techniques. By the time I was fourteen, I knew more than ninety-five percent of the nation's police inspectors about their own craft. I even studied my school lessons once in a while, just so I could graduate and get a real job.

"For the next four years I practiced on those hick cops. Lots of times I'd break into stores, safes, or government offices and not take anything. Some of my best crimes and escapes were never known to anyone but me."

"Poor you, the unsung hero," said Harry sarcastically.

Bumper shrugged. "Well, I kind of made up for it with the Golden Gate Bridge thing, don't you think?"

"I suppose you don't give a shit about Pierre's friends, but I saved your life too, didn't I? Can't you just leave us and go?"

"Pierre's friends? You think I don't know you? Harry, I know everything Pierre knows. He's the helpless shit who didn't have the balls to stick around when sweet Carmen ladled out the punishment. He didn't know anything about that part of our life. He'd check out and leave me to take the beatings and the torture, but I'm also the one who grew tough from it. And there are more of us here, Harry. You don't know the tenth of it. When the assassins cut Pierre down just before you happened along, what do you think he did? Huh? Take a fat hairy guess," Bumper screamed.

"You know what he did," Bumper went on. "He checked out and left me down and bleeding to die alone. *I* pulled my weapon and tried to return fire instead of cowering. It was me you saved, Harry, not Pierre. Me. It was even me that kissed you. Pierre wouldn't have had the guts for that either."

"And why were they trying to kill you? I never knew why."

Bumper let out a laugh. "Well, it seems I might have improved some evidence to solve one of Pierre's cases. It turned out I got the wrong guy, and his family took a dim view of it. My eternal gratitude to you for preserving my career, Harry."

"But what about the tap on Ratto's phone? Nate's fingerprint was on the clip, and there was the taped message that he had Alissa. Was Nate your partner?"

"Just when I congratulate you for being smart, you go dumb on me, Harry. You were right there when he put the print on the clip. When the clip was found in the telephone junction box at the Hall of Justice, I saved the clip after Nate held it. I'm kinda proud of the tape recording. I chewed my pencil here and balled up page after page of a note to you, and finally told Nate I wasn't satisfied it was just right. I made him read it out loud so I could make sure it sounded perfect for the history books. He caught on right after he read the part that said, 'I have Alissa.'"

Harry heard Nate's throat rasping as he sagged into the noose. "Since it was you I saved, how about paying me back by letting me live?" he said.

"Ummm, let's see. Nah," said Bumper with a fiendish grin. "Though God knows I did try my best to keep you clear of this. You just don't take *hints*, do you, Harry?"

"The problem is, you aren't getting out of here alive either, Bumper. I *will* kill you. And you want to live, don't you?"

"Well, it's like this. Do you think I ever expected to die in bed?"

"Poor impotent Bumper. You haven't had a moment's control in your entire life, have you?" Harry let the sarcasm hit the other man like a slap.

"What?" shouted the enraged gunman, jerking his pistol back up. "What? You really want to fuckin' die, don't you? Look around. I *am* the one in control here."

"I already told you I would have saved you if I could. You were what? Six or eight when she started on you? Nobody can defend himself at that age. She molded you with her viciousness, and you've been dancing to her tune ever since. It's Carmen who was the Hellhound. Every time you killed or tortured, it was Carmen's sick legacy that guided you. You were just the little robot that she programmed to spew out her own sickness and hate. When did you ever act independently of her, Bumper? When?"

Bumper winced but did not answer, so Harry went on. "Never. You never acted for yourself. Have you ever stopped to think why you've been killing women? Have you? It was to save other little boys, wasn't it?"

Bumper looked dazed. "What?"

"Everyone let that beast of a woman do you like that, when they should have saved you, and you knew that when you were only six. If you could save yourself at twelve, you could do much more as an adult, couldn't you? Wasn't that it? You were taking out other young females masquerading as sweet innocents, before they could grow into Hellhounds and bitches like Carmen and Rita. Wasn't that it? So you could save other little boys from torture and pain?"

Bumper began to look upset now. His mouth grew pinched. His eyes started to glaze over, and he was breathing hard as he forced out the words, "Ding dong, the Bitch is dead." He began to laugh weakly at his own joke.

"Is she really, Bumper? Or is she alive and well in her little robot?" pressed Harry. He nearly shouted at the other man, "Hell, you're repaying Carmen's cruelty by giving her immortality. How about it, Bumper, do you have a protege yet, so you can pass on Carmen's loving legacy?"

"No, I'm not—"

"Wouldn't you just once like to tell her to fuck off? Live as if she had never touched your life? Come on. Come on, be the friend you were years ago when you were at the point of dying. You loved me then. At that moment, you were free of Carmen. Be free now. Free yourself. You can!" Harry leaned toward him, urgent and demanding.

Bumper stood up straight and inhaled a deep breath. His rage seemed to vanish. He drew a switchblade knife from his pocket with his left hand, and pressed the button. It sprang open. He flipped it in his hand and tossed it to Harry, handle first. Then he spoke in a voice so soft that Harry could barely hear him. "Cut him down."

Harry drew the Derringer out of his pocket and kept it in his left hand. He put the knife between his teeth and jumped up on the barrel behind Nate. Bumper only stood there and made no move to shoot them. Harry cut the rope, and Nate collapsed. The two tumbled to the floor, Harry holding onto Nate to protect him in the fall. He dragged Nate to his feet and pulled the gag down so he could breathe more easily. Bumper walked over and sat on one of the barrels, watching them.

Then he began speaking in a strained voice. "Harry, did I mention how funny Carmen looked when she was running around the room with the whip sticking out of her eye? Slipping and sliding in her own blood? She had a challenge in pulling the whip out, with her arms lying on the floor and all. I never laughed so hard in my life."

The burly man stood up, took something out of his jacket pocket, and then unzipped the jacket. In his hand was a hand grenade, from which he pulled the pin with the pinky of his gun hand. Tucked in the belt around his waist were three packets of what appeared to be plastic explosive. Bumper looked at Harry with glazed eyes and said, "Life's just a bitch, Harry, and then you die." He let go of the lever on the hand grenade. It sprang away from him and bounced across the floor, starting the timer. He caressed his face with the grenade, holding it against his cheek with both hands, and then screamed out, "Fuck you, Carmen. Roast in Hell."

Harry yanked Nate's left arm around his neck and wrapped his gun hand around his waist to make a run for the giant truck doors. "Come on, run, dammit," Harry screamed into Nate's face. As they began to run, he took one look back. Bumper was still sitting on the barrel caressing the grenade. He gave Harry the merest trace of a smile.

Suddenly a collage of thoughts, images, and feelings flooded through Harry's brain: that smile; "act, don't react"; the jump off the bridge; Hansen screaming "you double crossing..."; Oz spilling out dead on his feet; the smile that wasn't right.

Harry stopped with a lurch. He knew. This drama, it was a *lie.*

"Run, if you don't wanna die, Harry," yelled Bumper.

"Not this time, Pierre." He dropped Nate's arm. "I'm not dancing to your choreography anymore."

"I told you never to call me that."

"For Chrissakes, Harry, help me," pleaded Nate.

Now Harry walked slowly toward Pierre, training the Derringer on him. "Then shoot me, Pierre," he said. "Pierre, Pierre, Pierre. You don't want to, do you? Who will testify to your deaths, if you kill me? It's why I'm here, isn't it?"

Nate frantically began to crawl for cover toward the racks of boxes.

Pierre and Harry faced each other at ten feet apart, their pistols pointing at each other. "Too late now, Harry. I don't have to kill you. We're both dead," said Pierre, nodding toward the hand grenade. Harry knew he was being invited to look away at the grenade, but locked his stare instead into Pierre's eyes. The pop of the practice grenade was lost as the piggybacked reports of the two pistols, first Harry's and then Pierre's, cut through the warehouse.

Harry's bullet found its target first. It sank into Pierre's left thigh, just below his abdomen. His body jerked with the impact, making his pistol hand swing wide. His bullet ripped through the flesh of Harry's left side and kept going. Harry grimaced as it spun him to his left. He caught a glimpse of Nate still crawling. He fired his second and last bullet. It struck Pierre hard in the right shoulder, and he recoiled backwards. His hand dropped below his waist, but the pistol did not fall. He grunted as he fought to raise his weapon back up.

The shot that had hit Harry made him stagger backwards. He now stood fifteen feet from Pierre. He dropped the Derringer and clutched his left side with his right hand as he took a step forward. A blaze of pain paralyzed him for a moment. He watched Pierre bring his pistol back up almost to waist height. Then Bumper flashed an insane grin as the pistol inched upward. He looked at Harry, and between gritted teeth said, "Just for that, old buddy, I'm gonna fuck little Alissa before I kill her."

Harry's launched himself forward and heard himself cursing. He let go of his side and bounded one step, then two, as Bumper pointed the Beretta straight at him. Bumper smiled and tilted his head. He had won. Harry knew he could never make it. Bumper tightened his trigger finger. Then, from over Harry's left shoulder, Nate screamed, "Drop it or you're dead!"

Bumper's hand jerked to his right. He fired before he could see Nate crouching with only the empty drain cleaner bottle clenched in his hands. Harry took his last two steps, landing on his left foot only three feet from Bumper, who was now turning the Beretta back toward Harry. Harry raised his right leg up so that his thigh was parallel to the ground and then snapped his lower leg up with all the force he could muster. He delivered this snap kick to the gun hand and carried it through into Bumper's face, catching him on the chin.

The Beretta flew straight up over their heads. Bumper staggered back but did not fall. Harry saw the pistol hit the floor some six feet to his left, and he went for it. The other man lunged forward for the gun too. They collided in mid-air, and then crashed to the floor on top of the pistol. As they grappled, Harry could feel Bumper's rock hard muscles tensing to throw a punch with his left fist, aiming for Harry's throat, but in the close quarters he hit Harry's collar bone instead. Harry countered with a thrust of the base of his palm up into the other's nose, breaking it so strategically that the cartilage was driven upward toward the sinuses.

Even as the blood flooded out of his nose, Bumper did not pause in his onslaught. He jerked his left knee up into Harry's abdomen, right into the gunshot wound. Harry's mouth opened in a painful gasp as he doubled up. As he clutched his stomach, Bumper scrambled for the pistol, his fingertips brushing the weapon. Harry drove his left fist into Bumper's shoulder wound, and as the madman involuntarily tried to protect his shoulder with his own left hand, Harry seized the chance to snatch the gun with his right hand. Bumper quickly rolled onto his back and kicked straight up with his right foot, and the pistol again went flying, lodging inside one of the racks of barrels. Rising to his knees, Bumper seized Harry's stomach with his powerful left hand and squeezed his wound. Bumper grunted into his face, "I always knew it would come down to you, Harry," as he twisted his hand. Harry tried to rise, but could only get up on his elbow. The pain was overwhelming.

Suddenly Bumper released Harry's gut and lunged to a new position. He threw his left forearm around Harry's neck and dragged him down to the floor, fiercely pulling him against his chest. Harry felt the crush of Bumper's arm on his throat, shutting off his airway, and whipped his elbow back forcefully into his attacker's stomach once, twice, and again. Bumper grunted, but the solid muscles of his stomach held, despite the wound just below them, and his viselike grip did not soften. Harry could not break his hold and knew he had precious little time before he blacked out. He shifted his hips to the side and raised his forearm as high as he could, making a tight fist that he brought down hard into Bumper's groin. The grip broke. Harry rolled over on top of him and pounded his fist into the thick neck with no effect. Bumper's left hand shot out and again seized Harry's throat. Grimacing through clenched teeth, he grunted, "That all you got, Dipshit?"

Harry felt a rush of emotion as old as life. He snaked his left arm past the other's strangling hand and then suddenly thrust it up, breaking the hold. He took Bumper's throat with both hands and steeled himself for a rain of punches to his bleeding side. But the blows did not break his grip, and he tightened his fingers, leaning down into his hands and squeezing with all his might. The punches to his stomach and side stopped. The hand briefly clawed at Harry's hands, and then fell away. Harry did not relax his grip.

Bumper's eyes remained open, and his legs thrashed while Harry kept squeezing, hatred in his mind. Then Harry shifted his hands, grabbing Bumper's chin in his right hand while he put his left to the crown of the man's head. In a voice that was half scream and half child's whine, Harry spoke the words in measured beats: "My-last-word-will-not-be-OOPS." At the last syllable Harry yanked Bumper's head around to the right as far as it would go. He heard a cracking noise, and a dead weight dropped from his hands.

Then Harry heard a noise that sounded like a billiard ball hitting the floor and rolling. He looked down and behind him to see Pierre's left palm, and a second hand grenade rolling away from it. The pin was pulled, and now Harry knew why the hands had quit their fight before the legs did. He rolled off Pierre toward the hand grenade and picked it up. He rose to his feet and threw it as far as he could toward the end of the pier. Then he spun around and ran.

He saw Nate ahead of him making his way to the door. He was stooped over and holding his neck and shoulder. Blood was seeping from below his hand, no doubt from a bullet hole. Harry took hold of him and continued his run for the door. "Come on, buddy, push those legs," he shouted at Nate. "Come on, come on."

Nate pushed himself as well as he could, with Harry half supporting him as they ran toward the silvery outline of the small door set into the giant one. They were almost to the front room through which they had entered the warehouse when the hand grenade went off. This was no practice grenade. They felt the concussion, but kept running toward the glowing escape hole.

Another explosion sent a wave of heat into their backs. Then another, and two more in quick succession, as the acetone barrels began to pop. The heat burned into their backs as Harry kicked open the door with all his might. Barrels were now going off like firecrackers. When Harry looked sideways at Nate, he saw that a roiling fireball was bearing down on them. He pulled Nate through the portal and cut toward the street. They were almost there when the entire warehouse was ripped by a blast that shook the ground. As the two of them rolled into the street, Harry could see the fire and blast debris extruding out the windows and doors of the warehouse, and then sections of the walls breached and flew outward. A choking fog of blistering acetone fumes enveloped them, and they lurched to their feet, staggering forward until they could breathe again. Reaching a parked Mercedes, they hid behind it to watch the fireball devour the area where they had been. Blast after blast exploded as they sheltered behind the car to escape the blistering heat.

CHAPTER TWENTY SIX

When the explosions finally stopped, Harry and Nate left the shelter of the car and retreated further down the street to sit down near the edge of the water. Sirens wailed as multiple fire engines arrived, followed by police cars and an ambulance. Harry found medical help for Nate, who was immediately given aid for his injuries and chemical burns. One E.M.T. got a plastic container from the ambulance and began drawing sea water off the wharf. While one worked on the bullet wound, the other poured the sea water over his chest, stomach, and legs to wash away the remaining lye solution. Nate moaned as the sea water hit him, but a second shot of morphine began to dull all sensation and soon he sank into semi-consciousness.

Harry could hear fire fighters shouting over the thunder and rumble of the fire. The conflagration had melted the corrugated steel roof, and they could not get close enough to douse the blaze, so they kept it under control and let it begin to burn itself out. The TV camera crews arrived and arranged their trucks to cover the firefighters as they worked on the spectacularly blazing pier.

Slowly the terror, the mad run, the broiling heat, and the bullet wound took their toll on Harry. His strength began to ebb, and he collapsed to the ground. His head became curiously heavy as the E.M.T. began to doctor his wounds. "You're going to be okay, sir," he told Harry. "The bullet went through the skin and fat layers, but it doesn't look like it hit any organs." He gave Harry a shot of morphine for pain and one for tetanus. When he was bandaged, he asked the paramedics if they had a phone.

One brought him a cell phone. Harry propped himself up onto his elbow and called his office, where Bridge answered. He could hear his own lethargic voice saying, "Hi, Bridge."

"Oaf?" she said. "Are you all right? Are you drunk?"

"No, but I'm alive, and that's almost as good. It's okay now. It's over." He thought a moment and added, "Really, this time. Any messages from Yvonne?"

"Yes. Yvonne called just two minutes ago, but she wouldn't give me a location or number. She said she'd call back."

"Was she the last call before mine?"

"Yes, why should...Oh, yes. I see. Hold on and I'll star-69 her, and see if it goes through."

"Bridge, if you reach her, have her call this number." He gave her the cell phone number, and then said, "Oh yeah, turn on the news." Then he hit *End*.

Yvonne rang him several minutes later. "Harry? You sound awful. What's that noise? Are you at a phone booth?"

"No, I'm at a fire. Lots to tell later, but what happened at the Cobbs' house? I found the door open and everyone gone."

"Mrs. Cobb said she noticed a car pass slowly by the house several times, and she pointed it out to Mr. Cobb. He took a look and said it was an unmarked police vehicle. He could tell by the tires and the antenna, he said."

"Yes, I warned him it could be a cop."

"The car started to pull to the curb a couple of houses up from us, and Mr. Cobb said we all had to get out. He grabbed Lissa, and we all ran out the back and straight into a neighbor's back door. We hid in the basement until the neighbor took a walk around the block and said it was clear."

"Where are you now?"

"Is it okay to say, Harry?"

"Yes, and you can go home. It was Pierre. I killed him. I think he'll stay dead this time," he said wearily.

"Pierre? Oh my god," she gasped. "At least that explains why he couldn't catch the Hellhound. Mr. Cobb took us to the place he said he knows the best, the docks. We're hiding in a warehouse on the Embarcadero."

"Small world. Can you look out a window from where you are? Go look. Can you see the fire?"

"God yes, the smoke is blacking out half the sky. What about...Did you do that?"

"Is Lissa there? Put her on."

Distantly Harry heard "Daddy, Daddy. Is it really him?" Then she was on. "Hi, Princess," said the tired voice. "Daddy loves you very much. You're safe now. I'll see you soon. Gotta go. Bye." He clicked the phone off and closed his eyes. A hand grabbed it just as it slid out of Harry's hand.

The ambulance took Harry and Nate to San Francisco General Hospital, where a doctor confirmed that the bullet had passed only through skin and fat and barely scored some muscle tissue. Several hours later, after Harry had been stitched inside and out and was ready to be discharged, the E.R. nurse told him that Nate was being admitted for probable skin grafts, but that his bullet wound was not serious. It seemed that a doctor friend of his was coming in on her day off to tend to him.

Rico and Ratto arrived just as Harry was released. They led him out a shipping entrance just beyond the view of the lurching mob of reporters. Rico would not let him go home or to his office until the bomb squad had checked both places out.

"You don't have to do that, Rico," Harry said.

"Yes, I do. I don't want him killing you with a booby trap after he's dead. I can just see myself explaining to your sister how I delivered you to a goodbye bomb from Pierre."

Rico went home with an unmoving Harry sprawled in the back seat.

CHAPTER TWENTY SEVEN

At their table in the rear of the "He's Not Inn," Harry was sipping beer and Bridget her chardonnay. Tyrone had a double Stoli martini, and Rico sipped a mineral water, while Doctor Paschov nursed his cabernet. Tyrone took a slug of martini and asked Harry, "Are you sure Pierre didn't know what he was doing? Maybe that Bumper stuff was just an act."

"I don't think so," said Dr. Paschov. "I doubt that Pierre had any memory or consciousness of being the Hellhound. I must admit he had me fooled. As rare as partner serial killers are, multiple personalities are even more rare, despite what the movies suggest."

"Then if Pierre was really trying to catch the Hellhound, why didn't he ever uncover any evidence?" Rico asked.

"Because whenever the danger of discovery loomed, Bumper took over in their common mind and covered up to protect himself. Self-preservation always surfaces. Afterwards, Pierre was only aware of searching and finding nothing, or of seizing evidence that turned out to be useless. He could never understand why he kept coming up empty handed."

"I understand the multiple personality thing, Doctor," Harry said, "but why would Pierre have explosives on him to take to the Belford mansion at all?"

"It would have been Bumper who hid the explosives on himself, but Pierre who went to the Belford mansion. Then at some point Bumper took over again and planted the explosives. When Pierre left, he was honestly anguished at the ensuing tragedy and mystified as usual how his nemesis could outfox him after he had just checked the house over. You see, Bumper could pop up whenever he needed to, and then leave just as suddenly."

"But Dr. Paschov, how could Pierre not be aware of blank periods?" Harry asked.

"Who says he was unaware? But what would Pierre see as more likely, that he was a psychotic serial murderer and just never noticed it, or that he had just been working so hard he was falling asleep on his feet?"

Heads nodded all around the table, and the group fell quiet. Then Bridget cocked her head and said, "I'm curious about the gifts he left for the little boy whose sister he murdered. Was Pierre always kind toward children? Did you ever get a chance to see him with kids, Harry?"

"Only once or twice, but when he was with them he seemed as gentle as you could ask. I'm positive he beat bloody hell out of one guy he saw abusing his daughter."

"I thought so," said the doctor. "That rather confirms what Harry had already suggested to Bumper or Pierre before he died, that in his sick way he was trying to protect other little children as he had never been protected."

"And I'm afraid that hurting innocent girls was just more fun for him than killing old women," said Harry, "but the hatred and rage were real enough. Anyone who saw the Texas shack would agree with me on that."

"Speaking of the Texas incident," Rico said, "the esteemed Captain Ratto has been demoted. He was just getting Judge Kellogg's signature on the arrest warrant for Nate when the reports came over the radio that it was Pierre. That was about all that the judge or the Chief could do. Tiny will be taking an early retirement. He and Alquiza can play checkers in the park together." Everyone laughed.

"The good news is that when Nate gets out of the hospital, he'll be sporting Lieutenant's bars and taking over Pierre's job," Rico added.

"All that for getting shot?" Tyrone asked.

"Heck no. Nate was actually the one who first figured out it was Pierre," Harry said. "I told the Chief about Nate's heroism, and with my current celebrity the mayor and the Chief didn't want to go against the popular tide."

"Speaking of which," Bridget interrupted, ringing her glass with a spoon, "Ta-Daaaa, I want to be the one to announce that Harry will be the cover story in the next issue of *Newsweek*."

The group applauded.

"What about Hansen?" Tyrone asked.

"He was probably innocent of any of this," Harry said. "Pierre was the last one out of Hansen's apartment after the warrant search. It would have been easy for Bumper to grab some items with Hansen's prints on them to plant at Fisherman's Wharf. My guess is that Pierre promised to clear him if he cooperated. Maybe the poor bastard thought he was rescuing Alissa when I arrived."

"Not bloody likely," Bridget said. "Have you forgotten that he drew a gun and tried to kill you?"

"Actually, it wasn't me. Pierre was right behind me. When we all arrived with guns drawn, he figured out he had been set up. He was acting in self-defense, knowing he was going to be killed to silence the patsy. At that point though, it didn't matter. When he drew on me, I had no choice."

"But what about the Wildman girl he left alive?" Rico asked. "Pierre went to interview her with Nate. How could he take that chance? Was he trying to get caught by then?"

"I feel stupid on that one, since I was there," said Harry. "At the time, it seemed to be just consideration for the victim, but every time Pierre spoke, he dragged Nate or me off to some quiet corner to talk. I'm sure the girl never heard Pierre's voice."

Bridget's pager began beeping. "Oh, no. Him again. Harry, will you *please* call Mr. Tolliver back? He's driving me crazy."

"Bridge, didn't I tell you to get rid of him? His case is really complicated, and I'm behind in all my other cases because of all this Hellhound stuff."

"Well, luv, I did as you told me. I told him you were so busy you'd have to charge him $20,000 to put other cases aside and take his." She opened her purse and handed Harry an envelope. "So here is the certified check for twenty thousand that came by Fedex this afternoon."

Harry turned the envelope over in his hand. "Bridge, didn't I tell you to always put a good client like Tolliver straight through to me when he calls?" Boisterous laughter followed, with Dr. Paschov's chuckle heard close by.

"Oh geez," Harry shouted, "I really have to run now. I've only got twenty-five minutes to get to the hospital to see Nate before visiting hours are over." He jumped up, and Bridget joined him in his rush for the door.

"Harry," Tyrone called after him. "You forgot your briefcase."

Harry rushed back to the booth and grabbed his briefcase. He carefully zipped it and walked out into a beautiful, clear San Francisco day.

www.ingramcontent.com/pod-product-compliance
Lightning Source LLC
Chambersburg PA
CBHW050517260626
47157CB00004B/1368